CONCERT OF
GHOSTS

CAMPBELL ARMSTRONG

CONCERT OF GHOSTS

HarperCollins*Publishers*

HarperCollins books may be purchased for educational, business, or sales promotional use. For information please write: Special Markets Department, HarperCollins Publishers, Inc., 10 East 53rd Street, New York, NY 10022.

FIRST EDITION

Designed by Claudyne Bianco

Library of Congress Cataloging-in-Publication Data
Armstrong, Campbell.
Concert of ghosts : a novel / Campbell Armstrong. — 1st ed.
      p.   cm.
ISBN 0-06-017946-5
I. Title.
PR6052.L25C66   1993
823'.914—dc20   92-54423

93 94 95 96 97 ❖/HC 10 9 8 7 6 5 4 3 2 1

This book is for Rebecca,
who found light in the darkness

*Thanks to Marymarc Armstrong for
her generous assistance, and Noel Fray,
lapsed hippy, for his contribution to
stalking ghosts in San Francisco*

Most of the newcomers were less interested in gleaning philosophical or creative insight than in getting stoned as often as possible. They smoked or swallowed anything said to be psychedelic, and when the visions grew stale they turned to other drugs, especially amphetamines. . . . For these people Haight-Ashbury was the last hope. They had nowhere else to go. They were the casualties of the love generation. You could see them in the early morning fog, huddled in doorways, hungry, sick and numb from exposure, their eyes flirting with vacancy. They were Doomsday's children, strung out on no tomorrow, and their ghostlike features were eerie proof that a black hole was sucking at the heart of the American dynamo.

—*Acid Dreams,* Martin A. Lee
and Bruce Shlain

1 Daily, from first planting until final harvest, Harry Tennant attended his crop with the patient devotion of a man who has grown weary of society and wants nothing to do with the outside world. He'd go deep into the woods where the plants grew and with great care would pluck a leaf or bud, crushing it tenderly between thumb and forefinger to release the scent of resin. Eyes closed, he'd smell the liberated perfume of the plant. If he was pleased, he'd say something to Isadora, the Great Dane who always accompanied him. When he wasn't happy, he'd frown, and the dog, recognizing the expression, took to sulking among the trees.

The crop dominated Tennant's life. Whatever change in weather affected the plants affected him too. He was sensitive to frosts, to periods of extreme dryness, to the excessive rainfalls that came unfailingly to this part of upstate New York in late summer.

During one such monsoon he put on his mackinaw and an old Stetson and went down through the rattling trees to the crop. The Dane plowed after him with the kind of duty that transcends sodden discomfort.

When they reached the place where the crop grew, Tennant

experienced an uneasiness he couldn't quite understand. Was it the way the dog, her snout quivering, had begun to scamper back and forth as if in pursuit of something unseen, a mystery? Or was it merely how the plants bent under the force of the rain? They looked fragile to him. In weather like this they could lose their potency, and there wasn't a damn thing he could do to save them. You had to recognize how powerless you were: The elements made you helpless in the end, as helpless as the plants themselves.

He walked back to his house in the clearing, pursued by echoes of the monsoon that crashed in a boisterous rage through the trees. At one point he stopped and wondered anxiously if he heard something other than the roar of rain, the muted engine of a small plane, say. He looked up into the dense clouds. He saw nothing. Perhaps the sound had been that of a tractor droning in a distant field.

He continued to walk. He thought: *Farmers don't plow fields in weather this savage.* When he reached his house, he went inside the kitchen and took off his hat and mackinaw and stood for a long time looking across the clearing at the woods. With wet fingers he lit a cigarette. The sky over the trees was gray and turbulent and finally mysterious, as if it concealed all manner of hidden menace. He wondered how many times he'd stood in this very place and observed the trees and the sky in the manner of a man assailed by the inexplicable instinct that something wasn't quite right with his life, that he stood on the edge of a revelation that, should it ever come, might emerge from an unlikely combination of leaf and cloud.

Bullshit, he thought. My life is fine, just fine.

That night he awoke fully clothed. It was raining still, though the sound was softer now. He had a sense of the axis of darkness having shifted in a slight way, as if something in the woods had changed. The notion disturbed him. His bedroom was cold and damp, the window open. He'd had a dream filled with images of a city that might have been San Francisco; the architecture was strangely angled and dreadful, the streets depopulated. An eerie emptiness had prevailed.

He didn't move for many minutes. In the lower part of the house a board creaked, and he thought of Isadora turning in her sleep on the sheltered porch. Then there was the sound of the screen door flapping gently against its frame, and he pictured the dog entering the house the way she often did during the night.

He got up, looked down the staircase, saw nothing because the night was moonless and cloudy. The air still held the smell of the eggs he'd fried hours ago for supper. His heartbeat had a clock's certainty. He called out the dog's name. No response, no thump of tail upon wood. He put his palm on the handrail and began to descend.

The first flashlight went on at the bottom of the stairs. A second flicked on immediately after. Tennant stood very still as the disks of light played against his face. He saw a dark coat streaked with moisture, the gloss of two black shoes beneath the slick wet garment, and he had an impression of Isadora, barely touched by either light, lying in the hallway, eyes closed, her tongue hanging from her huge jaw.

"Harry Tennant," somebody said. "You're under arrest."

Hands cuffed behind his back, Tennant was dragged away from the motionless animal and led out onto the steps of the porch, where rainwater dripped from the roof into his hair. The two cops who cuffed him had shot the Great Dane with a tranq gun filled, so they jovially said, with enough dope to bring down a bull elephant.

The woods beyond the house were astonishingly transformed by lights. Lurid blue and red lamps of cop vehicles strobed the darkness, flashlights and lanterns created fantastic shadows. Tennant was blinded by the extravagance of it all. Voices echoed through the trees. How many guardians of law and order had come? The noise suggested fifty, sixty, a preposterous number for an operation as insignificant as his. No—the night magnified sounds, and the restless flashing lights gave the impression of frantic activity. Ten men, a dozen at most. Some from the county sheriff's office, a few from the state police, perhaps an agent or two from the Drug Enforcement Administration. The specific affiliations of law enforcement officers meant nothing to Tennant. They were all heat, no matter what their badges said.

He had a sense of inevitability. Luck was a string; his had broken. A major thrust of adrenaline was going, but he wasn't sure yet if it was fear. He was distanced from events, a dazed spectator.

"What's going to happen to my dog?" he asked.

"She'll have a mother of a hangover," one of the cops said.

Tennant regarded this cop under the porch lamp. He was fiftyish and had sunken cheeks. He looked generally disappointed with life. Milky rings circled his dark pupils.

"If she wakes," said the other cop.

"What's that supposed to mean?" Tennant asked.

"She took a fair dose." The second cop was young, concave beneath his mackinaw. Tennant was sure he'd seen this one before—a local shop, a barn auction in Sterling Township. "She's a big un. Should be okay. Dog like that."

"I fucking hope so," Tennant said. "What happens next?"

The young cop said, "We wait for Sheriff Grabbe."

"Yeah, that's what we do," said the other. "Wait for the sheriff."

Tennant thought he had a memory of seeing Jack Grabbe election posters nailed months ago to telephone poles in the district. He couldn't be sure because he rarely paid attention to political hucksters. Politics was for people who bought into the system. Let the people be heard. Let them choose between one nondescript candidate and another in secret ballot. Tennant lived in that fringe place where politics had no dominion.

"Here he is," said the tall cop.

Sheriff Grabbe walked between the illuminated trees in the direction of the house. He had a small man's strut. He was wearing an ordinary raincoat and a dark suit. His thin hair was plastered by rain to his scalp in streaks so symmetrical they might have been drawn on his head by a finicky child with a black waterproof marker. When he came up on the porch, he squinted at Tennant.

"Harry Tennant?" he asked. "This your land?"

Tennant said it was. His voice wasn't quite right. He had to keep it lower. Firmer.

Grabbe flashed a piece of paper in front of Tennant's face. "Search warrant," and he jerked a thumb in the direction of the woods. "Looks like you got yourself a fine old plantation of cannabis. Lemme guess. You haven't a clue how it got there, right?"

Tennant stared into the trees, the carnival of light and shadow. He wondered how he could walk away from this mess. The cops had him cold.

"I haven't a clue, you're right," he said, and tried to sound bewildered.

"Maybe some campers came along and just tossed a few seeds around and wouldn't you know—there's a crop in your own backyard," Grabbe said, and smiled like a man who knows the score. "Something along those lines, Harry?"

"Could be. It's news to me. I don't go into the woods."

"I follow the letter of the law around here, Harry. No drugs. No dealers. No pushers. No growers. That's it. Straightforward as you can get." A rivulet of rain slithered along Grabbe's eyebrow like a quicksilver bug dissolving. "It's going to take some daylight calculation, Harry. But our first assessment is you got a real good harvest out there. Ten kilos. Maybe fifteen. Lotta reefer."

He stood on tiptoe and pushed his face forward. "You peddle the stuff yourself, Tennant? You hang around schools?"

Tennant said, "I wouldn't sell dope to kids. I wouldn't sell it period."

Grabbe shrugged and looked unexpectedly sympathetic. "'Tween you and me, I don't see much harm in cannabis in moderation. All kinds of people smoke the stuff and it don't seem to do them a whole lotta damage 'cept red-eye and a big appetite. They don't go out like crack addicts and mug folks. They don't get behind the wheel of a goddamn car drunk outta their skulls on seven martinis and kill pedestrians. Just the same, Harry, you're in some kind of shit, because Judge Stakowski don't share my private view. Stak says guys like you should be skinned and gutted, then deep-fried."

"I'll need a lawyer before I get cooked," Tennant said dryly. Stak. The abbreviation was ominously suggestive of a small-town clique, a private club of law enforcement officers and judges, secret agreements, whispered deals.

"Oh, you'll get one. Don't worry."

"When?"

"Soon's possible."

"How do you define soon?" Tennant asked. "An hour? A day?"

Grabbe ignored the question. He looked at the two cops. "Take him away. Lock him up nice and tight."

Lock him up. *Lock.* Finally. Tennant felt a distinct chill.

The notion of being confined in a small space filled him with dread. Locks turning, key rings rattling. Styrofoam plates. Plastic spoons. The sound of food being slurped. Whispers in the dark, people whimpering in their sleep. No. No way. There was an excess of nightmares in restricted places. People dreamed mad dreams. The concept of insanity terrorized him, those great shapeless prairies of the mind, the interior wilderness without boundaries. He had a great pressure inside his head, an urge to break free and run. He wasn't going to be stuck inside some awful airless room. Under no goddamn circumstances. An uneasy sense of familiarity touched him. Locked rooms. Small windows. Walking from wall to wall, pacing, counting every step only to find the arithmetic never varied.

If he'd been uncertain before, he knew now beyond a doubt: He was afraid.

The cops led him down the steps. The black muddy ground sucked at his boots. He tried to resist in a mulelike way by refusing to move, but one of the cops, laughing, clenched his fist and drove it into the base of Tennant's spine. Tennant went down on his knees, head slumped forward. Maybe the same cop, maybe another, struck him on the neck, a swift, stabbing blow. Pain roared in Tennant's brain. He was dragged to his feet and shoved against the side of a police car where, stunned, he was dimly aware of how the frame house had tilted to one side and the sound of the night rain had become a dull ringing noise. Confusion and pain. He barely felt the last assault, a knee jacked up into his groin. He couldn't breathe.

"Now you behave yourself, Harry," somebody said.

He was thrown into the patrol car. The cuffs cut into his skin.

"Judge Stakowski," said the hollow-cheeked cop who drove.

"Wowee," his spindly young colleague said.

Was that enthusiasm in their voices? Was Stakowski their hero? Was Stak somebody they admired? Or was their tone of awe a kind of put-on to further upset Harry and make him think he was going in front of a hanging judge? Cops played rough games. Only you never knew what the rules were or if it was really a game at all.

There was silence and rain and the blacktop gleaming in the headlights. A scent of onions was blown on the squall, flying out of dark fields where here and there a trailer sat, visible only because of pale blue TV lights that sometimes fell sadly from windows on the outline of a rusted tractor, the edge of a battered pickup, a child's swing, and on one occasion a solitary man smoking a cigarette on his stoop. A landscape of the lost, Tennant thought. The damned.

In this census he included himself.

He expected to be driven directly to the lockup in Oswego, but somewhere along narrow back roads the car went off on an unfamiliar route. He'd been studying the darkness anxiously and felt the change, not as a tangible switch in bearing, but as he might experience an unusual sensation. He looked from the window. Now the countryside was only a dark monotony of fields unbroken by either trailers or houses, the sky starless.

"Where are we headed?" he asked.

Neither cop answered immediately, and Harry had one of those moments of unease layered with deadly potential. He might be driven to a dark field, a drainage ditch, and shot in the back of the head. Obvious, simple, logical. Who would miss him? And if anybody ever inquired, he'd been killed trying to escape. Wasn't that the way things happened in the anonymous little counties, where officers were no more than licensed vandals, that constituted the Republic? People vanished, unclogging the legal system. Unidentifiable bones turned up years later. Nobody cared. To whom would an old skeleton matter?

He asked his question again.

The younger cop said, "Just you relax back there, Harry, unless you want more of what you got before."

In a voice strained by pain, Tennant said, "Why aren't we going straight to Oswego?"

"We're driving a different route if it's okay with you."

"Which goes where exactly?"

The cop with the unhealthy eyes said, "To the goddamn jail, Harry. What the hell do you think?"

Tennant said, "I think you're driving around half the county to unsettle me."

"Boy's got some funny notions, don't he?" said the older cop. "Probably smokes too much of his own product."

The cops laughed at this for what seemed to Tennant a long time. Rain rushed against the windshield and the wipers squeaked, and still the cops laughed in modulations that continued to change—now a murmur of merriment, next a higher tone of mirth that exactly resembled the sound of the wipers. The night was charged with lunacy and violence, Tennant thought, strange arrangements, human sounds syncopated with those of machinery.

Trying to forget his pain, he shut his eyes and listened to the scampering rain on the roof, and he imagined tiny bedraggled creatures, bats, birds, alighting briefly on the car only to be sucked away in the wet slipstream. The cops were no longer laughing. The young one whistled "Pennies from Heaven" and stared to the side. In back, Tennant might have been forgotten by his captors, like an old joke that didn't bear repeating. He saw no future in pursuing the matter of the car's direction or destination. He was a prisoner, and his questions could be answered or ignored as the cops chose. And if they decided to put a gun to his skull—

You die in a rainy field. One bullet was all it took.

His fear turned black, a spider in his head spinning a surreal design, infinite and complex.

Be still. Seek the center. The quiet eye of the cyclone. From what corner of his mind had that worthless little whisper of advice emerged? Some random discharge of electricity, the brain in turmoil, nothing else.

He squirmed in his seat, legs cramped and numb, stomach and head throbbing. He was over six feet tall, and weighed about 175, and it was goddamn hard to find the quiet eye of anything in the back of a cop car, especially after you'd just been casually beaten.

The car turned, turned again. A green road sign was abruptly illuminated but vanished before Harry could read it. He wasn't quite sure why in the absence of landmarks, but he had a sense of familiarity again, as if having traveled off the edge of the world the vehicle had found its way back. Houses appeared now, big Victorian homes set in large lots, places of ornate substance that rose up and up by means of steep narrow staircases into the darkness of attic rooms. These steadfast houses somehow reassured him, and the panic he'd felt before subsided—slightly, as a tide quietens when the wind drops for a while. But you know the wind will come again.

He recognized Oswego, the outskirts of which had seemingly loomed from nowhere. Pale lamps, quiet leafy streets, here and there a neighborhood tavern closed for the night. The blue oval of a Genesee Cream Ale sign floated in a window like a distorted electric kiss. Near the railroad tracks a couple stood beneath a tree, the man's surprised white face and the woman's parted lips caught for a moment in headlights.

"Took us a shortcut, Harry," said the older cop. "Surprised you, heh?"

"You got a bad case of nerves there, Harry," the thin cop remarked.

Tennant thought of maps, the veins of old roadways, blue reservoirs, creeks. He marveled, more from relief than admiration, at how the driver had found Oswego by this unknown route. The countryside could be slyly inscrutable, concealing from outsiders facets known only to the locals. Tennant felt the alienation of the stranger. After nine years in his wooded acres, he really knew very little about his chosen county.

Now he remembered his absolute certainty that he was going to be walked into a darkened field and shot through the skull. It was funny, if you knew how to look at it the right way. The detached way.

The car stopped outside City Hall, in the basement of which the jail was located. Harry's panic, subdued so briefly, came fluttering back. There was nothing comical about jail.

The cell smelled of a certain cheap disinfectant that was meant to be redolent of pine needles but instead suggested a pot-pourri of caustic chemicals. Alone, overpowered by the scent, clutching his neck where it hurt, Harry sat on the narrow bunk and gazed at the wall. Graffiti had been written and then partially erased. Old messages, jokes, obscenities. Here and there an isolated word could be read.

He didn't know how long he'd been in this room—an hour, two; he wore no watch. How long before he could call a lawyer? Authority loved the sadism of mystification, the silences and secrets. Authority's victims lived like specimens suspended in murky liquid. You heard nothing, you waited, you floated in stillness.

Tennant was afraid to close his eyes. It was like locking the shutters to your skull, in whose passageways he had no urge to wander. The trick was to concentrate on the walls. The graffiti could have been written by a person to whom English was a third language. Words combined in odd phrases:

DIPSHIT BLACKBIRD CHUCKEE

For a moment he wondered if there might be something significant in these words, a hidden meaning, but that was a dangerous game to play. You look long enough you can find almost anything.

He walked around the cell, conscious of how the walls pressed against him; he had a suffocating sense of space dwindling. He wondered about his dog. Was she unconscious still, or had she risen, alone in the dark house, half-drugged, baffled? He clenched his hands: Confinement angered him. He wanted out. He wanted a lawyer. Bail. He walked to the door, smacked it a few times with his fists, called out.

Nothing happened. A great silence prevailed.

Goddamn. He'd sit down, think of nothing. He wasn't going to let this room undo him. He managed to sleep briefly. When he opened his eyes a man was touching his shoulder.

"Harry. Frank Rozak. Attorney."

Tennant's mouth was dry. "Whose attorney?"

"Yours if you want me."

"I didn't call you. I don't even know you."

"I keep my ears to the ground. I have that good old Yankee initiative for drumming up biz, Harry. Besides I'm the only insomniac lawyer in town. Solitaire till dawn. They call me the Vampire. I heard they brought you in. Figured I'd offer my services. If you prefer somebody else, okay with me."

"I don't know anybody else."

"Yellow pages, Harry. Let your fingers do the walking."

"I haven't even seen a telephone," Tennant said. "I was under the impression I had some right to a call as soon as I was arrested."

"Ah. They come off as hicks around here about that kind of thing," Rozak said indulgently. "You want your call, I'll see to it immediately."

Tennant shook his head. He let the matter pass. What was

he supposed to do—pick an attorney out of the phone book? A lottery. He studied Rozak, a gray-haired man in his mid-fifties with purple sacs under his eyes, leaden pouches large enough to contain small handwritten messages. His hands were blood red and arthritic, knuckles swollen, the joints of the fingers ugly bulbs.

"Two other things. The cops worked me over. And I didn't get my rights read."

"Bless my soul, Harry. I'm shocked to the core." Rozak laughed in a bronchial way. "First, they'll say you were resisting arrest so they were obliged to squash you. And second they'll claim they read you your rights anyhow. That's a winged horse people in cells are always trying to jump. Didn't read me my rights, so please can I fly out of here? This isn't TV, Harry. Forget all that rights crap. Let's see if we can spring you as soon's possible." Rozak looked at his watch. "It's five A.M. You'll go before Judge Stakowski at ten. We better talk bail."

"How much are we looking at?" Tennant asked.

"You own your property, Harry?"

"Free and clear."

"Market value—what?"

"Sixty. Maybe seventy. More."

"My guess is bail will be set around twenty. You ever been in trouble with the law before, Harry? Any outstanding warrants? Serious priors?"

"Nothing," Tennant said.

"You don't sound too convincing there, Harry."

Tennant gazed at the man. "Nothing I remember," he said.

"You want me to defend you, you come clean. You don't hide shit from me. That's the way I play ball." Rozak took a prescription bottle from his jacket and swallowed a maroon capsule. "Painkiller." He gestured with one brutalized red hand.

"Okay," Tennant said. "Maybe there's a traffic violation I overlooked years ago. Something like that. Who remembers that stuff?"

Rozak smiled. "I don't want surprises, Harry. I don't want

to suddenly discover there's a bench warrant out for you. Know what I mean?"

Tennant nodded. Traffic ticket, some unpaid fine, how could he know? The trivia of his life, the building blocks out of which a world is constructed—these things seemed intangible to him.

"Here's the next thing. The county attorney is a hard-nosed maggot called Flitt. If he's down with his ulcer, which is often the case, then we'll have to deal with a fellow by the name of Kant—one of your all-time major misnomers—who has an IQ that so far hasn't registered on any known instrument. Kant would be better for us than Flitt. Any questions?"

"How did they discover the crop?"

Rozak said, "How else? Somebody informed. I saw the search warrant. Ironclad."

"And that's it?"

"An anonymous person drops a dime, Harry. A cop checks out the information, sees the crop, gets a warrant."

An anonymous person, Tennant thought. A ghost in the woods. Somebody, perhaps, in a low-flying plane. A walker in the forest.

"So. You want me to represent you, Harry?"

"You'll be fine," Tennant said.

"Lord, I get the biggest kick out of your enthusiasm. I'd shake hands on our association, Harry. But pressing the flesh is obviously awkward for me." Rozak paused, walked around the room, looked thoughtful. "I don't give a shit whether you're guilty as hell, Harry. My job is to show you had nothing to do with the crop. So I'm going to need some kind of evidence about how you live, your income, stuff like that, which will demonstrate you didn't need dope money to survive."

Evidence about how you live, Tennant thought. Exactly how did he live? He grew dope in the woods. That was it. That was his whole life. That was how he defined himself.

"Understand this. The prosecution will want to know how a guy can survive on air. I need whatever you've got relating to sources of income."

"I'll do what I can." He wondered what. He had no bank account, no savings in any financial institution, no inheritance. He'd have to invent something plausible. Such as?

"I also need background. Family. Character witnesses."

Background. Family. Character witnesses. These were knots on a string of personal identity. How did you begin to unravel them? Tennant looked at the attorney as if Rozak had just addressed him in a defunct language.

"You got a problem with any of that, Harry?" Rozak asked. "I take it you have family somewhere. Father. Mother. Brothers maybe. Sisters."

Tennant felt cold. Rain had seeped through the soles of his boots and his socks were wet and the chill had begun to spread through his body. "My mother's dead. I don't have brothers or sisters."

"What about your father?"

Tennant hesitated. "What about him?"

"Is he alive?"

Alive? Tennant shrugged. "I guess so."

Rozak sat down on the bunk. "You guess?"

"I haven't seen him in a while."

"A falling out," Rozak said, shaking his head. "Happens. Father and son don't see eye to eye."

"You could say that."

"You want to tell me where he lives and maybe I can contact him?"

"Washington somewhere," Tennant said. How vague, he thought. But nothing specific came to mind, not even his father's face, which floated away from him even as he tried to recall the features. How long was it since he'd even thought about Rayland Tennant? "Look, I don't want him involved. I don't want you going near him."

Rozak sighed. "That's up to you, Harry. But I still need to know I can call on somebody to swear blind there's a halo round your head. A family priest? A doctor maybe?"

"I don't have anybody like that."

"Okay. You're not religious. Me, I'm a card-carrying atheist and I haven't been struck by lightning yet. But everybody's got a doctor somewhere, Harry. Nobody goes through life on an apple a day, for God's sake. Gimme the name of somebody who treated you for *something,* even if it was only tonsillitis."

Tennant closed his eyes, leaned back against the wall. He had from somewhere a memory of a caring man in a herringbone tweed suit, a physician with an easy manner, but if there was more to the recollection, it evaded him. "I guess I had one when I was a kid, but I don't remember his name." He looked at Rozak. "I don't see how a doctor who treated me for— Christ knows, a cut, a cold, whatever, more than thirty years ago—could say anything remotely relevant about my character."

Rozak patted Tennant's knee. "Hey. Cool down."

Tennant said, "I'm jumpy."

"Sure you are. You don't need to be."

"I don't want to go to jail."

Frank Rozak stood up; his skeleton creaked. He walked round the cell. His expression was pensive. He examined the graffiti in the manner of a man attempting to break an impossible code. He said, "I'll be straight with you, Harry. You can forget jail. That's the last place you're headed."

"What makes you so certain?"

Rozak smiled. He had a good smile, no fake dazzle, no used cars to hawk. "That's a toughie to answer, Harry. Just trust me on it. You'll walk. No two ways about it. Forget any charges. They'll be dropped and you can go back to your little house in the woods. Free as a hawk. All you gotta do is sit tight."

"I don't see how you can be so damn sure," Tennant said. "You must know something I don't."

Rozak shrugged. "I get paid to know things." His expression, suddenly sly, mystified Tennant. "Like I say, just sit tight."

"What if this character Flitt has different ideas?" Tennant asked. "What if he decides to throw the book at me?"

"In order to throw the book, my friend, first he's got to find it."

"Meaning what?"

Frank Rozak winked. "Get some rest, Harry."

"Wait," Tennant said. He got up.

But Rozak was already stepping out of the cell. The door was shut behind him. Tennant heard a key turn in the lock. He returned to the bunk, sat down, pondered Rozak's statement. Okay. Okay. What was he—some flashy hotshot lawyer who knew how to drive a tractor-trailer through loopholes in the law? Or was he just doing his lawyerly thing, showering a client with optimism, a bit of positive reinforcement in the dead of night?

Puzzled, Tennant listened to the silence of the cell. It occurred to him that he should have asked Rozak to find out about the condition of the Dane. Now it would have to wait.

Tennant was taken before Judge Stakowski at 10:00 A.M. Frank Rozak was not in court. Tennant sat alone at the defendant's table and wondered what had delayed the attorney. The courtroom was dark, old-fashioned, empty save for a couple of uniformed cops, a court reporter, two or three spectators, and a man in a cheap suit, who stood at the prosecutor's table.

Stakowski turned out to be a midget whose black robes engulfed him. As he climbed to his judicial bench he gave the impression of something inky and formless rising, as if the garment contained nothing but playful currents of air or balloons. Only when he was seated, seemingly on a column of cushions for height, did Stakowski's face emerge from the robe. He had solemn eyes. He looked about the court in the fashion of a minister surveying his church. Had the pews been waxed? Were the stained-glass windows clean? Was this a fit space in which to play the game of law? Then let us pray. Satisfied in a gloomy kind of way, he directed that proceedings for the day begin. His voice was surprisingly deep, a big man's voice.

"Who is representing Mr. Tennant?" he asked.

Tennant stood up. "My lawyer hasn't arrived yet."

The judge frowned. "And who exactly is your lawyer, Mr. Tennant?"

"Frank Rozak."

"Rozak?" the judge asked. He looked at the prosecutor. "Is Frank Rozak known to you, Mr. Kant?"

Kant shook his head. "No, Your Honor."

The judge turned his attention to Tennant. "In what circumstances did you appoint this man?"

"He came to my cell earlier this morning."

"And he offered to take your case?"

"He did."

The judge was silent for a time. "Is he a local man? Somebody from another town? An import?"

Tennant, who kept glancing at the door, said, "He told me he lives here."

"Peculiar," said the judge. "I know every lawyer in this town, Mr. Tennant, and I've never heard of one called Rozak."

Tennant thought: They'll clear this up in a moment. They'll see a mistake has been made. Why wasn't Rozak breezing into court right now, apologizing for being late? Did I imagine the man? No, Rozak had been real, all the way from the pain-swollen hands to the big open smile to the supreme air of confidence.

"Is it possible you got the name wrong?" the judge asked.

"It's possible, I guess."

The judge looked at his watch, tapped his fingers. "Did he give you a card? A phone number?"

Tennant shook his head. "He said he was called Frank Rozak. I didn't ask for ID, he never offered any."

Stakowski spoke quietly to one of the uniformed cops. Tennant couldn't hear what was being said. The judge, dismissing the cop, stared curiously at Tennant.

"It seems there's no record of anyone visiting you in your cell, Mr. Tennant. A visitor would have been logged. There's no such entry."

In a dry voice, Tennant said, "Obviously there's been some kind of . . . oversight."

"Or some kind of mischief," said the judge.

"Mischief?"

Stakowski ignored Tennant's question. "In the circumstances, which I find somewhat odd, the court will appoint an attorney on your behalf. At least until your Mr. Rozak decides to show himself."

Bewildered, panicked, Tennant heard himself try to explain that Rozak was simply delayed, he'd turn up any moment, it was just a matter of time, but the legal proceedings, like a circus performed solely for the benefit of the clowns and acrobats themselves, went on as if he'd ceased to exist. A small bald man in a brown suit, a certain Harcourt McKay, was produced from among the spectators and appointed Tennant's attorney of record. Much conferring went on around the judge's bench between McKay, Kant, and Stakowski, three men who whispered in the manner of conspirators. Tennant, deflated, disappointed, puzzled, sat down. Rozak had vanished. But the show had to go on.

As if he were listening to words being ferried toward him by a frail breeze, Tennant heard bail being discussed. Figures were bandied around. He had the impression he was, in some kind of auction room. A hammer would come down when agreement was reached. The house and land were acceptable collateral for bail, although Kant, plagued by the peculiar syntax of a man who can't see the end of any sentence he begins, grumbled about the accused's reliability. Mumble mumble. Drugs. Mutter mutter. Serious business. McKay, who had a pompous delivery, claimed he needed time to study his client's case and the nature of the charges.

Judge Stakowski, seemingly weary of a business that had upset the smooth running of his court, and unwilling to perplex himself further over the mystery of Frank Rozak, set trial for a date six weeks hence. Tennant was enjoined to remain at his present place of residence and appear on the appointed day and time. In the meanwhile he was not permitted to leave the state, and if he intended to travel beyond the immediate vicinity, the court had to be notified. That was the end of the thing.

Some papers were signed and Harcourt McKay, whose hands were sweaty little plump paws, led Tennant out of the courthouse.

Tennant blinked in the hard light of the morning. He looked along a stretch of Bridge Street. Bleak downtown Oswego was not his place of choice. Nearby was the sound of the Oswego River, which poured vigorously into Lake Ontario. The smell of freshly fried donuts drifted in the air.

"So who the hell is Rozak?" Tennant asked.

Harcourt McKay, on whose upper lip lay a band of sweat, shrugged. "Maybe some joker. You get guys—clerks, shoe salesmen, nobodies—pretending they're something else. Lawyers. Doctors. Gives them the old ego boost, I guess."

"Terrific joke," Tennant remarked. "He sounded like he knew what he was talking about. He mentioned Kant. He knew the name of the county attorney, Flitt. He was pretty damn convincing."

Harcourt McKay had a strange mannerism, drawing his neck down deep into his shoulders. "I'm no psychologist, Harry. Who knows what gives some guys a kick, huh? He imagines he's a lawyer, so he sounds like one. I was you, I'd write this Rozak off as a basic loon and concentrate on the biz at hand."

"Yeah," Tennant said. The biz at hand. The prospect of jail. But he couldn't get Rozak out of his mind. He could see the maroon painkiller go from hand to mouth, he could still hear the voice. *Everybody's got a doctor somewhere, Harry.* So what was Rozak's game? A loose nut at a loose end, nothing better to do than make believe he was a lawyer? But the guy had had a certain authority about him, a sincerity that suggested he was more than a mere imposter. And his confidence about the outcome of Harry's case had been absolute. Way too good, Tennant thought, to be true. He was depressed.

Maybe McKay was right. The world was filled with oddballs. And Rozak was one of them—what else?

McKay said, "We've got a bunch of work to get through, Harry. My diary's stuffed for the day, so we'll talk tomorrow.

My office at noon. You want me to drive you home?"

He turned down McKay's offer. He thought he could thumb a ride back to Sterling. Besides, he had an urge to walk for a time, to clear the jail out of his head. He wanted to think.

McKay handed him a business card. "Tomorrow noon. See you then."

"One thing. I don't want to do hard time," Tennant said.

McKay scrunched his neck down. "Who said anything about time?" He smiled—a quick flap of lips—and walked to his car, a wine-colored Buick rusted by the severity of Oswego's winters.

Tennant watched him drive away, then moved along Bridge Street in the direction of the state university campus, a scattering of windblown buildings on the shore of the lake. He figured his chances of a ride were better where there were students. He walked past stores, bars: the Cameo Café, Gentile's Cameras, Byrne's Dairy. In the distance were the monstrous stacks and electric wires of the power plant that dominated this small city.

The morning was already humid and uncomfortable. When he reached a bar called The Woodshed, he was picked up by a dirt farmer in an old Dodge flatbed, who dropped him about two miles from home. Tennant, fretting again over his dog, hurried along the edge of the blacktop.

He'd gone about a mile when a red Cadillac, brilliant as a wax apple, pulled up alongside him. The girl behind the wheel lowered her window. "Can you help me? I'm looking for somebody called Harry Tennant."

2 Tennant had lived for nine years in a quiet green world, a limited universe that made no demands other than the need to harvest his crop. He had his small white frame house and the secrecy of the trees and a mailbox at the end of a dirt road. He rarely received mail except for discount coupons and items addressed to Occupant. He had no phone, and his electricity came from a generator; few bills arrived for him. When he wanted groceries, he drove his pickup truck past barns and onion fields to the township of Sterling in Cayuga County. He didn't know the owner of the grocery store, nor did the owner know him. He didn't even know the name of his nearest neighbor. An isolated life, but a regulated one—until the bust.

Until the appearance of the girl, a stranger in a Cadillac convertible.

She was small, thin, her black hair cut short to her scalp and parted boyishly to the side. She wore black jeans and a loose-fitting sweater, careless and casual, unaffected. A single earring, a silver hoop, hung from her left ear. But these details were extraneous, impressions Tennant barely gathered, because what captivated him was that aspect of her face that surely struck a response in everyone who saw her: She had the marvelous eyes of a torch singer. Large, cryptic, sad, as if they'd been witness to heartbreaks and atrocities and might never again see anything worth a damn in the human condition.

"Why do you need to see Harry Tennant?" he asked.

"I'd like to talk to him."

"About what?"

The girl smiled. "You his social secretary?"

She opened the car door. Tennant saw she wore scuffed tennis shoes. She tilted her head to the side and looked at him frankly. "Or are you Tennant?"

"I'm Tennant."

"You don't look much like your photograph. A little maybe. But not a lot."

"Photograph?"

"Look. Are you in a hurry or have you got time to talk?"

Tennant's mind still echoed with the word *photograph*. When did he last have a picture taken? He couldn't imagine what she might be referring to. For a moment it occurred to him that she could be an agent of the law, an official of some sort following up on the bust, somebody with questions to ask.

"What's on your mind?" he asked.

The girl didn't answer directly. "Is your place nearby? I need a drink. This humidity's a killer."

Tennant pointed. "About a mile up the road."

"Get in. I'll drive you."

He opened the passenger door. He wondered why he was obeying her so readily. Surprised, he thought. Too perplexed to refuse her. It had been a morning of perplexities.

As he sat down, he asked about the photograph.

"Here." She dug inside a large lizardskin purse that lay on the seat. She produced a scrap of yellowed newspaper.

He looked at it with a lack of concern. A blurred newspaper photograph of five young people, taken—if the bell-bottom pants and headbands and hairstyles were any guide—sometime in the late sixties. He had an odd jangling sensation in his mind, a buzzer sounding in a darkened recess, but then it passed. He wasn't in any mood for strangers who came bearing ancient bits of paper. The other pressures upon him, the law, the disappearing Rozak, the prospect of jail—which, with Rozak's vanishing act, had come to seem tangible—made him more than impatient. The notion of imprisonment tended to make everything else insignificant by comparison.

"Well?" the girl asked.

"Well what?"

"You just dismiss it?"

"You show me some old picture. What am I supposed to say?"

"You can't be serious. Look again."

He sighed and did what she asked, studying the photograph more carefully. His eyesight had lately begun to diminish, and he hadn't bothered to get glasses because it involved too much; when he examined the picture a second time, he had a nervous sense of looking into a distorted glass in which lay a puzzling image from some other reality.

"What's wrong?" she asked. "You look like you don't remember it."

"I remember," he said.

The lie came to him before he had time to think about what he was saying. He couldn't take his eyes from the picture. He might have been looking at a counterfeit whose validity he desperately wanted to believe. The hand that held the paper wouldn't be still. Something weird. He was gazing at an unmistakable image of himself from more than twenty years ago, but there was a void between Harry Tennant and the photograph that had nothing to do with the passage of time. He had a feeling of displacement, a sensation a man might have in the middle of an earth tremor. Fault lines, he thought. Cracks in my personal landscape. Why the hell couldn't he remember the picture? What was wrong with him?

"Well?" the girl asked.

"Well what? It's just some old photograph," he said defensively. "I don't see anything especially interesting about it."

"It's more than just some old photograph."

"Is it?" He stared out at fields that were flat and colorless in the midday light. Two mournful brown mares in a fenced meadow regarded him without much interest. He let the paper flutter from his hand to the seat as the big car turned past the mailbox on to the narrow dirt road.

The girl braked when the house came into view. "We need to talk about this." She picked up the clipping and held it toward Tennant.

"Some other time."

He got out of the car. He was reluctant to enter the white frame structure from which ancient paint peeled like sunburnt skin. It seemed smaller than it had yesterday, and shabbier, a crabbed little dwelling. The windows were without reflection, like rectangles of dank water. The porch was in shadow and lifeless.

No Isadora stood there, no great welcoming whip of a tail lashing the air.

Crows cawed and a buzzard flapped with sleek purpose in the sky. There was all the noisy serenity you find in thick wooded areas. Crickets, the busy fretting of blue jays—a harmony of sorts, but misleading now. The woods looked gaunt, stripped of their secrecy; a process of defoliation might have gone on in the hours of darkness—the trees uprooted, then transplanted in unfamiliar configurations. Tennant, who'd been able to find his way in these woods blindfolded, realized he no longer belonged in this place. It wasn't home. Perhaps it had never been. Perhaps he'd spent the last nine years lying to himself.

He considered calling the dog, but if she was awake, she'd already be rushing happily down the steps of the porch, driven by the frantic energy of her love for him. He felt an exhausting wave of despondency. He took a few hesitant steps toward the house, conscious of the girl some paces back. What did she want anyway? What possible importance did she attach to an ancient photograph? He had more on his mind than a picture he couldn't remember.

Rubbing his palms apprehensively on his jeans, he climbed

up on the porch. He suddenly knew there would be grief. He knew you could never be prepared for it. What was a dog anyhow? You could always buy another one, right? In the great scheme of things a pet was expendable. You replaced an animal with a snap of your fingers: just like that.

He pushed the screen door aside.

What struck him immediately in the gloomy interior was how badly the place had been trashed. The cops had gone through it like a hurricane. They'd pulled drawers from cabinets and dumped the contents on the floor. A sofa was overturned and slashed, disgorging the stuffing. Pictures, cheap little Victorian things he'd picked up at auctions, had been yanked from the walls. Broken glass lay across everything as though it were a form of congealed rain. For some reason a wall had been punched out and the slats of frail old lathework made visible.

He moved across the floor. The guitar he'd tried for years to learn stood in a corner, neck snapped. The books he'd spent a long time over—books that at first had intrigued, then finally failed him—were scattered here and there, brutalized. Mystical works mainly—Gurdjieff, Ouspensky, Huxley. Explorers of hallucination, voyagers in misty perceptions, dabblers in the unsayable. What had he ever hoped to discover in those voices— a system by which to live? All he'd found were puzzles, spiritual acrostics, mind-trips—his hobbies in isolation.

None of these games mattered now.

Worse than fruitless mysticism, than a broken musical instrument, worse: The dog lay at the foot of the stairs where he'd last seen her. She was still and cold, large in death because the process had not had time to diminish her. He knelt beside the animal and placed a hand upon the big skull. It amazed him that life could leave any creature so vital as Isadora. His sorrow was a sudden winter in his heart—icy, dark, merciless. When he'd bought Isadora as a pup, she'd been an animal of great joyful clumsiness, anxious to please, slow to learn. What he remembered were the enormous paws and the floppiness of the body. She loved to walk with him in the woods. He'd fallen into the habit of conversing with her about the composition of the soil, the state of his plants, the head-clearing whiff of the buds. Like many people who have only animals as companions, he believed she listened and in her own way understood.

"Jesus Christ, Harry. What the hell has happened here?"

Harry. An easy familiarity. He hadn't heard the girl enter the house. Now, as she saw the dog for the first time, she gasped and said, "Oh God." She placed a hand on his shoulder while he crouched over the animal. He was grateful for the touch, the sympathy. How long since anyone had shown him kindness?

"Who did this? Who did all this, Harry?"

"We call it law and order in this country," he answered. There was a break in his voice.

He stood up. He thought: I'll bury the dog among the trees. Yes. His eyes were wet, and he drew the cuff of his shirt across them. He walked past the girl and stepped into the kitchen, where he took a bottle of Jack Daniel's from a cupboard. A long hit.

Canisters of flour and sugar and coffee had been dumped on the floor. Cabinets lay open, assorted items of china upturned, broken cups, saucers. The kitchen window was cracked. Foodstuffs had been dragged out of the refrigerator. A jar of honey spilled on the floor had already drawn a congregation of ants.

The girl entered the kitchen. "I'm sorry," she said. "For what it's worth I'm really sorry, Harry."

The Jack Daniel's made Tennant's chest warm. He drank again. The girl stood with her hip against the table. In her black sweater and black jeans, she might have been fading away into the shadows around her. Her pale, expressionless face belonged exactly in this dead house. Even the solitary earring had shed luster.

"They trashed the place," he said. "Okay. That's bad enough but it's only stuff. Things. You can always replace things. But the dog, the poor fucking dog . . ."

The girl touched his shoulder again. "I know."

"They could have gutted the goddamn place without harming the goddamn dog."

"The pigs aren't renowned for their delicate sensitivities, Harry. They're licensed for brutality. Nothing gets in their way."

Tennant wanted to roar. To explode. He experienced an impossible clot of sensations and urges, frustrations that couldn't be dissolved in one swift gesture. He thought about getting the gun he kept in the attic—if the cops hadn't found the weapon—and shooting something, anything. It was an old Taurus revolver he'd fired maybe a half-dozen times at stationary targets in the woods—soda cans, rotted tree trunks. He had no affinity with the weapon, which had come from Bobby Delacroix. "You never know when you might need a piece, Harry," Bobby had said in his conspiratorial way, his hand fingering the sterling silver death's-head he wore round his neck. Bobby, who purchased Tennant's crop every year, was all flash and secrecy and hidden weapons. Guns made him complete. But the Taurus was a needless gift so far as Tennant was concerned. Unlike big-time growers in California and Oregon, who protected massive acreages with machine guns and land mines, Tennant had nothing in these woods worth killing for. He harvested a small crop that brought him more than enough for his needs.

Death had no role in his size of business.

Now he sat here in this broken house with a dead dog and a girl he didn't know. He set the Jack Daniel's on the table. He was dizzy and it was only midday, but he felt time had slowed. He lit a cigarette and coughed. He needed to be sober, clearheaded enough to make decisions. What next? How to act? He couldn't just sit here and get wasted. No, he had to move, get his blood going. He had to bury the dog. That was the first thing, the most difficult.

He went back to the foot of the stairs. The girl followed him. She picked up a length of thick curtain the cops had hauled from a window, and she laid it across Isadora in a gentle manner. Tennant studied the dog a moment, then walked outside, found the wheelbarrow, and dragged it ponderously up the steps to the porch. Then he entered the wretched house again.

The girl said, "Let me help you, Harry."

He was dizzy again. He hated the sensation of drinking on an empty stomach. The day was rushing away from him like a train he'd missed. "I appreciate the offer, but there's not much you can do."

He stooped, caught the dog by her paws, and dragged her considerable weight halfway across the floor. He tried to imagine her as refuse to be hauled out, a piece of furniture beyond repair. There was no other way he could get through this. This struggle. This misery. His eyes were wet again. Without asking, the girl reached down and slid her arms under the animal's body and, with an enormous effort, helped Tennant raise Isadora from the floor. Tennant kicked the front door open. With the girl's help he managed, somewhat clumsily, to slide the animal into the wheelbarrow.

The curtain that covered Isadora slid away, snagged on a door hinge.

Tennant found himself staring at the Dane's head. He experienced a moment of slippage. All his perceptions were scattered like random atoms. The smell of fur struck him, a deep musk reminiscent of damp places and wet black-brown soil. He walked to the end of the porch, where he stuck his finger into his throat and tried to throw up. Nothing came except some sticky fluid, but his head cleared. When he turned around, the girl was covering the dog again with the drape.

"Are you okay?" Her voice was very quiet, the kind reserved for terminal wards.

"I'm fine. I'm sorry about that." He gestured loosely toward the end of the porch, embarrassed.

"It happens. It's nothing to be sorry about." The girl leaned against the porch rail and stared out into the trees. "Maybe you want to bury your dog alone, Harry. If you need my help, fine."

Tennant said, "I want to get the thing done. That's all."

He lowered the wheelbarrow down the porch steps in a series of awkward clunking maneuvers. Then he stopped. The wheel was sinking into the earth. It would take all his strength to get to the woods. He fetched a spade propped against the side of the house, then laid it across the curtain. He was suddenly conscious of textures—the rusted metal of the spade, the rose-colored fabric of the curtain, the tan fur of the dog's hind legs. The details startled him in the dull light.

The girl walked down from the porch. "I'll come with you."

"Sure," he said. He didn't like to admit it to himself; he wanted company, her company.

The grave he dug for Isadora was four feet deep in a place near the ruins of his tall plants, which had been unearthed and hauled away by the cops, leaving broken stalks and fibrous pieces of root and a scattering of leaves. Appropriate—bury the dead in a dead place. When the hole had been dug, the girl helped him lower Isadora into the ground. A paralysis struck him; he couldn't bring himself to replace the earth. He sat hunched on the edge of the grave. How undemanding it would be to sit here in a zone of stillness and wait until Rozak came to take him to trial.

The girl took the spade and worked silently at filling the grave. Tennant watched her, wondering at her energy.

"I don't know your name," he said.

"Alison Seagrove."

"Thanks . . ."

"For what?"

Tennant shrugged. Alison Seagrove leveled the earth with the head of the spade, then placed the implement in the barrow. She was breathing heavily.

"They busted you for your plants," she said. She'd seen the ruin of his crop.

Tennant nodded. He stood up because he didn't want to linger in these forlorn woods. He walked away from the grave, beset by the intuition that he was turning his back on more than some broken stalks and an abandoned wheelbarrow and a dead dog. The girl fell into step beside him.

"You have to hand it to the cops, Harry. They've got their priorities in the right place. Rapists go free and guns fall into the hands of schoolkids—but when it comes to the demon reefer, hell, they're right on the ball."

Tennant forced a small smile. He longed for lightheartedness, a charge of flippancy, an infusion, say, of helium to his brain.

As he emerged from the trees, he heard a car on the dirt road. A gray Ford, solid and bland, came into view. The driver, a bulky man unknown to Tennant, got out. He wore a navy suit and an unbuttoned fawn raincoat whose belt hung loose. Tennant and the girl walked toward the stranger, who had parked halfway between the woods and the house, and now stood with his feet spread belligerently apart and his hands on his hips.

3 The visitor introduced himself as Ralph Flitt, county attorney. He was pleased with his title. A smile, a firm handshake; Flitt bore the stamp of one who'd been to more than a few management courses. He pushed himself at people, thrusting, hand forward, unlikely smile fixed, eyes made electric by sheer effort. He had a certain raw stage presence. Tennant half expected him to break into song. Flitt's white skin, though, was unhealthy and belied the robust surface.

"I tried to be in court for your arraignment, Harry," he said. "Held up. Story of my life. Busy as all hell."

Tennant stepped back. Flitt's breath was rancid; sour milk, diapers, crypts.

Flitt glanced at Alison Seagrove but didn't ask for her name. He shifted his position and gazed toward the woods. "Heard all about your bogus lawyer, though. Funny kinda business, guy turning up claiming to be an attorney. Weird."

Flitt looked back at Tennant and smiled. "It's a good feeling to be free, huh? Makes you want to go down on one knee and praise the system, Harry. America the bounteous. Turn criminals free. Let dope dealers stroll the streets. Give a pusher an even break. Yessir. Something to be said for that. In Turkey, now, you'd be hanging by your heels. In Saudi Arabia you'd have your hands cut off. Perchance, Christ, your balls. Good country this is. So why the hell do people who live in it abuse it, Harry? Breaks my heart. I think, ingrates, ingrates."

This spray of words was delivered rapidly. Each little expulsion of breath sent a putrid pocket of air toward Tennant.

"Got an answer for me?" Flitt asked.

Tennant said, "I don't think I've abused anything."

"No?"

"You found some marijuana growing on my property. Prove it was mine."

"Hi-diddle-dee. I didn't graduate law school this morning. The dew ain't dripping from my ears. I know you. I know your type. You broke the law, mister."

"Even if I did, it's a stupid law. Grass should be legal. It's like the Dark Ages." This was more than Tennant wanted to say, but Flitt provoked him.

"Dark Ages! No way! You gotta love America, Harry! How can you bad-mouth a country where even criminals can freely criticize the laws of the land? What a deal we got here. Smell that air. Whooo-eee. That's liberty. You think air smells like that in Iran or Turkey?"

"It's goddamn hard to love a country where the cops trash my house and kill my dog."

"Line of duty."

Alison, who had looked uneasy and impatient, said, "Line of duty, my ass. You want to look inside this man's house? You want to see the dog? Then maybe you can define duty for us."

"I don't know your name, missy, or what you're up to here. But you're walking straight into a heap of trouble by hanging around, lemme tell you."

"I'll take my chances, Mr. Flitt."

Flitt turned his attention back to Tennant. "What am I doing standing here listening to an angry doper and his chick? Guys like you. Sewage. I don't need this."

"Sewage," Tennant said, and laughed.

Flitt leaned toward him and gripped his shoulder. "Laugh, Harry. Enjoy. Here's the kicker. Here's the punch line. You're going to jail. You know that, don't you? You're clear about that, I hope."

"That's un-American of you, Flitt. Sentence a man before trial?" Alison said.

Flitt dropped his hand from Tennant's shoulder. He glared at the girl. "I'm just stating a fact, missy. A trial's for press and public. PR. Lookee here, taxpayers of the county, your system's at work! Smile and be joyful, drones. Harry better face it. He's going down. Two years minimum."

The certainty in Flitt's voice filled Tennant with disbelief. How it contrasted with the forceful optimism of the phantom Rozak. "I imagine my lawyer has other ideas," he said.

"Sure. Sure he has. McKay's full of them. Gets well paid for them too. Just don't kid yourself. Harcourt's a good man. But when it comes right down to the buzzer, he knows you're going away and he can't do a goddamn thing about it."

"I'd like his opinion on that."

"He's your lawyer. Go talk to him. He's all ears and his meter's running. He'll be happy to chat until hell freezes. But the outcome's the same no matter how you slice it. You're about to become a guest of the great Empire State, where accommodation is free but disagreeably unwholesome. Still feel like laughing?"

"Why don't you get the hell off my property? Next time reach me through my attorney." Tennant turned and started to walk away.

"Wait now, Harry. Don't go slamming doors. Don't go off in a funk. I think we've got some room for negotiation." Flitt suppressed a belch. His stomach rumbled in a remarkable manner, the sound of a door creaking on stiff hinges.

Tennant stood still. "Negotiation? What are you talking about?"

Flitt walked toward him. "I take back that sewage remark, Harry. I have this mean ulcer and it bites like a crab, and I get cranky, and sometimes I say things I don't mean. You're probably an okay guy. Misguided, sure. But you don't strike me as your common or garden doper. You're smarter than that."

"What are you trying to say?" Tennant stared at the man, noticing how the whites of his eyes were tainted a little by yellow.

Flitt shoved his hands in his coat pockets. "Harry, you were growing maybe fifteen kilos here on your property."

"Something you still have to prove."

Flitt ignored this. "Fifteen keys is a goodly amount. But it's not fifty, and it's not a hundred. So I draw this conclusion— you're small-time. On that account, maybe, just maybe, a guy like you deserves a second chance. Probation. Some drug counseling thrown in. A little community work. Raking lawns for people in wheelchairs. Working the Salvation Army thrift store. Something decent."

Tennant knew. He knew where this was going now.

Flitt sighed, harassed by his ulcer and the burdens of office; a pity-me sound. "Look. It would save me the trouble of a trial and you the certainty of jail, if you could see your way to *assisting* me, Harry."

"You want names, don't you?" Tennant said.

"Quick thinking, Harry. Yeah, I want names. I want to know who takes the dope off your hands. I want to know the moneyman. The distributor. Bottom line, I don't want you. You're a tadpole. You're an amoeba. You're a flyspeck, sweetheart."

"I can't help you."

Flitt shrugged, turning his face back to the house. "Lemme tell you what happens when you're found guilty at your trial. Not only do you go to the slammer for a while, which is tough, but you also lose this property." The county attorney swept his arm greedily in an arc. "All this green and pleasant land, Harry. The federal government confiscates it on account of how it was used for profiteering in the drug market and probably even purchased with illicit income—which leaves you, Jack, with zippety-do-da. Bite on that one. Hurts, huh?"

Tennant looked at the house. He felt disconnected from the property anyway, but the idea of the feds taking it away galled him. What was going on in the land of the free? Men in uniforms, officers, constables, came and punched holes in your walls and hacked your possessions into tiny pieces and walked away unaccountable. He experienced an oppressive cloud in his head. What had Flitt said? Line of duty? Duty was a tarnished word explaining nothing. A buzzword.

"The land's nice, Flitt, but the house needs work after last night's wrecking crew. Good starter home for a young couple maybe. Do-it-yourselfers." Tennant tried to sound unconcerned, even cheerful.

"You may jest," Flitt remarked. "But unless you negotiate with me, my hearty, you go in the toilet. Just say the magic password and pleasant stuff starts to happen. Lo! The sun shines on Harry."

"It's shit," Alison remarked. "If that's the system, it's complete shit."

Flitt belched brightly. "Best shit in the world though."

Flitt went back to his car and waved cheerfully as he drove off. Tennant looked at the girl, whose expression was one of anger.

"I can't stand guys like Flitt. They come off as half-assed gods. They've got their own little patches of America and they think they can do anything they like with them and the rest of us have got to lie down and roll over. You better call your lawyer, Harry."

Tennant, who found himself admiring the flame in this slight girl, said, "Yeah, I better."

He walked to his truck.

"You don't have a phone here, do you?"

"Never needed one. Anyway, it's only a few miles."

"Let me drive. My gas guzzler's probably faster than your pickup. The sooner you make this call the better."

Tennant was agreeable, ready to be activated by somebody else. He didn't feel much like driving right then. He was lacking a certain coordination; he wanted to be a passenger, to sit with his eyes shut and be taken away.

"What was that stuff Flitt mentioned about a bogus lawyer?" she asked.

Tennant told her about Rozak, about the man's confidence. It was a puzzle already diminishing in his mind, obscured by other matters.

"If he wasn't a real lawyer, how did he get access to you? And how come there's no record of his visit?"

"I guess he slipped past the front desk. Maybe the night cop was snoozing. I don't know. He sounded like he knew what he was talking about. He'd seen the search warrant. He said."

"It was probably some kind of dirty trick. He could have been one of Flitt's people sent in to probe a little. Do some exploratory work. See how you were reacting. See if you were in the mood to cop a guilty plea. I wouldn't put that kind of thing past Flitt. The blow below the belt."

"Yeah, but he was adamant I wasn't going to jail."

"I think they call that lulling you into a false sense of security, Harry. Like softening you up. Getting you to lower your guard. Give you something with one hand, whip it away with the other. Suddenly, you don't know where you stand. You're confused. It's an old trick, but it's still a nasty one."

"Could be." Tennant stepped inside the Cadillac and gave the girl directions. She drove, in the kind of silence that suggests controlled outrage, two miles down the highway to a country store that smelled of New York cheddar, cider, cinnamon. From the call box outside the shop Tennant dialed McKay's number. The attorney answered on the first ring.

"I just had a visit from Flitt," Tennant said. "He wants names. If I don't talk, I'm going to jail. So he says."

McKay was quiet in a way that was troublesome. Tennant could hear in the silence an echo of a cell door closing. He could see himself trapped between four miserable walls.

"What do you say to that, Harcourt?"

"I'll defend you, Harry. I told you."

"Flitt says you can defend until you're blue in the face. If I don't speak, I'm going down. How much of what he says is bullshit?"

"Harry, the quid quo pro would guarantee you your freedom. You'd get a sizable fine, probation maybe two years. You don't give him names, he'll throw everything he's got at you. Since he and Stakowski are like Mutt and Jeff, I'd be a fool to predict the outcome. We're talking about cultivation of a controlled substance, a toughie. The only promise I can give you is I'll defend you to the best of my ability."

"How good are you, Harcourt? What's your track record against Flitt? What's the bottom line?"

"Look. No two cases are alike. Yours is different from any other—"

"Just give me the scoreline."

McKay laughed quietly. "It doesn't work that way."

"Have you ever won against him?"

"Sure."

"And you've lost too."

"Like they say, the ball bounces back and forth."

"So give me a tally."

McKay said, "Off the cuff, I don't know. Maybe we're even over the years."

"Then again maybe he's slightly ahead."

"It's not a contest. I don't keep track."

"I've got a fifty-fifty chance at best? Would you say that?"

"Yeah. Well. In there at least."

"I don't like the odds."

"Nobody in this town will give you better, Harry."

"I don't like the idea of jail."

"Jail, jail. Look on the bright side."

"Is there one?"

Tennant put the telephone down. His quarter came spitting back out at him, rolling over his foot. A lucky omen, he thought. He needed some luck. If he couldn't get any, he'd make his own.

He walked back to the Cadillac. Alison Seagrove was

drumming her fingertips on the steering wheel. Tennant thought: This is getting to her. My whole situation *means* something to her. He had always regarded his world as one of comforting self-sufficiency. Now something had altered, but there was no way of knowing the extent of the change.

"Well?" she asked.

"Put it this way. I'm not encouraged."

4 He took a beer from the refrigerator. His hands and fingernails were filthy from digging in damp earth and his shoulder muscles locked solid. He sat at the table, massaging his right shoulder. He drained the beer, set it down, and looked at Alison Seagrove's face. She had an irregular loveliness, all the more delightful because it wasn't bland in an age of the homogenized bimbo. If you weren't suckered in by the enchanting darkness of the eyes, you noticed the small mouth and the crooked tooth and the slight asymmetry of the nose; but the high cheekbones quickly drew you upward from these minor imperfections and into the eyes, where you were pleasantly lost. He wondered how many people had gone astray there.

She moved around the kitchen, shaking her head at the wreckage of the place. She created unfamiliar echoes in a house whose rooms hadn't reverberated with any human noises except his own for years—unless you counted the cops. But he didn't want to think about the gendarmerie for a moment. The whole process of law burdened him, lay on him like an iron weight. It was an odd thing how the law could imprison you even before you'd been tried for any crime—but that was what

he felt: trapped, restricted, denied liberty. What was he supposed to do? Sit here and wait until Flitt slammed the cell door
in his face?

"I can't do it. I can't give them names," he said. "Even if I
could, I wouldn't. It's something you just don't do." He wondered if he was being honest. To spare himself jail time, would
he have named names had he been in the position to do so? He
didn't like to think so. There was an unspecified code between
outlaws like himself and Delacroix, and even if you'd never
seen the rules written down, you understood them anyway.
You said nothing, kept your mouth shut.

Alison picked up a broken cup and set it down on the sink
counter. "It's a slimy proposal. But then Flitt's a slimy guy.
And your lawyer doesn't sound much better. It happens in these
small towns, Harry. One attorney lives in another's pocket. They
lunch together. They play golf. They play bridge. Old pals.
The law's just another game for them. The client gets shafted."

Shafted, Tennant thought. He gazed around the kitchen,
remembering how tidy the room had been, towels folded neatly, canisters labeled Tea and Coffee and Sugar placed just so
on shelves. A fastidious bachelor's kitchen: He'd often been
struck by the possibility of becoming an old man cemented in
his ways, doctrinaire and mechanical, performing every function to an undemanding schedule. But that prospect, which
had been strangely comforting to him, was no longer an
option.

His eye picked out the dog bowl in the corner. It contained
the crusted remains of canned meat. A fly, disgustingly alive,
hovered over the relics.

"Consider your situation, Harry. Maybe McKay will come
through for you and you'll get probation. More likely he won't.
It's a gamble no matter how you slice it. Look, I really wish I
could help you in some way. I'm just not sure how. Can you
think of anyone else you could turn to for advice?"

He shook his head. Her question disturbed him. He was
reminded of Rozak's request for character witnesses. *Anyone
else?* "Not really."

"What about old friends? You must have them somewhere. What about school? College?"

He shut his eyes. He said nothing. Friends, he thought. Acquaintances. He was drawing one blank card after another. He remembered a few faces from high school, but they belonged in another time, strangers to him now. And he'd never gone to college. There was Delacroix, but he wasn't a friend. "I can't think of anybody."

"That's about the saddest thing I've ever heard." She sat down and took the newspaper photograph from the pocket of her jeans. She dropped it on the table in front of him. "Then who are these people? What role did *they* play in your life, Harry? Were they perfect strangers? Did you just happen to come together?"

The mysterious picture: Tennant glanced at it. He felt defensive all at once: Who was this little girl with her difficult questions? "What's your interest in this thing anyhow?"

"A story."

"You write."

"Yeah, I write," and she mentioned the name of a magazine only vaguely familiar to him. *A journalist, sweet Christ. Who else would penetrate his isolation like this?*

She opened the refrigerator and took out a can of beer. "You mind if I help myself?"

"Feel free."

She sipped the beer, then ran the back of one small hand across her lips. "When you looked at it before, I got the distinct impression you didn't remember it," she said. "Does San Francisco in 1968 jog your memory?"

He didn't speak. He looked out the window. Somebody turns up with an old photograph of you, and you don't recall it ever having been taken. You don't remember the people in the group, the day the picture was shot, the circumstances—everything gone. His head had begun to ache; his throat was parched. He found a fresh beer and popped it open and drank hastily.

"Harry," the girl said.

He looked directly at her. The lapse in his memory humiliated him.

"You really don't remember, do you?"

The girl touched the back of his hand in a sympathetic way, and he recalled how sweet she'd been when they'd dragged the dog out of the house, the way she'd helped. Death created tiny bonds. "How could you have forgotten?"

"I didn't *say* I'd forgotten." He picked up the flimsy piece of creased paper. "I'll look at it again."

The photograph depicts five young people. A girl, beautiful in a delicate, lacy way, dominates the center. Her long black hair hangs against her peasant blouse. She wears a big floppy hat and fancy hand-stitched moccasin boots. On her right, close to her, is a young man with a Mexican-style mustache and frizzy hair. The eyes are spirited, a bandit's face. On this young man's left stands a fat girl in a paisley shawl, big round granny glasses upon her eyes. Something about her suggests a healthy outdoor upbringing, clover meadows and milk pails. She looks as if she might never have heard of grass or acid, but her clothes betray that impression, and the small smile, when you study it, is more spaced-out than jolly. Beside her, big and bearded, dressed in Osh-Kosh B'Gosh dungarees and a plaid shirt, is a man with a congenial expression on his hairy face. Unflappable, good-hearted, that's the impression he gives. Tennant himself, in bell-bottom jeans, denim stitched with tiny zodiac conceits, is standing at the edge of the group, as if he were the photographer's afterthought, included only to balance the composition.

Five hippies—the word sounded odd to Tennant; an extinct species. Each face strikes something of the same attitude. The expressions are those of people who have sensed, like some spore borne on the wind, freedom. But there is also fragility if you look for it, a spidery crack in the Day-Glo-painted eggshell. Explorers in a dream, they look as if they've been given passports to a fabulous place where liberty was anything you wanted it to be.

Tennant looked away from the image. Rain had begun to

fall quietly in the woods. The sky turned dark. The beer in his mouth had a stale taste. How was it possible to look at a likeness of your younger self and fail to locate it in place and circumstance? Who were these strangers standing around him? And yet—didn't he also have a thin shiver going through him, something that was neither recognition nor familiarity, but spectral, indefinable? He was beset by a sense of loss he couldn't explain to himself.

"Admit it, Harry. You're baffled. Why?"

He shook his head, determined to cling to some little raft of obstinacy. It was only a matter of time and the memory would return and everything would be just fine, everything clear. But even as he looked at the five faces, they seemed to recede. He remembered San Francisco—how could he not?—in a series of cameos that were not always sharp. He remembered the drugs, the patchouli musk rising from the flesh of girls on warm afternoons, the street scene in the Haight-Ashbury, the music day and night, the bells and cymbals that rang with the consistency of a sound track. Faces came and went in these flickers, but none he could assign to this goddamn photograph. But why should he recall this one picture anyway, when for most of the time in San Francisco he'd been high, zonked, zoned, indifferent to his existence in the careless manner of the time? You lived to get stoned. You got stoned to live. It was wow time. Bring on the carnival. Uppers. Downers. Pot. Thai sticks. Cocaine. Acid. What was a mind if not for blowing? Hey-ho, those were the days. How could you recall every detail of those burnt-out times?

He said, "Okay. I guess it escapes me. There's something . . . slightly familiar about it, but I can't get a handle on it. Sorry."

"You can do better than that," she said. "Try. Try a little harder."

How could he try harder? He pushed the clipping across the table toward Alison. As he did so, he happened to glance at the lovely girl in the center of the photograph, and his head throbbed and he wondered if, in the neon clamor of his drug days, he'd been attracted to her, if he'd known her. The idea, the spark, slipped away. He'd remember anyone with those features, wouldn't he?

"Who took this shot?" he asked.

"You don't even remember that much? The photographer was called Sammy Obe."

"It doesn't ring a bell." He finished his beer. *Sammy Obe.* "What's the big deal about the whole thing anyway?"

"I'll run it past you. Maybe you'll understand why your failure of memory surprises me. The photograph was taken in June 1968. Chinatown, San Francisco, to be exact. It became one of those pictures that collect a certain amount of fame because it captured—I don't want to sound pompous—the *essence* of a place and time. The hippie culture. The *look.* Some pictures do that accidentally. Capa took a shot of a soldier dying in the Spanish Civil War, John Filo photographed a woman called Mary Vecchio kneeling over a student shot by the National Guard at Kent State—these things take on a certain spirit. They become icons."

The girl paused and gazed at Tennant as if she felt a profound pity for him.

"Obe's photograph was like that. It was reprinted scores of times around the world. You'll see it in histories of the sixties. It was even turned into a poster, but by that time the mood was beginning to change and the whole Haight thing was going down the tubes. The poster had a short shelf life, Harry. But for a moment that photograph was famous. And you say you don't remember it?"

Famous. Tennant, who found this hard to accept, walked to the window and looked out into the rain. Where was this girl leading? Didn't she understand he had more pressing things in his life than what was obviously a case of drug-induced amnesia? No, that didn't quite cut it: He was evading his own failure of memory. He suddenly wanted to be graceful and weightless, to float like a hawk through the rain, free.

Don't flee from stuff, boyo. You cope by standing still.

Boyo? Another upstart voice in his head, a bastard that

didn't belong in his mental apparatus. How did you get like this? Did the drugs really fuck you so royally?

"It's a blank," he said. "You've got to keep in mind the way things were back then. Too many acid trips. Sometimes you took trips so goddamn intense you never quite made it back from the stratosphere. You left parts of yourself in orbit. Some things have been deleted from my tapes, that's all. Black holes." As some people are said to feel the presence of an amputated limb, so Tennant imagined just then that his dog was brushing against his leg. A strange illusion.

Alison Seagrove picked up the clipping and held it in the palm of her hand. "They must be enormous black holes if you can't remember anybody in this picture."

"You weren't around in those days," he said. "A lot of bad acid hit the streets towards the end. Organized crime moved into the Haight. Those gangsters didn't give a shit what kids swallowed. People freaked out. I was unlucky enough to be one of them. I live with that. Some people live with a disability. I think of it that way." *If I think of it at all.*

"An incomplete life."

"I never really considered it like that."

"Exactly how *did* you consider it, Harry? Or did you just hibernate out here in the boondocks and grow your dope?"

Tennant ignored her question. He wasn't going to admit to the plodding, clockwork way he passed his time. Okay, so the failure of memory was disturbing, but he had an explanation for it, and if she didn't like it, that was her problem.

"I'm waiting for the rest of your story," he said.

She sighed, irked by his evasive manner. "It's simple really. I started out doing one of those fluff pieces—'Where Are They Now?' That kind of thing. It's filler, Harry. Faces from the past. How are they living these days. Blah blah blah. But when I started to dig, something happened. It began to get interesting." She laid the cutting in front of him. "Two of the kids in the picture seem to have vanished. And the other two are dead."

"Dead?" Tennant wondered why his heart was wired with

dread. If he couldn't recollect his companions in the picture, why should he be troubled by the knowledge that a pair of them had died? "Which two?"

She pointed to the photograph. "The kid with the Mexican mustache, Carlos Carlos, was killed in a motorcycle accident. December 1968."

Tennant looked at the boy's slightly wasted smile. *Carlos.* Did the name mean anything to him? It was hard to tell.

"Who else?" he asked. He couldn't swallow. The kitchen felt like a clammy box in which he was suspended. Alison Seagrove's index finger, in the manner of a pointer crossing a Ouija board, moved over the surface of the photograph for a second. "This one," she said, and she touched the fat girl with the granny glasses and the fringed paisley shawl. "Kat. She jumped from the Golden Gate Bridge, March 1969."

Tennant felt a curious relief that Alison Seagrove hadn't singled out the long-haired girl in the middle of the shot, although he wasn't sure why. Dread, relief—he was being dragged through some odd mixture of emotions.

"You said the other two have vanished."

"Gone. Disappeared."

"This girl in the middle . . . you haven't found any trace of her at all? Absolutely nothing?"

Alison Seagrove sat down at the kitchen table. She picked up the newspaper, and something in the way she touched it suggested an obsession she was beginning to resent. She'd been living with the story behind those five faces for some time now, and her quest was frustrating. She looked at Tennant with regret, as if she understood that by coming here she was disturbing ghosts that were not her own, but his, only his.

"Absolutely nothing," she said. "It's like Maggie Silver never existed."

5 He couldn't comprehend the relief he felt when Alison had pointed to the plump girl and not to the one called Maggie Silver. It was as if some kind of thread attached him to a person he must have once known—but that knowledge was so incomplete as to be worthless. Yet there was no denying the emotion, which must have been lying in wait somewhere in his brain—that place of absences and silences.

"There's some easy explanation for people vanishing," he said. He managed to sound eminently sensible. "They move and they don't always leave forwarding addresses. You're looking back a long way. The Haight was a transient society. Kids changed their names. They dropped acid and went off into psychedelic realms, and they came back with a new name, a whole new personality."

Tennant wasn't exaggerating. After a couple of monumental acid trips, scenic routes through light shows and into the vortices of the cosmos, who would want to be called Clyde Bullington or George Kryzaminski or some such thing? People became Sunshine Halo and Plenty O'Trips, outlandish names that now seemed ludicrous. He had the mildewed scent in his nostrils of an extinct generation.

"I managed to find you at least," Alison Seagrove said.

"Yeah, and I've been wondering how."

"Through your father. Indirectly."

Good old Rayland. He'd had no direct contact with his father for—how long? He couldn't be sure. Years.

"Indirectly?" he asked. "What does that mean?"

"I got to know a young lawyer in your father's firm," Alison said. "I understood from him that you and your father have been estranged for a long time."

Estranged. Tennant thought that a mild word. "We don't talk, if that's what you mean. We don't have contact. I don't want to see him. I don't even want to think about him."

"Am I allowed to ask why?"

Tennant was agitated. He knew he didn't have to answer this young woman's questions: All he had to do was close the door on her, treat her as if she were no more than an unwelcome purveyor of encyclopedias or somebody conducting some useless statistical survey. But he wanted to talk, as if to set free something trapped too long inside him. He walked around the room, his hands plunged in his pockets. He rattled loose change as he moved, a sound reminiscent of a light chain that echoed with every step he took.

"What can I tell you? We had a big-time disagreement. Call it a philosophical difference, if you fancy euphemism. Rayland defended a guy I considered indefensible. Worse than indefensible. A fucking monster."

"Did the monster have a name?"

A name, Tennant thought. He couldn't bring himself to utter it easily. Some sounds, innocuous in themselves, assumed pernicious meaning by connotation. He sat at the table. "Noel Harker. Colonel Noel Harker."

"Ah yes. The butcher," Alison Seagrove said.

"You got it. The butcher." Tennant was silent a moment. He might have been listening to the house as though it were a temperamental clock he expected at any second to tick. "Any guy who gives the order to massacre innocent Vietnamese women and kids isn't somebody you'd want to sit down with at

Sunday lunch, never mind defend in a court of law. Which is what Rayland did. And he did it goddamn well, if you can appreciate that kind of performance. Poor Colonel Harker. The heart bleeds. Rayland got him off on the grounds of diminished responsibility caused by 'battle fatigue.' The jury had seen photographs of babies burning, for Christ's sake. They'd seen pictures of bayonetted women lying in ditches. And Harker walks out free."

"That was—what?—1967," Alison said. "You haven't spoken to Rayland since?"

"Sure. Once maybe. Twice. I don't know. His defense humiliated me. I told him he was fucked up. He argued that the system gives any man the right to the best defense available. Christ, we fought bitterly. For the first time in my life I was ashamed of my own father. What was more agonizing was the way he began to appear on TV shows whenever there was any discussion about American brutality in Vietnam—voilà, there was Rayland on the box, defending the actions of men in war. He'd become an expert in the art of justifying atrocities. Jesus, he was smooth. He was good at it. By the time he finished you wanted to shake his hand and thank him for pointing out that sometimes brutality was more than justified, and God bless it."

Harry stood up, restless. Exhuming his relationship with Rayland was an exhausting business even now. It should have been a corpse, long interred, but it still came back to haunt him. "I didn't want to see him after all that. I wanted absolutely nothing to do with him. He was a dead man where I was concerned. I went off to San Francisco. I threw myself into a life-style that was directly the opposite of Rayland's. And that infuriated the hell out of him, which in turn delighted me. Sometimes . . ." He paused by the window and the girl looked at him.

"Sometimes what?"

"The thing is, he was terrific when I was a kid. My mother died when I was about eight, and Rayland—the only word I can find to describe him back then is devoted. He spent all his spare time with me. We went places together. Ball games. Movies. It was like he didn't want me out of his sight. He was considerate. Generous. You couldn't have asked for a better father. He could have shipped me off to some expensive school, but he didn't. He kept me at home, he made himself constantly available, no matter what his schedule was like. That's the Rayland I like to remember. The other Rayland's a guy I don't begin to know."

He stared out at the darkening woods. He had an image of his mother, the first in a long long time. Lily, who had died of kidney failure, had had an anarchist's attitude to the society in which her husband was obliged by business to move. Addicted to five o'clock martinis, she'd dissect Rayland's acquaintances, saying they were terrific arguments for the legalization of euthanasia. *Thieves and villains, I swear. Every man jack of them. You want to watch out for them, Harry. Power's all they think about.* Lily, with her wide lipsticked mouth and overrouged cheeks and fanciful hairstyles, an eccentric who made her foibles attractive.

Tennant looked at the young woman. "I'd say the final break with Rayland came about a year after the Harker trial. We met in San Francisco. I was stoned out of my gourd at the time, which didn't help the situation much. We were speaking like people from different planets. He mentioned he'd given up the day-to-day practice of law and turned his talents to something I found just as laudable as defending ghouls: high-powered lobbying on behalf of the goons who make arms. A whisper in the right congressional ear. A discreet cocktail with a senator in some quiet bar. You know how it works. Rayland's a persuasive man. And by the time he defended Harker, he'd made a bunch of new pals in the military, and no doubt they saw Rayland's potential. Want to bulldoze some useless new trillion-dollar high-speed tank through congressional appropriation committees? Rayland's your man. He's on intimate terms with all the best ears in town." Tennant was quiet a moment. "We had a real bad scene in the bar of the Mark Hopkins. There he was in his dark three-piece while I had on this leather

vest and faded jeans and my hair down to here—and I dumped
a drink on him and tossed peanuts into his face and he slapped
me. It might sound amusing now, but at the time it was god-
awful. Rayland isn't big on unseemly behavior in public
places."

"He was the warmonger and you were the hippie pacifist?"

"The way I see it, dope beats the hell out of war any old
day of the week," Tennant said.

There was a silence. Tennant wondered if, having told the
story of his relationship with Rayland, he'd actually unbur-
dened himself of anything. Probably not, otherwise he
wouldn't feel the way he did, weighed down, depressed.

"So you met a friendly lawyer in my father's firm and he
was kind enough to provide you with my address?" he asked.

"It took some small persuasion and a great deal of patience
on my part. But he told me eventually." She smiled then, perhaps a little slyly, a gesture that caused Tennant to wonder
about the nature of this intimacy. It must have been enough to
turn the lawyer's head around, because Rayland's private files
were sacrosanct, rumored to contain damning information
about prominent men.

"Funny," he said. "I had no idea Rayland knew where I
was living. That was naive of me, I guess. He always did have a
network of informants and private detectives. I can see how
he'd get some satisfaction knowing my address. He has this
dark side that enjoys information gathered in secrecy and
stored in locked cabinets. It gives him a jab of power."

Tennant, dismissing the memory of his father, discarding
the sense of betrayal Rayland inspired in him, stretched a hand
across the table and let it fall upon the newspaper clipping. In
the dimming light he could no longer make out the details of
the picture, and he felt indifferent to the faces now, as if the
falling darkness had stripped the images of any ability to surprise him. Even so, there was a charge in the air, a sense of
impending ambush, like a stillness trapped between canyon
walls. He had the instinct that something else was about to
happen.

Alison Seagrove picked up the picture and looked at it. "So you don't remember anything about this picture because you were too fucked-up on drugs and the whole San Francisco scene. Is that your story, Harry? A casualty of the times. One of the walking wounded. Maybe you blame your father for driving you off into an alternative life-style?" Was there sarcasm in her voice?

"Blame him? I might have gone to the Haight anyway with or without his contribution. How would I know? I can't go back and point to the exact spot in the crossroads and say why I took one particular direction instead of another. You can't always reconstruct things, for Christ's sake." He heard irritation in his voice; why did she have this knack for sliding under his skin?

"You're not exactly a whiz when it comes to reconstruction, are you, Harry? Maggie Silver, for example. You can't reconstruct a memory of her at all, can you?"

He shook his head. He wondered what constituted a recollection in any case. Did you require precise images? Or would a solitary inexplicable emotion suffice?

"Listen. I can't help you with your story. It's museum stuff anyhow. It's old record albums. Janis Joplin. Country Joe and the Fish. Jimi Hendrix. Peace symbols. In thousands of attics you'll find trunks crammed with hippie clothes. Beads. Headbands. They all smell of mothballs. Tell your editor you gave it your best shot. Write about something else."

"Why?" she asked.

"I told you why. Old hat." He didn't like her persistence, but he was enjoying, in unexpected ways, the presence of another human being in the house.

"Ah, but it gets better, Harry. Take the photographer. Sammy Obe was represented by an agency called Cygnet. I got the names of all the people in the picture from the agency files. There were old addresses for three of the participants, but none for you or Maggie. I didn't expect them to check out after all this time, and I was right. I thought I'd ask Obe if he knew the whereabouts of any of the subjects. I figured, say, a fifty-

fifty chance. After all, that photograph made him famous. Maybe he was still in touch. It was worth a try. But I didn't get further than a phone call to his wife, who says he sits in a room in an institution somewhere in Iowa. On good days, according to her, he can just about weave a few strands of a basket. On bad days, he tears up newspapers and babbles. He's been in the same joint since 1968. Nobody's quite sure what happened. One day he was seemingly okay, the next . . ." She snapped her thumb against her middle finger, suggesting the sound of a mind breaking like a fragile twig.

Tennant opened the kitchen door and turned on the outside light. Small flares of moisture hung like gases in the reaches of electricity. He liked the rich sound of rain in the woods.

"Two dead kids, a photographer who's lost it, and a couple of people I haven't been able to trace. . . . That's what I call all the elements of a good story, Harry." She stood directly behind him. He could smell her perfume, mellow as a newly punctured peach.

Flippantly he said, "Maybe the picture's jinxed." The rain was harder, the trees buckled. He wanted to step into the core of the thunderous noise. Suddenly the downpour slowed and the dark shed its turbulence.

"Yeah, right," Alison Seagrove said. "Don't you wonder at times? Don't you *ever* ask yourself about your black holes or whatever you call them? Is this your whole life, Harry? These woods. Your precious plants. Is this all? It's not much, is it? Was it ever enough?"

"It was okay," he answered. "It was a life, and I lived it, and I lived it quite happily."

"How long have you been here?"

"Nine years. A little more."

"Before that? Did you grow dope someplace else?"

"Before I came here you mean?"

"Right. Between the time you lived in the Haight and the time you came here, what did you do with yourself?"

"I . . ."

And he stopped.

It was as if his mind were a room plunged suddenly into stillness. He walked to the end of the porch and breathed the wet air deeply. He wondered why he was struggling so to get his lungs going. The darkness in his head was bleaker than anything in the woods out there. "Well, Harry? Or have drugs rubbed out all that too?"

He didn't speak. He scanned his mind frantically, trying to bring back some memory that would enable him to answer the girl. He felt as if he were rubbing sticks together in the brain in the hope of creating the friction of recall. A tiny flame. Anything. *You'll be okay boyo. You'll lead a happy life.* That voice. Did madness lie in this direction—amnesia, voices, messages from your personal ether? He shut his eyes, frowned in desperate concentration. Nothing came back from the void. It was a gulley without echoes. Go back, Harry. Back before this place. Back and back. What do you come to? "I don't . . ." He opened his eyes and looked at the woods and he thought: *Nine years in this place is all I have. Where is the rest of me?* There was slippage going on; more than slippage. He was slithering down a slope, kicking up nothing but scree.

"You don't know, is that it?" she asked.

"Wait. Gimme a minute." He gripped the porch rail, felt rain blow against his face. "Gimme a minute," he said again. Why was he having this difficulty in fixing that part of his history? The surge of panic he experienced threatened to consume him. Control, Harry. Slow down.

"Okay. I was in San Francisco," he said.

"Until when?"

"It must have been . . . 1968, '69, I guess."

"And you came here in what?"

"April 1981. The twenty-second." Such precision. Such surprising precision.

"That leaves about *twelve* years, Harry."

Twelve years. Something in his chest flapped and fluttered. He was suddenly frail, a scrap of paper in the night rain, a kite freed from its line and set adrift across the trees.

"What do you remember of those years, Harry?"

"Look," and he was talking quickly now. "I did all that acid, I told you, I dropped hundreds of tabs of the stuff, I lost count, and the last batch was criminal, and it did something to my head, it did something bad to my fucking head."

"Calm, calm down," she said. "Relax."

Relax, right, relax. He was afraid. He had a sudden memory, sharp as ice, of tripping on particularly vicious acid for days. Day after day of terrors. Volcanic eruptions threatened to burn his eyes out of his skull; disgusting reptilian shapes, disturbed from subterranean slumber, slithered among his bedsheets. Some scratching furry thing lived beneath his floorboards. From the window of a room he watched traffic passing along Schrader Street toward the Panhandle and it created an unbroken sinew of lava. Inside the Conservatory of Flowers—he'd no notion of how he'd reached the place—the humidity had devastated him. He might have been drowning in an ancient swamp. A giant imperial philodendron hung above him, its huge fronds flying at him like prehistoric birds. He'd been drawn into massive, gnarled twines, which suggested tortuous freeway systems leading, in directions too complicated to reckon, to the secret center of the planet itself. And what lived there, in fold after fold of shadow, was too dreadful to contemplate.

How could he remember the specifics of that trip and yet be unable to place it in time? Nor could he bring the room on Schrader back with any clarity. Had he lived there? Maybe it had been nothing more than a place where he crashed one night; you were always sleeping on somebody's floor in those days.

He stepped back from the girl and thought: Twelve years and it's like I never lived them. The thought might have been a meteorite crashing through the fundaments of his life.

"You had to be somewhere, Harry. You didn't just dematerialize. You didn't go out of existence circa 1969 and reincarnate in 1981. You had to be somewhere, for God's sake."

"I don't know. I don't know."

"You don't remember the photograph. The people in it.

You don't remember a whole chunk of your life. Think, Harry. Were you in a hospital? Did somebody look after you? Think."

A hospital? He had no such recollection. "I don't know, goddamit, I don't know." Lost, he turned his face away from the porch. The only life he ever really knew lay dead in the woods.

"Harry." The girl took his hands and drew him back inside the house. She made him sit at the table. She poured him a glass of Jack Daniel's. He sipped it, but it did nothing to dispel the chill inside him.

"Why did you never ask yourself about your past, Harry? Why did you never wonder about those years?"

He shook his head. "I don't know." It was as if he'd come into existence in this place in April 1981 and he'd started growing dope in the woods and every now and then he flashed on the old days in the Haight and that was it, that was all. Amnesia—the word was monstrous.

Alison sighed. "Maybe you don't want to remember. You know, something you buried, didn't want to look at. Something that happened in San Francisco."

"Like what?"

"I don't know. If it was me I'd kill to find out. I'd want to know where I'd been and who I was with. I'd want to know why I can't remember."

"I told you. Drugs and more drugs."

"Drugs, okay. But drugs don't necessarily kill your curiosity, Harry."

Tennant turned his empty glass upside down and tapped it with his fingertips. Sure, he was more than curious; who wouldn't be? But fear held him back. Fear of movement, of discovery. His past twelve years were blanks and he'd lived so long without even pondering them. Why blow the clouds away now? And yet: *I always had this odd feeling, this sense of something without a name that lay in the landscape. But I never let it trouble me because . . . because I was too busy.*

"Here's something for you to consider, Harry. You're in a bad situation. You sit around here, you stand a good chance of going to jail. Right?"

"Right," he said.

"Face it. You're carrion for guys like Flitt and this Rozak character. They've got your number."

Flitt and Rozak, he thought. Were they accomplices? Was Alison correct in her assumption that Rozak was part of the general game? Tennant's mystification turned to something else; it was as if he'd stepped into a river and the currents were eddying unpredictably around him. Flitt, Rozak, Judge Stakowski, perhaps even Harcourt McKay—he had the weirdly illuminating notion that they were all part of a scheme to imprison him, that they met in the back room of some local restaurant and discussed how to manipulate his fate. He recognized paranoia in this line of thinking, but sometimes paranoia, in the absence of any facts to the contrary, was the only reliable compass. He felt panic again. His brain became crowded with bad possibilities, images of conspiracy, Rozak whispering to Flitt, Flitt playing a round of golf with Stakowski, Harcourt McKay having a quiet cocktail with Rozak—permutations that had only one outcome: Send Harry Tennant to jail. He glimpsed, on one level, that none of this was clear thinking, but his brain wasn't operating logically. Fear, a familiar cumbersome weight, pressed back in on him.

"I should get the hell out of here," he said. "I should skip."

"Exactly. Unless you want to sit around and wait until they come for you, Harry. The idea of being a fugitive is a damn sight more attractive than the county jail. I couldn't hack that."

I couldn't either, he thought. It was more than the dread of confinement now. It was the prospect of brutality. A guard who didn't like him. An inmate bored to the point of sadism. How could he tolerate that?

She sat next to him at the table. "Let's say you run."

"Let's say."

"Let's say I go with you."

"You want your story."

"I'm not going to deny that. Maybe there's a connection between your loss of memory and whatever it is that happened to the people in the picture—"

"How could there be?"

"I don't know, Harry. But I'm not going to be happy until I find out. And I don't think you're going to be happy either."

For a moment he considered an alternative to flight. He'd call his father, who would surely arrange for some slick smart-ass in the firm to defend him in place of the bumpkin McKay; but this idea was a measure of his desperation. Contact Rayland? No way.

"What the hell have you got to lose?"

He gestured vaguely at the house. But he'd already lost that.

"Think about it, Harry. What can possibly keep you in this place?"

She's right. There's nothing here. Maybe there never has been. Mirrors, clouds, deceptions. Nothing. If more than twelve years of his life had vanished, why should he lose even more time behind the bars of the county slammer? He got up from his chair. Somehow he'd come to a decision, but the fear hadn't left him. He was still cold.

He went up to the attic, where the cops had forced open some old suitcases that had been in the house longer than Tennant. Clothes styled in the fashion of the late 1940s spilled from the cases. A sweet aroma of decay filled the attic space.

The gun was still in its hiding place, a space behind a wood panel. He'd never liked guns. He wondered why he wanted it anyway. Protection, sure—but from what? Everything was happening too quickly. What was he doing, agreeing to fly off into the night with a girl he hardly knew? It wasn't altogether rational—but nothing made sense to him anyway.

In the same concealed compartment as the gun were two Maxwell House coffee cans stuffed with money. He removed the cash, which amounted to some six thousand dollars in hundreds and fifties. He was ready now, as ready as he'd ever be, even if he wasn't sure of anything except trepidation—such as a visionary on paper wings of his own design might feel flying from a high cliff down to a fretful sea.

6 Tennant kept expecting the Cadillac to be pulled over. Whenever he saw a highway patrol car, he waited for sirens, but nothing happened. Alison drove with one hand resting lazily on the wheel. Sometimes she smiled at him, as if encouraging him to relax. On Interstate 90 towns floated past in the night—Oneida, Utica—communities forged in the same dreary foundry.

Alison said her first stop was New York City, where she had a minor lead—minor was an overstatement, she admitted: Skimpy was probably correct—to the man known as Bear, whose real name it seemed was John Sajac. "It's not much, but it's worth checking out anyway. I've investigated five or six different leads about Bear in the past few months, but none amounted to anything. I'll say this for myself. I've got all the instincts of a hound dog. Failure's a kind of fuel for me. It keeps me in overdrive. And if this one turns out a bummer I'll still go on looking. Sooner or later I'll find Bear Sajac. Or Maggie Silver. Or both."

"Compulsive," Tennant said.

"And ambitious," she said. "You don't get to be a features writer at my age without a heavy dose of determination. Competition's fierce. The world's full of cutthroats."

Tennant thought: She chases whispers. She stalks by smell candles long blown out. What had begun as an innocent little foray into sweet nostalgia had changed for her into an affair with intriguing, even sinister, echoes.

For his part, Tennant was anxious to get New York State behind him. He longed for the Pennsylvania line, or New Jersey, places beyond the reach of the New York highway patrol. Now and again, when he stared into a passing streak of dark greenery, he would try to force his mind back to that empty time before he'd come to the white frame house, but he might have been wrestling an eel. And sometimes, when his head ached from the effort of this, he'd think about Obe's photograph. Taken, Alison had said, in Chinatown. What did he remember of Chinatown?

Maybe once or twice he'd gone there to score some opium from a young Oriental head, but this was as vague as anything else. The condition of my world, he thought, is zero. Below zero. A mind in permafrost. He considered the faces of Maggie Silver and the others, but if Maggie provoked a thin response in him, the rest of the group meant nothing. Maybe he was imagining the response anyway. A lovely girl in an old photograph: He wanted to believe he'd known her. He pondered the vastness of the continent and wondered where the girl might be. Take any valley. Any mill town or large city. An obscure farmhouse. She could be anywhere. If she was alive. If she hadn't expired inside the structure of Alison Seagrove's "mystery." How old would she be by now? Early forties, like himself. Probably she wasn't even recognizable; he could pass her on the street and fail to relate her face to that in Obe's picture.

"Tell me something, Harry. Do you still get high?"

He shook his head. "If you count booze."

"You never smoked the stuff you grew?"

"I had to prove I could refrain. I was running a test on myself. I passed."

"But the old days were different."

"Ah. The old days. If it could be swallowed or smoked or

snorted, I tried it. Blindfold me and I could have told you the difference between . . . hell, Rangoon Red and Mauie by touch alone. I could tell you the cut in coke just by smelling the stuff. Give me a button of peyote and I might have been able to pinpoint its place of origin from the taste. It's the kind of knowledge that doesn't add up to much in the end. Talent of a misspent youth. It won't get you a lawful job. It doesn't impress on a resume." Once upon a time, he remembered, the drugs had been fun. Owsley's Sunshine, Orange Wedge, amazing acid. Innocence. Then the fun darkened along the way, the colors bleached and ran. Bad dope, created in malignant laboratories by quick-buck artists or corrupt men with connections to the law, hit the streets. The free clinic in the Haight had been overwhelmed by casualties of these narcotics. Nights of bedlam, kids sobbing without knowing why, baying at the moon, screaming incomprehensibly from the horrors that had been inflicted on them. He remembered this much.

He gazed at the outline of a rusted silo, an abandoned farmhouse. The skyline of Albany came into view. He wondered if there was an office somewhere in the bureaucratic density of the state capitol that dealt with bail jumpers; he pictured his name popping up on a computer and being sent at impossible speeds to various law enforcement agencies. But it could be days before his flight was discovered. McKay might wonder at the missed appointment; or Flitt might visit the house to ask more questions. But Harry's absence in itself wasn't enough to persuade anyone he was a fugitive. Gone for groceries, a long walk, anything. This understanding relaxed him a little. He'd bought time, though he didn't know how much.

"How hard did you look for Maggie Silver?" he asked.

"I went to the Haight. The obvious place to start. I didn't have an address for her. There wasn't one in the old Cygnet files. I don't know why. Maybe it had been removed. Lost. Who knows? All I got there was a name, nothing else. I asked around. There are still some leftovers from the sixties in the neighborhood. Nobody remembered her. Nobody could tell me anything. I tried Social Security—I have a few connections in low places. No luck. No Maggie Silver. I tried the motor vehicle people. I thought she might have a license. Another big blank. The trail was stone cold. Either she's dead or she changed her name."

Dead. He shut his eyes, listened to the rhythm of the big car's engine. He thought about the window of the room on Schrader Street and how he'd watched traffic roll toward the Panhandle. He had an intuition that the room—even if the details of the place were out of his reach—was something more permanent than a bed or a floor where he'd crashed one night. How could he feel that? Was his amnesia like a gray lifeless pool on the surface of which there appeared, every now and then, a ripple from a bottom far below? He thought of wreckage lying inert under opaque water. Twelve years of wreckage—perhaps even more. Pretend you're whole, you're complete, you're just cruising the night with a pretty young woman.

"Tell me about the lawyer in my father's office," he said. "Did you sleep with him to get my file?"

"That's privileged information." She concentrated on the road.

Harry said, "He wouldn't give you my address for nothing. Attorneys aren't famous for freebies."

"We had dinner a few times," she said.

"And then?"

"Piss off, Harry."

"You've been digging into my life. Tit for tat."

"I don't remember any reciprocal agreement."

"You ask all the questions, I try to answer. Is that the rule?"

"I find your particular question objectionable."

"One rule for you, one for me. Very democratic."

"I never said I was democratic. When it comes to my work I can be a dictator. If you don't like that, I'll turn the car around and take you back."

"I don't think so," Harry said, a little amused by the discovery that Alison Seagrove could be piqued.

She drove off the freeway to a roadhouse surrounded by

ugly gas stations and fast-food joints. As she parked she said she needed a drink, something to eat. She walked ahead of Harry inside the building, a busy place decorated with license plates from all the states of the Union. A Mexican plate from Sonora was the only incongruity. A jukebox played Merle Haggard; the cornball riff of a fiddle rose in the air then died. *I'm always on a mountain when I fall. . . .*

Alison took a booth at the window. Harry sat facing her over the menu, a ketchup-stained sheet of paper contained in plastic.

She said, "I didn't have to screw him, Harry. He was too busy drooling over the possibility to realize he was being . . . let's say quietly used."

"Am I being quietly used too?" he asked.

"You're different. I consider our relationship mutually beneficial."

"I'm relieved." Conversation, chitchat, surfaces. You could make believe an ordinary life. If you worked at it.

He looked at the menu. He had no appetite. A teenage waitress wearing an outsized crucifix and a badge reading JACKI came for their order. Alison wanted a cheeseburger and a Bloody Mary, Harry asked only for a beer. When the waitress left, Alison leaned across the table.

"Well, Harry? Anything to report from Brain HQ?"

So we're being lighthearted, Tennant thought. He needed that, even if it was an effort. "Everyone in head office is on strike," he remarked. "Unsanitary working conditions. Poor pay. A real industrial dispute."

"Ungrateful bunch," she said. "I would have figured the short working hours might have been compensation."

"Apparently not." He wondered how long you could keep that shuttlecock of levity in the air. The waitress came back and set down the food and drinks. Tennant raised his glass but didn't drink at once. He turned the glass around in his hand, studied the tiny bubbles that broke on the surface. "I'm sitting here and I'm thinking I don't know the first thing about you. Background. Education. What got you into journalism."

"What's to know?"

"A brief bio might help."

She was quiet for a while, as if she were considering how much to tell him. Was she editing material in her head? "I was raised in Tonawanda. You ever heard of the place?"

"It's a suburb of Buffalo," he said. "You were born there?"

She stirred her Bloody Mary and looked pensive. She didn't answer his question. "It's the kind of place you want to get away from. My parents are decent people. Dad's in banking. Mother once had ambitions to go onstage. An old story. All the will in the world but no talent." She paused, looking as if she intended to say more about her mother, but she didn't. "We lived in a ranch-style house on a street of homes that looked exactly alike. People flew flags on their lawns on the appropriate patriotic days. You could always smell barbecues in summer. I always had this weird feeling like, I don't know, I didn't *belong* there. I was from outer space or somewhere."

"When did you leave?"

"Three, four years ago. I did some journalism courses in high school. Then a year in college." She drew the celery stick from her drink and bit into it. "College wasn't the real world for me. I wanted action, Harry. I wanted the smell of ink on my fingers and a phone that wouldn't quit ringing and deadlines you had to bust your ass to make. I got lucky in New York. Two months in the typing pool before I turned in a story about a large quantity of cocaine that had somehow mysteriously disappeared while in the possession of the NYPD. I got rescued from the typing pool after that one." She put the celery aside. "Like I say, I had some good luck. And an editor who believes in giving his writers as much freedom as they need. He's the old-fashioned sort."

"You keep in touch with your parents?"

She shrugged. Something in the gesture suggested to Tennant a shadow in her history; perhaps, like himself, she'd distanced herself from family. Perhaps there had been disagreements, arguments about her career choice—who could say what ghosts rattled behind the walls of respectable ranch-style houses in Tonawanda? He watched her sip the Bloody Mary.

"I haven't been home in a while," she said.

"And that's all you want to say?"

"That's all I'm going to say, Harry."

"You don't get along with your parents, is that it?"

"Harry. Enough."

The bare bones of a life, Tennant thought. Small evasions that kept the skeleton unfleshed. He wanted to know more. "Is there a man?"

"You ask too many questions."

"Then we've got something in common, don't we?"

She flashed a smile at him. "I've had my moments of the heart, let's say."

"Is there a current man?"

"Christ, Harry. Gimme a break."

"I read that as a no," he said.

"Read it how you like. I'm about to eat this burger and you're going to leave me in peace, right?"

"For the moment."

He slid out of the booth and went in search of the men's room, which was located near the entrance. He stepped inside, urinated, washed his hands. In the mirror his reflection was pale. He needed a shave. The face that had been gaunt in Obe's photograph had fleshed out and creased; lines made small grooves around the corners of the eyes and across the forehead. The dark hair showed few signs of either graying or thinning. The eyes were brown and somber and, Tennant thought, older than the face in which they were set. If he'd seen himself on the street, he might have thought: That guy looks burdened, he should joke more.

He tugged at some paper towels and dried his hands. An overweight man in dark glasses and a fiery red baseball cap stepped into the room, glanced coldly at Tennant, then walked inside one of the cubicles where he issued a damp farting sound.

Tennant wondered what he'd done to merit the chilly look. Wait. Hold on. Was that a fugitive's thought? From now on would he attribute hidden purpose to the casual expressions of everyone? Faces, even the most innocent—were they to conceal jeopardy? A man in the men's room, a stranger in a motel lobby, a driver in the car behind: It was a hell of a way to live.

He thought: *It isn't too late to go back to the wreck of my house, the possibility of jail.*

But it is. It's far too late. All that is over.

He moved toward the table where Alison, her head tilted to the window, was gazing out. Something in the pose, in the angle of chin, caused him to stand still. He couldn't say why, but he had an edgy sensation, a hot wire around his heart, as if some cruel revelation were about to occur, a correspondence he couldn't take. The air became heavy, barely breathable, a sudden vacuum. An odd suffocating moment, disconnected from the thick flylike buzz of diners all around him; but then it passed and Alison turned toward him and smiled, and whatever had fallen out of sequence so briefly clicked back in place, like a lock closing on the door of a secret room.

And now Manhattan, where the rain created a grubby weave joining concrete and sky in a seamless leaden way. This city of hard angles, which Tennant had always found too abrasive to sustain more than a facsimile of human life, was traffic jammed, streets locked by motionless cars, drivers leaning on their horns, an angry chorus of the impatient waging war against the immutable.

The windows of the Cadillac fogged, and Tennant rubbed a spyhole for himself. He felt like a hick. How long since he'd been here? Ten years? Eleven? The Hudson, sluggish and muddy, was visible briefly between buildings; surrounded by rainy spray, a ghostly barge was laboring across the surface. Then the river was gone, and Alison had found a parking place for the Cadillac, a slot between two delivery trucks into which she maneuvered with ease.

Tennant took his bag, got out of the car. Head bent against the angle of rain, he followed Alison along the sidewalk to a small hotel in whose old-fashioned lobby a smell of wet umbrellas hung in the air. What now? Was this where her trail to Bear Sajac led? He had a sense of having cut himself adrift, of having jumped too easily into the young woman's slip-stream. She steered, he followed. She persisted, he acquiesced. What was to stop him from saying *Live your own life, babe,* and turning around and going back into the street anyway? Did he think he'd be even more lost without her if he just upped and strolled away? Or was it that thing he had no heart to face again: solitude?

As he walked behind Alison to the reception desk, he resented the tiny sense of dependence he experienced. He could go where he liked, for Christ's sake. He didn't need this young woman nor any involvement in her story; he didn't need to feel like a character trapped inside her private fiction.

He saw her put a credit card on the desk. She signed a form and was handed two keys, one of which she gave to Tennant.

"Just for one night," she said. "Adjoining rooms, if that's okay with you."

Inside the elevator he said, "I wasn't expecting to stay in the city. I thought we'd check your lead, then get out of the state."

"Lighten up. It's not as if I gave them your name at the desk, Harry. It's not like I said, 'This guy's a fugitive, call the cops.' Tomorrow we're gone."

Where? he wondered. But didn't ask. He realized he hadn't asked enough questions from the start. Destinations. Plans. He'd been made content by the relief of flying out of Flitt's range and the menace of imprisonment; he'd assured himself that details would come later. Alison would explain her leads, her dead ends, her possibilities.

On the seventh floor, before they went to their separate rooms, Alison said she'd freshen up, then meet him in the lobby bar. Tennant was agreeable.

He unlocked his room, which was long and narrow. The window overlooked an airshaft filled with damp newspapers, fast-food boxes, scraps of old linoleum cut in different shapes—the random collage of a city's wind-tossed trash. He sat on the bed for a time, canvas bag on the floor between his feet. The room was plain, an Alpine landscape on the wall, TV, bathroom; he felt, as he'd always done in hotels, an unsettling anonymity, as if he'd left his identity at the front desk. *What identity?* he wondered.

He checked the box-shaped bathroom, the old-fashioned tub, the lime deposits that had hardened around the shower nozzle. It was a good room for a suicide. It didn't welcome you nor invite you to linger. If you wanted to snuff yourself, you couldn't find a better place. And if suicide wasn't your thing, you could work up quite a claustrophobic lather here.

He moved toward the locked door that separated his room from Alison's. Was that her voice he heard? Maybe she was speaking on the telephone to somebody, an editor, a friend. Was she talking about him? About how she'd found him? He pressed his ear to the wood and listened. In an old hotel like this, where doors were thick and insulation sturdy, sounds were readily absorbed into oak and masonry. He made out no distinct words; he wasn't even certain if the voice had Alison's pitch, muffled and distant as it was. It could have come from some other source, up or down through the passageways of ancient ductwork that riddled the building. It had a mysterious quality, such as you might hear at a séance, otherworldly, bringing news and advice from beyond.

When finally the sound stopped and an impenetrable silence fell, Tennant moved away from the door. He felt as eavesdroppers often do, foolish, embarrassed, glad not to have been discovered in the ridiculous act. He stepped into the bathroom, laid out his shaving kit, ejected the old blade from the razor, and inserted a new one.

He was about to splash water on his face when his telephone rang. He went to the bedside table and picked up the receiver. It was Alison to say she'd meet him in the bar in five or ten minutes. After he hung up he realized he hadn't answered a telephone in years. Once, in the bad old drug days, phone connections had sometimes meant terror, dark electric absences in which nobody spoke and the only sound was that of something sighing in deep space, a weird connection between Tennant's mind and a monstrous phantasm whimpering in another reality.

He shaved, changed his shirt, then left the room. He knocked on Alison's door. Since there was no answer, he assumed she'd already gone down to the bar. He stepped inside the elevator and felt a brief lurching of the car as it began its descent. He imagined thick cables rising and falling in the black shaft. *L* for lobby.

He walked inside the bar, a brown-paneled room where an eternal dusk prevailed. Green-shaded lamps glowed on the counter and stubby little candles, imprisoned in orange glass, flickered on circular tables. Tennant so far was the only customer. No Alison. He took a table with an uncluttered view of the front door and the lobby. Rain fell on the dark streets; lamps shimmered on the sidewalks. People moved back and forward in the lobby, bellboys carried suitcases, a grinning man zoomed past in a motorized wheelchair—a sense of flurry, lives being lived.

A waitress took Tennant's order for Scotch and soda. From some hidden recess taped music kicked into life, a Simon and Garfunkel tune squeezed out of a synthesizer. "Bridge Over Troubled Waters."

Tell me about that bridge.

He sipped his drink, waited, watched the door for Alison. He'd lost his sense of time: Had he been sitting here ten minutes or twenty or what? When he was halfway through his Scotch, he used the bar phone to call her room. No answer. He sat down again, fussed with the drink.

Okay. Consider the possibilities. She had an unexpected errand to run. Or she is stuck in the elevator. Or locked in the bathroom. Or or or. You could sit here all night playing the disjunction game. He went back to the phone, tried again. This time the number was busy. She was calling somebody. Or somebody was calling her. He put the phone down, waited a minute, picked it up again, dialed her room. Now the line rang, but without answer. Had he called a wrong number before when he got the busy signal? Or had she finished her call, hung up, then left the room hurriedly? He set the receiver back, then ordered a fresh drink at his table where the fluttering candle threw a sickly complexion on his face.

This is the place, he thought. This is where a mild uneasiness comes in. She will appear in a second. She will say she has been delayed somehow, and it will be perfectly plausible. End of story. What other explanation could there be anyway? Only if he attributed subterfuge to her, something beyond her desire for a story, only then might there be something sinister in the busy signal. You have to trust her, he thought. You're like a man who needs to trust his guide to lead him through a swamp.

He accidentally spilled his Scotch, which flooded across his paper napkin. The waitress hurried over, scolding him in a jocular way, bad boy, tossing booze around, where are your manners?

He smiled absently. Go with the flow. Live in the moment. He breathed deeply. He was calmer now.

The waitress brought him another drink. He took a fresh napkin and tore it into thin strips. He placed one of the strips inside the jar that held the candle, and it caught flame immediately. Then he dropped the paper in an ashtray, where it flared and died. Playing with fire. Yes indeed.

Fire. Crackers. Had he gone once to Chinatown during a festival? Every question he asked himself led him inside a kind of tomb where the past lay locked. Without access, Tennant, you might as well be a dead man. What was personal identity if you had no fucking memory? How could you ever say with certainty who you were? How could you check the reality of the past if you couldn't relive it? He was uneasy again; that brief calm had dissolved in a flare of panic. He finished the Scotch, burned another paper strip, watched it curl and smoke.

"You'll burn yourself, Harry."

He looked up to see the girl approach the table. She wore a short black dress and an unbuttoned black raincoat.

She sat down beside him. "Sorry I took so long."

He waited. She would surely make an excuse, say she had calls to make. But she didn't.

"You want to get moving?" she asked.

He had a moment of indecision. Okay, she has a private life I know nothing about, a group of friends, she has her profession, and colleagues—was it a crime to call somebody? *Only if thinking made it so.* And you've just been doing some thinking of the twisted kind, Harry. Trust her. You have to. There's nobody else. Without this girl, you're the loneliest man in the world.

He got up from the table. The strip of paper napkin clung to melted wax and smouldered blackly.

7 "This guy calls himself Alphonse Trebanzi," Alison said. She drove the Cadillac through the streets of the lower West Side where a few delicatessens and bars glimmered in the rain. "Bear Sajac had given Trebanzi's apartment in the Haight as his address in 1968. It was probably nothing more than a crash pad. Trebanzi, naturally, has moved around since then—a dozen times at least. His trail kept running very cold. Nothing on Social Security. Motor vehicles, zip. Sometimes I have a flash of inspiration. I figured drugs. He was probably into them years ago—maybe he hadn't changed. So I checked with hundreds of drug rehab centers. I got a break. He'd undergone some drug rehab in New Jersey about four years ago. What I have here, after mucho research, is his last known address. It's a shot in the dark, I admit. But I don't have another link to Bear. I don't know if Trebanzi's dead, alive, what."

Tennant considered the complexity of connections, the accidents of place and time that joined people across years. Two decades ago John "Bear" Sajac shared a pad in the Haight with somebody called Trebanzi; by a fluke of the gravity—destiny, absurdity, whatever—that alters our tides, Bear had appeared in a photograph with Tennant and Maggie Silver and two other kids. Accidents, whimsical crosscurrents. Now, years later, Bear was a possible connection to Alison's riddle of missing people and dead kids and a deranged photographer. And maybe a link to Maggie Silver.

If Bear had survived. If *Maggie* had survived.

Tennant had a disjointed and slightly unpleasant awareness of traveling into his own mute history, a passageway where here and there a fluted whisper might be heard or a fragment of song—and it was alien to him, a journey that could take him places he had no desire to go. What persisted as he stared out at the black streets of lower Manhattan was a weight of anxiety, something leaden in his heart. His past had become a country for which he might no longer have a visa. Perhaps, like some miserable Third World republic, rotted by humidity, filled with the screech of mysterious birds, it was the kind of place for which no visa was needed anyway because no tourist ever went there—a shantytown of the mind, leprous little shacks wherein people died young and weary to the bone.

He gazed at storefronts; a drunk, oblivious to weather, shuffling along, a bag lady pushing a trolley filled with the sad stuff of her life, two cops lingering in a doorway, one slackly slapping his nightstick against his thigh.

Tennant had the Taurus in the pocket of his raincoat. Its weight made him uncomfortable, and he really wasn't sure still why he'd brought the thing; at best you could say the presence of the gun consoled him in a way it had never done during his years of crop cultivation. He put his hand inside the pocket and touched the weapon as Alison swung the Cadillac along a darkened street.

Tenements, here and there an unvandalized lamp, a crone of a tree: It wasn't a street that suggested a community, a neighborhood. You couldn't imagine block parties being held here—only the surly passage of people who lived in close proximity to one another without benefit of friendship. Tennant had the thought that the men and women who endured in this place collected welfare, food stamps, government handouts—

dehumanizing rituals; ah, how the bureaucracy, the *Sturmbann-führer*s of the Republic, imposed humiliation on impoverished souls.

The pall of the neighborhood depressed him. He had absolutely no desire to get out of the car when Alison parked, but he did so anyway. They climbed a short flight of steps to the doorway of a tenement, where a sequence of buzzers were located; each had a name attached, many illegible, faded, altered. Residents came and went here, and they left nothing in their wake. It was a good street for fugitives, men who'd fallen behind in child support, small-time hoods, failed con artists, drunks.

Alison struck a match and held it to the buzzers. She studied the little cards. "Alphonse Trebanzi. Where are you? Where the hell are you?"

Tennant looked along the street. Windows reflected the subterranean blue of TV screens. Sometimes a figure would pass in front of the box and eclipse the room. An upraised voice might now and then be heard; a small act of verbal domestic violence. A place like this bludgeoned the spirit, he thought.

"Gold!" Alison said. The match burnt her fingers and she dropped it, but struck another one immediately. The flame illuminated the name Trebanzi. Even as Alison exclaimed her delight, Tennant continued to look the length of the street, watching, expecting God knows what, but he had his hand in the pocket that contained the gun. Nobody moved in the rain. His anxiety created faces out of the light that struck the few trees. He was a mere step away from hearing rain make leaves whisper in understandable phrases, or discovering a Morse code in the noise of water falling on plastic trash bags along the sidewalk. Random sounds—but if you were in a precarious state of mind they could be made to yield meanings; statements, propositions, anything you liked.

He gazed at Alison. In her small determined features he might find an anchor to something substantial.

She pressed Trebanzi's buzzer. She looked at Tennant with

such a profound expectancy that he hoped Trebanzi would not be a waste of time for her, that all kinds of information would come tumbling, by preposterous magic, out of this one man's mouth. Bear's address? Sure, no sweat. Maggie Silver? Hey, got her phone number right here. Harry Tennant's memory? No problem. Got it in my attaché case. What else can I do for you?

In dreams, Tennant thought as Alison pressed the bell again. The tenement was weirdly quiet, as if unoccupied, every buzzer disconnected.

"Answer, come on," Alison said, keeping her finger attached solidly to the bell. "Come on, Alphonse. Answer. Talk to me."

A fuzzy sound came from the speaker. "Yeah?"

"Mr. Trebanzi?"

"Yeah." The voice was distant, as if it might have traveled all the way from a high turret.

"I wonder if you could spare a few minutes to speak to me," Alison said. "We've never met. My name's Alison Seagrove. I don't need much of your time."

"What you want to speak about?" Trebanzi asked.

"I'm a journalist. I'm writing a piece on San Francisco, the late sixties."

"How come you're ringing *my* goddamn buzzer, lady? What makes you think I'd know anything about San Francisco?"

"Look, it's cold and wet down here. Can we talk face-to-face? Can I come up?"

A long silence. A car passed slowly down the street. Tennant observed it, aware of two occupants who showed no apparent interest in Alison or himself.

"It's important to me," Alison said. "I wouldn't trouble you otherwise."

"You alone?"

"Sure." She glanced at Tennant, who indicated with a gesture of his head that he'd follow her inside as soon as Trebanzi pressed the button to open the door. Instant complicity: Tennant liked it.

"I don't know about this," Trebanzi said. "I lead like a real quiet life here, you unnerstand? I don't want my name in some scuzzy rag."

"I promise. No publicity."

"You wanna give me that in writing?"

"If you like."

"Okay. I'm on the third floor. You got five minutes."

The buzzer sounded, the front door opened, a hallway of closed doors stretched toward the stairs. A solitary bulb, slung high overhead, was the only source of light. Tennant stepped in quickly behind the girl and followed her toward the staircase, which rose up through tiers of darkness. He had the odd impression again of emptiness, as if the sole occupant of the house was the man called Trebanzi. Every other door led into vacant unfurnished rooms. A spooky setting, a haunted house: How appropriate to be tracking his past in such a place.

Quietly, he followed Alison to the foot of the stairs, conscious of the corrupt odor of damp wallpaper. The arrangement of the stairway made it possible to see up between the handrails to the blackened skylight at the top of the house, beneath which was a scaffolding of the sort workers erect, a short spidery arrangement of metal tubes and planks. Perhaps some form of renovation was going on.

He put a foot on the bottom step.

Which was the moment it hit him, the flash, the rolling away in his mind of thunder and thin lightning, a shift in the gears of his brain. Strength went out of his legs. This house. The smell. The clamminess that choked him. Either he'd been in this place before or it brought back to mind, with ghastly precision, a house very similar, one in which he'd been skewered, crucified. And somehow Maggie Silver was there, a lovely burning cinder in his head. Why?

He looked upward toward the skylight.

It wasn't the house. It wasn't the damp perfume.

The scaffolding. *Something to do with the scaffolding.*

"Harry, for God's sake, are you sick, what is it?"

His eyes watered as he gazed at the assortment of tubes and

planks that, hardly touched by the reaches of electricity, resembled an insane sculpture, something hammered together in a nightmare.

"Are you ill? What is it?" Alison placed a hand against the side of his face. Aware of her concerned look, he caught himself and reached for the handrail. Support. Something solid.

"You're white, Harry." And she touched his forehead, checking him for fever. She was almost nurselike in her worry. He shook his head from side to side. He heard himself say something about a dizzy spell, something to convince the girl. But it wasn't that. It was more. A dizzy spell didn't cut it. Didn't go anywhere near cutting it.

"We can go outside," she said. "You need air."

"I'm fine."

"You're sure?"

"Sure."

"You don't sound sure."

"No. I'm fine."

"You scared me, Harry."

I scared myself. What for Christ's sake had happened to him? Some kind of acid rerun, an image he'd brought back from an old trip through the jungles of consciousness? An enigma grounded in some very ordinary alignment of metal pipes and planks of wood—what kind of sense did that make? Where did that belong in his life? Scaffolding beneath a black skylight. It was slippage, spillage from another time. A discharge of the brain; the mind's knavery.

Maggie Silver, he thought. What did the commonplace structure above have to do with a girl he couldn't remember knowing? He wondered if he was doomed to move in the same purgatorial circle of amnesia all his days. You can't get out, Harry. Sorry. No exit.

He moved cautiously up the stairs, fearing another attack. There was a buzzsawing pain deep in his skull. He followed Alison, who kept glancing back at him as if to reassure herself that he wasn't about to lose his balance again. He had an odd sense now of treading through warm syrup, struggling as he climbed.

On the landing he stopped. The pain dissolved; a tiny liberation. Breathing hard, he again glanced up at the scaffolding. It was badly rusted. Some absentee landlord had apparently abandoned a renovation project long ago, and now the matter was forgotten. An ancient bankruptcy, a change of ownership, whatever; the construction rotted, beyond any practical use. He didn't want to look at it. He couldn't risk absorption in the sight of the thing.

Another flight of stairs. Another landing. The air was cloying. He was more acutely aware than before of the great silence of the house around him, no TV, no crying baby, nobody coughing. The only scents were those of decaying wallpaper and rotted wood—nothing of food, fried meat, boiled vegetables. What did they do, all the people whose names were inscribed under the buzzers outside? Did they never eat, sleep, make love, argue? Unsettled, he stood very still. As if she too had become conscious of the same absences, Alison stopped halfway across the landing.

This was the third floor. Trebanzi's floor. There were four doors on the landing.

"There's something bizarre about this," Alison said. She was whispering.

"Think of it as a game show," Tennant remarked. Keep it light. Goose feathers. "Choose the correct door, you win the three-piece living-room furniture plus—and this'll make your mouth water—the propane barbecue grill."

Although each door had a number, none had a nameplate. If anyone lived in the rooms beyond, they worked at anonymity. Why hadn't Trebanzi come out to meet Alison anyhow? Why hadn't she been directed to a specific room number?

"Go on. Pick a door," he said.

The voice came from overhead, from the floor where the scaffolding was located. *"Yeah. Listen to your pal, lady, and pick a door."*

Tennant, surprised, stared up.

"Trebanzi?" Alison asked.

A shadow was visible among the struts and cylinders. "You

think I'm fucking crazy, lady? You think I open my door to anybody that comes calling? 'Ooo-eee, glad you dropped in, have a glass of boojolly with me, let's remember the good old days.' It ain't like that, sweetheart. Plus, you lied to me. You brought company when you said you was all alone."

Tennant put his hand in the pocket that contained the gun.

Trebanzi said, "I wouldn't be thinking that way in your situation, jack." And he came forward from the shadows of the scaffolding. He held a shotgun, the barrel of which he directed down at Tennant, who immediately lowered his hand to his side. He had no expertise in a situation like this. What was he supposed to do? Go for a quick draw? The shotgun was fat and lethal.

"You got a name?" Trebanzi asked.

"Tennant."

"Tennant. Tennant." Trebanzi, seeming to savor vowels and consonants as if he'd been deprived too long of speech, stepped into the light for the first time. He had a large bald head that sat in an ungainly way on a body that might once have been fleshy; skin hung loosely from his forearms. The man was either very sick or maintained himself, for reasons of vanity or psychosis, on a malnutrition diet. He moved a little way forward, and his features caught the light. The left side of his face was mauve and puckered, as if a skin graft had been attempted and failed. One eyelid was smooth and permanently shut, the upper lip locked in an oddly sad look. It was a disfigurement you could both fear and pity.

"Tennant," Trebanzi said again. He spoke hoarsely. "So explain yourself. I'm listening hard. What the hell brings *you* here on a night like this, huh? What's your connection with our scribbler friend—if that's what she is."

Tennant glanced at Alison, but she was looking upward, hypnotized by the shotgun. He said, "I'm a research assistant," which sounded feeble even to himself. He pondered the possibility of a more detailed fabrication—he was, say, her photographer as well, blah blah blah. But Trebanzi, in that unsettling voice of his, would have commented on the absence of a camera.

"You're the assistant, Tennant. The scribbler's pal. Is that it? You carry her notebooks and sharpen her pencils with a little tool, huh?"

"Something like that."

Trebanzi laughed. An odd sound, a wheeze, an old accordion. "I ain't in a buying mood, Tennant," he said, and turned to look at Alison. "Show me what you got, lady. Lemme see some paper."

Alison tossed her wallet up and Trebanzi seized it deftly; he flipped the plastic inserts, checked her ID, then let the wallet fall from his fingers.

She caught it. "Satisfied?" she asked sharply.

"Let's say you're a writer. What brings you to me?" Trebanzi asked. "What makes you think I got some association with San Francisco in the time frame you mentioned?"

"You knew a man called Bear. Bear Sajac."

"Yeah?"

"According to my information."

"Your information sucks, lady. I never heard of any Bear Sag . . . Saje . . . whatever you said."

"Sajac. He lived with you in the Haight."

"I never set foot in the place. I never met any Bear. You got the wrong end of the stick."

A silence. The big house retained sounds in a miserly way. Nothing echoed. Nothing reverberated. A dead house—and it made Tennant more curious than ever. With an impulse he couldn't deny, he reached for the door nearest to him and pushed it open. Through uncurtained windows a street lamp cast a flat, spectral light. The room was bare. No furniture. No inhabitant. Nothing. Lifeless.

"*Asshole! What you playing at?*" Trebanzi shouted.

He fired his shotgun. Tennant, amazed by the roar, heard the air collapse around him; a black hole, an implosion in his eardrums. The shot ripped through old woodwork, and for a moment the air smelled like that of an abandoned sawmill. The cartridge had come too close, far too close; Tennant had the feeling that if mortality was a telephone line, he'd just committed the number to heart.

"Don't go wandering around, Tennant. Don't think you're an invited guest here, because you ain't. Shut that door. Do it now."

Tennant didn't move. He wondered what perversity made him disobey Trebanzi's order. Was it the stubbornness Rayland had attributed to him? Was it—sweet Jesus—an off-center wish for death? Suddenly he resented Trebanzi and his goddamn shotgun. He hated being ordered around. He despised Trebanzi the way he despised Ralph Flitt and his threats; he begrudged the loss of his house and land, his dog, how all the safe chambers of his life had been violated and destroyed. Now this sad-looking bastard with a shotgun was menacing him, and he wanted to strike back somehow. "What's got you running scared, Alphonse? You live here all alone, don't you? The names outside. The buzzers. The pretense of tenants. It's a mock-up. So what's happening? What are you hiding?"

"I ain't scared, Tennant. I'm a hermit, okay?" Trebanzi said. "I like my own company in my own goddamn house. The human race is slime. You don't take this"—and he touched his face with a gesture of contempt—"out on the streets too often. I mind my own business, asshole. This scumbucket of a house belongs to me and if I don't want to rent rooms there ain't a law in the land says I got to. Okay? You *absorbed* that?"

Alison looked up at Trebanzi. "Listen, if you'll turn the gun to the other side, we'll call this a mistake and walk out of here. The end. You won't be troubled again."

"Hold your horses, lady. The party's not over."

"I think it is. You didn't know Bear. We've got nothing to say to each other. Good night."

"I said hold on." Trebanzi leaned against the handrail. "The way I see it, we got unfinished business."

"What would that be, Trebanzi?" Alison asked.

"I'm interested in how come my name cropped up. I mean, how did you stumble across some connectorooni between me and this, this *Bear?*"

"I did what I'm usually good at," Alison said. "Research."

"Research, huh? Tell me how that works."

"There's always a trail, Trebanzi. You leave signs behind no matter how fast you keep moving. You left yours in a drug rehab facility in Atlantic Beach." Alison had a small confident smile on her face, as if she sensed that, despite the shotgun, she had the upper hand with Trebanzi. She sighed and added, "Clearly, though, I made a mistake in your case. Unlikely as it seems, there's got to be another Alphonse Trebanzi walking around, and I got confused. I took a wrong turn in my research. No biggie. I'll get out of your hair and start again."

"Too easy," Trebanzi said.

"What's too easy?"

"You. Your friend Tennant. You can't walk."

"I'm good at it," Alison said. "One foot before the other. Like so. Been doing it for years, Alf."

"Funny lady. Unnerstand this: I lost my sense of humor some time back. So just don't fucking move. Both of you stay right where you are. You got a gun, Tennant, take it out and put it on the floor where I can see it."

Tennant pulled the weapon from his pocket and laid it down reluctantly.

"Good," Trebanzi said. "I'm coming down now. Just remember I can watch you through the rail. And keep in mind I got this mean-tempered baby in my hands."

Trebanzi descended, trailing the barrel of the shotgun over the handrail. He wore an old green-red plaid shirt and blue jeans about two sizes too big for him. He was somewhere in his forties, and taller than Tennant had thought. His jowls hung like empty sacs; if he was sick, it was with some ungodly wasting disease. The one good eye was dull, a dark space inside which light, when it entered unawares, was trapped. A dead eye, a dead house. Trebanzi had a quality of stagnancy; if Tennant had believed in auras, he might have found Trebanzi's a gray, lackluster mist.

When he came to the landing, Trebanzi pointed the shotgun at Tennant. "Okay. I got one question. Who sent you?"

"Nobody sent us," Alison said. "I told you. I'm writing a story. You're not the guy I'm looking for. Sorry. Beg pardon. Adios," and she turned away, but Trebanzi prodded her in the spine with the shotgun.

"Hey." Alison stared at him angrily. "Watch where you put that thing, Trebanzi."

"I'll ask again. Who sent you?"

"What makes you think somebody sent us?" Tennant asked.

Trebanzi said nothing. He gazed past Tennant toward the staircase; a thin shadow of the scaffolding fell across his face, distorted where it touched the ridged surface of his skin. Fear, Tennant thought. The man lives in terror. The facade of this house, the pretense of inhabitants, the shotgun, the aggression. This was way beyond your common dread of New York City; this was another level, a fresh dimension. He had a memory of dread from the drug days: He knew how it created its own momentum, how it spawned itself in the hours of darkness, whispering. You sat up waiting for dawn, your brain rattling, you imagined daylight had the power to dissolve all the monsters. Did Trebanzi, his mind sprinting in terror, his senses assaulted by half-seen shadows and phantom feet on floorboards, sit in one of these rooms with the shotgun on his lap and long for the sun to come up over the tenements?

"I'd like to know what you're afraid of, Trebanzi."

"Shit! I already answered that, man. I asked a question of my own so don't keep me waiting for a fucking answer. Don't sidestep me, Tennant. No fancy footwork. This lizard"—and he indicated the shotgun—"will explode in your face."

Alison said, "My magazine sent me. Does that ring your bell, Alf?"

Trebanzi smiled. The inflexibility of his upper lip made the expression ambivalent; you couldn't say if there was mirth in the look, or something beyond interpretation. The face was a book written in an obscure foreign language. "Magazine's don't mean *that* to me. I need something specific. A name. Names."

"The features editor is called Hewson. The editor's Burford Blackburn. But they didn't exactly *send* me, Alf. It doesn't work that way. I sent myself."

Trebanzi looked incredulous. "You expect me to believe that, lady? What about your boyfriend here? How come he tagged along? And don't feed me any guff about how he's your assistant. You came here to get me, right? You came here to take me away. All the rest is crap."

Listening to how Trebanzi's voice rose, watching the stressed cords in his neck, Tennant had the thought that Alphonse was a candidate for Straitjacket Hall. The man lived in a state of siege. There were devils congregating in his dark corners.

"What were you planning to use? A needle? Maybe you were just gonna shoot me right here," and Trebanzi kicked Tennant's gun across the landing. "Yeah. Why not? Kill me in my own goddamn house. Assholes. Assholes. My own goddamn house." Curiously, a tear formed in his eye and slid over his cheek; it was the last thing Tennant expected, and it was upsetting in its own strange way. A one-eyed tear.

"Nobody's going to kill you," Alison said. "I told you the truth, Alf. I'm following a story. That's it. If somebody's after you, maybe we can help."

Trebanzi seemed not to hear her. "Christ, I was safe here. I really thought I was safe here. Now I gotta make plans. I gotta throw some stuff together and split. Then there's the problem of you pair. I don't want to kill you. I don't want to hurt anybody. But you gotta unnerstand, it's you or me. And I'm so goddamn tired. Jeez, am I tired." Trebanzi wiped the tear with his cuff. "Now they know where I'm located. *They know.* I gotta move. I gotta move on." And he paced the landing in a restless, confused way.

"Who are *they*?" Tennant asked.

"Don't fuck with me. How long you been on their side, man? From the git-go? Maybe that explains why you're still walking. I gotta think fast. I gotta figure this."

Tennant took a step toward Trebanzi and spoke patiently.

"You're not coming through loud and clear, Alphonse. You better clarify this for me."

"Clarify." Trebanzi repeated the word as if it were unfamiliar to him. Waving the shotgun, he herded Tennant and Alison across the landing to the other side. "What's to clarify, Tennant? You know what's going on. Don't play mind games with me. That door at your back. Open it."

Tennant, seized by an urge to disobey, didn't move. He stood directly under the scaffolding, whose shadow seemed darker and heavier to him now, and threatening, as though it were about to collapse, to fall through space and crush him. He thought he could smell the rust of pipes. From somewhere he had a memory of clutching a rotted metal cylinder and then looking at how rust adhered like flakes of old blood to his hand.

"Open the door," Trebanzi said again.

Absorbed by the scaffolding, Tennant felt his mind drift to a recollection of the room on Schrader Street. Che and Bobby Kennedy pictures and psychedelic Fillmore posters and tiny hash pipes and roach clips and an elaborate glass bong—these scraps scurried around without substance, conjured up seemingly from nothing.

"Somebody open the door, for Christ's sake," Trebanzi said.

This time Alison responded. The room beyond was clearly Alphonse's lair, a big stuffy space cluttered with crummy furniture, the floor strewn with newspapers and magazines. Blackout blinds had been drawn across the windows. On the old-fashioned oak mantelpiece, impossibly ornate with hand-carved cherubim and bunches of grapes, sat two pistols. A couple of beat-up sofas were covered with battered cushions among which a scraggy cat slept. Burnt-down candles had left bizarre patterns of wax on the floorboards. Ashtrays were stuffed with cigarette ends and the blackened, oily remains of joints. A two-gram bottle on the table was half-filled with cocaine. Alphonse, even in his retreat, obviously had a shopping list and a supplier.

"I gotta think fast," Trebanzi said. Shotgun under his arm, he strolled to the window, slid back the blind a little way, gazed down into the street. Then he turned to look at Tennant—who had become abruptly chill and was no longer thinking about the room on Schrader, nor the sudden image of hippies erecting a precarious scaffold against a house and painting a cheerful mural of pink suns and Day-Glo mushrooms and marijuana leaves; he wasn't scavenging the contents of this abrupt memory because all that was vague to him still, and his recall was shot through with sick impurities—

No. His attention was magnetized elsewhere now.

Shocked into the present, he was looking at the large black-and-white photograph on the wall above Trebanzi's mantelpiece: Obe's picture of five hippies in Chinatown in 1968. Maggie Silver, locked solid in time, gazed out at him. Her look said: *I got a secret, Harry, baby. And I'm not telling.*

8 Disturbed by Tennant's sudden move toward the fireplace, the cat bounded from the sofa in one sinuous, gingery leap. The picture, blown-up, glossy, unframed, was held in place by thumbtacks. Faces, the inalienable property of the past, were sealed inside the wretched prism of eternal youth. Carlos Carlos, Bear, Kat, himself; and Maggie Silver in the dead center. Alison stretched one hand up to touch the surface of the picture, as if she suspected it might be unreal.

"Some things you don't throw away," Trebanzi said, looking at the photograph. "Even if you know they're gonna come back and fuck you one day, Harry."

Harry, Tennant thought. He couldn't remember now if he'd mentioned his first name to Alphonse. He had a sense of surfaces shifting and changing. The photograph. The first name. This weird house, this *sham.* There had to be some form of key to his history here, if he could find it. He tried to formulate a question that might force an explanation from Trebanzi, but it was Alison—with the inquisitorial habit of her occupation—who spoke first.

"I suppose you just *happen* to have this, Alf," she said. "I daresay this is sheer blow-me-away coincidence."

Trebanzi peered from the blackout blind again, then let it drop. He ignored Alison. "How many others are with you?" he asked. "You got friends in the street, Harry? I mean, if I was to make a run for it, I'd be iced down there?"

What was this man talking about? Tennant shook his head. "Nobody's out there."

Trebanzi crossed the room, gazed at the photograph, then looked glumly at Tennant. "I expected more than two, I guess. I thought they'd send four, half a dozen. Maybe it don't work like that. Maybe they only send two. Economy, huh? What the hell, I hear we're in a recession," and he laughed. "Gotta cut back when times is hard."

Expected more than two, I guess. Tennant wondered about the bleak nature of Trebanzi's expectations, and how they dissolved into puzzles. He glanced at the five faces Obe had captured and thought it strange that if he were to meet his former self on the street, there would be no recognition. Harry Tennant now, Harry Tennant then: More than age separated the two. The fretful question of personal identity again.

"You ready to talk about the photo yet, Alf?" Alison asked, impatient with any further detour down the culverts of Trebanzi's dementia. She liked straight lines, arrows to the heart of a matter. Her hands were clenched determinedly; her dark eyes had taken on a formidable look. She wasn't going to be fobbed off by Trebanzi and his evasions.

"It's a souvenir, lady. What else?" Alphonse scoured the room, frantically moving papers and magazines around. He found what he was looking for, a bottle of vodka. Tucking the weapon under one arm, he drank carelessly, quickly. Liquid spilled over his chin.

"A souvenir of what?" Tennant asked. "If you never knew Bear, why do you have his picture on the wall?"

"Bear," Trebanzi said, his tone scornful. "Bear's dead."

"Dead? How? When?" Tennant asked.

Trebanzi set the vodka down on a pile of books; the bottle fell on its side. Booze trickled over the paperback covers. Alphonse paid it no attention. He was elsewhere now, wandering. "You already know all that shit."

"We don't know anything, Alf," Alison said. "Enlighten us."

Trebanzi strolled close to her; in the one good eye was a harsh light of rage. "I got your number, lady. Games. You like games. I ain't playing. Sorry." He turned, gazing up at the picture, consumed all at once. His expression became one of—what?—dejection? hopelessness? His hairless head, a smooth pink dome of skin that rose up from the purple wasteland of the face, seemed to belong to somebody else, as if a surgical miscalculation had occurred; opposites had been joined by scalpel and stitch in the hands of an apprentice butcher. Tennant followed the line of Trebanzi's vision: What did Alphonse see in that accursed photograph anyhow? Why did he have it? *Some things you don't throw away, Harry.* Meaning what? Briefly he considered the dangerous notion of rushing Alphonse for the weapon, but Trebanzi still held it menacingly.

Alison was cross, flustered. "Okay. We've established you don't like games. Forgive me for being obtuse, Alf, but I'm not exactly sure about the rules here. We can't all be as bright and insightful as you, can we?"

"Touchy little number, ain't we."

"Don't patronize me, Trebanzi." She looked and sounded fierce.

"Yeah yeah. You one of them *modern* chicks?" He made a flicking gesture, like a man scornfully brushing a fly away. The rage was still in his eye, and contempt too. For a moment Tennant thought that he was going to turn the shotgun on Alison and pull the trigger. Harry had the urge to step between Alison and Trebanzi, to protect her. But then Trebanzi subsided and looked almost composed. He leaned against the fireplace directly under the photograph. "Why the hell did you ever have to find me in the first fucking place? I had a life. It wasn't exactly fantastic, but I'd learned how to maintain."

I know the feeling, Tennant thought. He saw his abandoned frame house, the hushed woods.

"I gotta kill both of you. And the trouble is, I ain't a killer." Trebanzi shut his eyes and swayed a little. The big bald head seemed insubstantial, a balloon on which somebody had crayoned warped features.

"The only thing I ever killed was Bear," Trebanzi said.

The remark sucked life out of the room. The air was lifeless, barely breathable.

"Why did you kill him, Alf?" Tennant asked.

"Don't keep shitting me. You know what happened. You wouldn't be here if you didn't."

"Alf, you've got it wrong."

"Fuck wrong! Fuck it! Fuck both of you!" Trebanzi, enraged, fired the shotgun into the ceiling. The room, so hushed before, roared now, as if directly under the floorboards a subway had rumbled. Flakes of plaster settled like misshapen snow. Trebanzi aimed the gun directly at Tennant. "You cocksucker. You turd. Pretending you don't know shit. Harry, Harry."

An odd little sense of familiarity touched Tennant; it was the vague feeling you have when somebody passes you on the street and is gone moments after you've registered a memory— a face, a way of walking. And it's too late to turn around and check because crowds have already seized and devoured the person, and you're left with a slight shiver, an emptiness. A name on the tip of the tongue. Someone recognizable, yet with the quality of a figure in a dream. He had that experience now, but he didn't know why. He was certain he'd never seen Trebanzi before tonight. How could such a face be forgotten anyway? What was it? What was this awareness? Frustrated, he felt his eye reluctantly drawn upward again to the photograph, to the young faces whose expressions appeared reproachful now, as if their ghosts blamed him personally for the crash of all their buoyant hippie ideals. Bright young savages. His mind, so often a court jester in the past, became a prestidigitator now, pulling away one silk handkerchief after another, reds and blues, lemons and pinks, on and on, silk after silk, a sleight of hand so slickly performed that Harry, his eyes fixed to the picture, was blinded by incredulity. What the magician was showing him could not possibly be the case; another funny little connection in his brain had just come loose, that was all. Pop goes a synapse. A cow jumps over the moon. A brass band, all clash and thunder, struts past in the hollows of your cerebrum.

Trebanzi was taking shells out of his pockets and shoving them into the shotgun. A space existed, a moment in which Tennant might have taken a chance and charged, but it dwindled into nothing. Tantalized by the wizard in his head, bewildered, he'd missed the opportunity.

"What happens now, Alf?" Alison asked. "You shoot us?"

"You got it."

"Then you run and you keep running."

"Running and hiding, lady. It's what I do best." Trebanzi turned his attention to Tennant. "One thing I'd still like to know, Harry. When did they get you to come over? When did you take their side? Or have you been with them all along?"

Tennant, wondering what area he shared of Trebanzi's dark world, felt yet another silk shift inside his mind; a chiffon haze lifted, pulled gently away.

No. It just wasn't possible.

"I asked you a question, Tennant."

Tennant experienced the optical illusion that the photograph grew larger, dominated the room. The only face he saw now was that of Bear; the others faded. The big bearded head, the sweet, mellow expression; a solid, happy face. A good face. You just knew that Bear was the kind of man you could count on in a bad situation.

Tennant heard blood rush through his head. The photograph, like a box of tricks forced open, grudgingly yielded one of its mysteries: Bear Sajac wasn't dead.

Hammered by the realization, his heart suddenly cold in his chest, Tennant stared at Alphonse Trebanzi. He could see the resemblance, but only vaguely; you had to look beyond the ridges of disfigurement, the wasting body, the baldness. But you could see it still. You could see it.

"How did it happen, Bear?" he asked.

"Bear's dead, Harry. I told you that."

"Somehow you had the face rearranged. You took off the beard, lost the hair. You shed the pounds. But you're in there somewhere."

"You're outta your mind, Tennant."

"I don't think so, Bear."

Trebanzi stood very still for a time; his expression was one of panic barely controlled.

Tennant said, "You altered yourself. You took Trebanzi's name. You went into hiding. Why? Why, Bear?"

"You're whistling in the dark, pal. I should fucking kill you right now." And Trebanzi moved with unexpected speed, striking Tennant hard in the center of the chest. Tennant, his strength knocked out of him, fell to the floor. The pain in his ribs—a sharp turbulence—spread to neck and arms, then rushed in a violent red wave to his head. Gasping, he rolled on his back and stared up at the ceiling, seeing nothing. He was vaguely aware of Alison bending over him, footsteps rushing on the floor, the sound of the door opening and closing. It took an incalculable time—thirty seconds, two minutes, he wasn't sure, his inner timepieces raced out of control—before his breathing became easier. But he was groggy, like a man on too many Seconal.

Alison helped him to a sitting position. Propped against a sofa, he felt a broad band of pain go through his chest. He moaned.

"Do you think anything's broken?" she asked.

"It feels like just about everything."

"Don't move."

He ignored her. He clutched the sofa and drew himself up, an imprudent act; he had no air in his lungs. He felt remote from his body. His vision was filled with fierce dark lines. "Did our man split?" His voice came out odd, like something you might hear at a fraudulent séance.

"He split all right."

Tennant stumbled toward the door and out onto the landing, where he heard the sound of the outside door closing. Clutching the handrail, he understood he couldn't move any further, couldn't go after the man who called himself Trebanzi, couldn't chase. He shut his eyes. He was in some kind of bad dream. Trebanzi. Bear. Had he been mistaken? Deluded by his own urge to participate in the past, to see things that didn't exist? He shook his head slowly from side to side, conscious of Alison standing next to him.

"Let me get you to a doctor," she said.

"No doctors."

"Then let me get you back to the hotel."

He made no response. When he opened his eyes he was aware of the shadow of the scaffolding, the odd gridlike pattern it threw on the floor; a diagram without meaning and yet sinister. "Wait," he said. "I just want to stand very still for a minute."

"What you said about Trebanzi—"

"I'm not sure. I could be wrong." Throb of pain. His heart might have been a drum on whose thin skin some evil child was thumping. "I was looking at the photograph and I just . . . I guess I suddenly saw this resemblance. Not much of one, sure. But there was something. The way he spoke to me—there was a familiarity in that. Goddamn." He leaned upon the handrail. "Say Trebanzi died and Sajac took his name, then had some drastic surgery to his face. Or maybe he was in an accident. Whatever. What I don't get is all this," and he gestured in a puzzled manner at the house. "Hiding. Thinking we'd come to kill him. That we'd been sent by somebody. By whom? What the hell does that mean?"

"Whoever they are, they obviously scared poor Alphonse shitless. If he's really Sajac, he's gone to some astonishingly elaborate lengths to conceal himself." Alison picked up Tennant's pistol, which lay where Trebanzi had kicked it. She turned it over in her hand and frowned. "I keep coming back to the photograph. Carlos is dead. Kat's dead. Bear—if that was Bear—lives in fear of being killed. Maggie Silver . . . who knows? So the question's this: What's so goddamn special about the people in the picture? Did they know something that made them candidates for a violent death?"

Tennant, in a tentative gesture, touched his chest. The pain was easing, but only slightly. "Personally, I can't think of a thing that would make anybody want to murder *me*. I haven't done anything—"

"How do you know that, Harry?"

She had a point, a terrible point. He felt suddenly angry with himself. Twelve barren years. He said, "Okay. Assume the people in the goddamn picture knew something. What are you driving at anyway? Some fevered idea of a conspiracy?"

"I don't know," she said. "I don't know if I'm driving at anything. I'm just tossing stuff out."

"I mean, look at the thing. What do you see? Five kids, all of them probably dopers. The Haight was filled with a quarter of a million just like them. Why would anybody want to silence *that* particular little group? It doesn't add up for me."

And he thought of Maggie Silver again, almost as if she were standing somewhere nearby and he could sense her presence; an instinct from the days of ruin. Then he imagined her dead, and the idea filled him with despair. If she was alive, was she living the way Bear Sajac had lived? Underground, disguised, altered? For some reason he couldn't imagine Maggie Silver gone to earth like a mole hidden away in subterranean darkness.

"Why didn't he just shoot us?" he asked. "That's all he had to do. Two blasts of the shotgun. Stuff the bodies in the basement. End of the matter."

"For us, sure. But not for Alphonse. He kills us. So what?

It doesn't end his nightmare. So far as he's concerned, that would only postpone the inevitable. He's afraid of what's out there in the streets. The others. The people he thinks sent us. I don't believe he had the heart for murder."

Murder, Tennant thought. The word seemed strange to him, a new entry in his vocabulary. He moved to the stairs. He took the gun from Alison and put it in his pocket. He ached with each step.

"I didn't know you carried a gun, Harry."

"It's not something I do every day," he said. "Let's get out of here. This place spooks me."

"Can you make it downstairs?"

"Yeah. I'll be fine."

He descended slowly, hand on the rail. The pain had receded somewhat, but was still a constant in his ribs, a series of little fires. In the hallway he stopped. He turned, looked up, saw the shadowy scaffolding. But the recollection it had inspired had given up any clarity. Now the image was formless, another element in the mystery his life had become.

Back at the hotel he sat with Alison for a while in the crowded bar. Two Scotches eased him. A pianist was playing old standards. "I Can't Get Started." "Begin the Beguine." At tables, couples talked in the animated ways of people who have just about reached the martini limits. It was all so amazingly normal he found it hard to comprehend. He had the unsettling feeling he was a tourist in a world of absurdities. Alison, who sat in pensive silence and hardly touched her vodka cocktail, looked at him every now and then with an expression he couldn't quite read. When she asked how he felt, he said something banal about the whisky working wonders, the healing alchemy of a fine Scotch. It was surface talk under which were layers of fog neither he nor Alison were able to penetrate, as if they had stumbled haplessly into a shared illusion too complex for dissection. Ignore it, neglect it, it might simply go away.

Impulsively, perhaps for his own reassurance that some-thing in the world was tangible, he took her hand. She squeezed his fingers gently. A connection, an intimacy. He imagined making love to her. Through his muted pain, he wondered if being inside this lovely young woman might cre-ate—if not a logic—then a sense of reality. Affectionate sex. The thought, at first so casual, assumed a deeper resonance. He could be happy. He could give something of himself blindly. He could underline the fact that he and Alison had become, in the blackness of circumstance, partners. He could abandon any notion of recreating the past, a turbulent undertaking in any case.

"I don't want to think, Harry. My brain's quit for the day." She smiled in a rather sad way. That fine darkness in her eyes suggested strange mirrors, reflections in smoke. "I don't have any answers. And for once in my life I don't even have the right *questions.*"

He didn't have the right questions either. And he didn't want to think of murders. Of paranoia. Of *them,* whoever they were. Besides, he was absorbed by the contact of skin. She had soft small hands; the fingers were incongruously long. It was no great act of imagination to envision them on his body. He tightened his grip on her hand. He needed this moment. This girl.

He thought about the last time he'd had sex. In spring last year he'd gone to one of Bobby Delacroix's parties down in Auburn, a ten-keg affair attended by aged bikers, dopers in black glasses, and superannuated hippies, leftover gurus of this kind and that, and he'd met a strung-out girl called Daphne who went with him up into the loft of Bobby's house where an old four-poster bed, lacking a canopy, lay beneath a narrow window. He was drunk, and outside of himself, and the love-making had been protracted, a constant rearrangement of posi-tions, as if perfection between two total strangers were a possi-bility.

Concentrating on the dim possibility of mutual climax, Tennant worked hard and sweated hugely. Once, something made him laugh aloud, some stray drunken thought, and the sound froze Daphne. She pushed him away. Why had he laughed? What was so funny, so hilarious? She was deeply offended and too stoned to be objective. It was all so *intensely fucking personal.* He found her undesirable, right? She didn't have any tits, that was it, right? She was ashamed of her small tits. People were always talking about them. Get yourself some silicone implants, why doncha?

He'd forgotten the reason for his inappropriate laughter.

"I'm going upstairs," Alison said. "What about you?"

"Sure." Why linger here alone?

She rose, moved away from their table. Harry followed. When they reached the lobby she stopped, turning to him, putting her arms round him. Her need to hold was as great as his own. They stood motionless, clasped together, as if isolated from everything around them—people in the lobby, the thin sound of the piano, the elevator bell. A moment of fragile intimacy: Tennant was aroused by the girl's touch.

"I don't want to be on my own," she said. "Not tonight."

Loneliness. He too had had enough of absences.

They stepped inside the elevator. Tennant, his arm around Alison's shoulders, saw himself in the mirror. The girl was tiny beside him. Her face, pressed against his chest, had assumed a quiet vulnerability he hadn't seen before, another side of her. He kissed the top of her head softly, and she raised her face, smiling at him in a rather wistful way. It was as if she were saying, Protect me, Harry. Keep me from harm.

When they emerged from the elevator, they walked along the corridor rather slowly, two people balanced on the gyroscope of the immediate future. He had the thought: *I want her. I want her badly.* It was more than an anodyne against solitude.

He unlocked his door, fumbling the key. The girl followed him inside the room.

He was at once assailed in the darkness by an unpleasant scent he couldn't identify. He switched on the light. He heard Alison gasp.

He wished he'd let the room stay black.

The man who had called himself Alphonse Trebanzi lay on the floor. Electricity illuminated the red-purple skin. It lit the barbarous slit in the man's throat and brightened the blood that soaked his clothes. The lurid effect was of scarlet neon: blood, blood everywhere.

9 The girl kept saying "Christ" over and over as she slumped against Tennant, who held her as hard as he could, as if he might somehow eradicate the sight on the bed, conjure it away. *Seek the calm center, boyo. Don't get upset with things. Take control.* Yes, yes, whoever you are, whoever you are that speaks inside my head. *Take control. Cope. Boyo.*

How? How do you cope with this? This wasn't a dead animal to be buried, however sorrowfully, in the depths of a forest. This was a man Tennant thought he had somehow known in the lost years. Who could tell? The figure that lay on the bed might have been a friend back then, someone with more than a goddamn photograph in common.

How do you reach over the divide that keeps you from yourself? You need a door to the past; but it had shut tight with the murder of Bear Sajac. He looked down at the floor. The corpse seemed by some illusion to hover in dark red light.

Somebody had brought Bear Sajac here and killed him. Somebody.

Who and why? Of whom had Sajac been so afraid? *Them. The Faceless Ones.*

Alison, her expression that of somebody struck hard in the face, said, "The poor, poor bastard."

"Yeah, the poor bastard." Feeling nausea, Tennant went inside the bathroom and filled the sink with cold water, then dipped his face into it. His head buzzed. He opened his eyes under water. It was good to be briefly enclosed in a wet cool place. He permitted himself the luxury of thinking he'd dreamed Sajac's body the way he must have dreamed everything else. The bust. The girl. The lost years. Any moment now he'd come wide-awake, sweating in terror, fumbling his way toward relief. Ha! A nightmare! The mind darkly frolicking. Nothing more. *My mind.* I have lost it. Completely. I have a jellyfish in my skull.

He pulled his face from the bowl of water and reached for a towel. He dried his skin and went back into the bedroom. Alison took the towel from his hand and tossed it over Sajac's features. A white flag. We've had enough. We can't go on.

He glanced at Alison, then turned to the window. His legs were heavy, not his own. The airshaft below was a great black rectangle perforated feebly here and there by lights from other rooms. The shaft itself remained finally impenetrable; it might have gone down forever, down through the city, subways, sewers, to unfathomable places. Tennant experienced the odd urge to open the window and step out into the big black space and fall between the pale lights and just keep on falling. Pull yourself together, Harry. Get a grip on this. Don't let go.

He opened the window. Fuel, wet concrete, sodden trash—these were preferable to the smell of the dead.

He thought: I could part company with the girl. I could pack my bag and split, stroll out of the girl's life, abandon her to her own pursuits. But she'd taken the edge off of his loneliness. She had touched him. He couldn't run out on her. Besides, where would he go? He had no idea. She'd taken him over; she was in charge of travel arrangements, routes, destinations.

The towel around Sajac's face had become stained with blackened blood. It seemed preposterous now, a mask, a Halloween joke. At any moment Sajac would sit up, whip the thing away, laugh, and say, *Gotcha going, huh?* But it wasn't to be like that. There was no practical joke here.

"They kill him," Tennant said. "They dump him here. It's a warning. It's a message. It's a fucking note written in blood telling me to mind my own business. Go away, Harry. Leave the past alone."

"It's more than a message, Harry. It's a lock. Whoever killed Sajac knows you can't go to the police."

Tennant hadn't thought that far ahead. He hadn't considered police, the consequences, the legal ramifications. In shock you don't make plans. You don't manipulate the future.

"You'll be the prime suspect. It's your room. And there's a dead man in it. The fuzz will take you downtown, pop your name in the computer. Bingo. Out comes the drug bust. You're a criminal, Harry. Worse, a fugitive. A front-running candidate for a murder rap. You know how cops think. They see one crime and immediately assume you're capable of another."

"Okay, I don't call the police."

"More than that. You *can't* call them."

Tennant sat on the edge of the bed. A lock. Shackles. *They* had him straitjacketed. "How did they find me?" he asked. "How did they know I was here in this hotel?"

"There's only one answer. We're being followed. All the way from upstate, we're being tracked."

"Tracked. Yeah. By whom?"

Alison sat alongside him. For a moment he entertained a suspicion he didn't need: This little girl had somehow left a trail for the Faceless Ones to follow. Inadvertently or otherwise. But he didn't like the otherwise. It was that question of trust again. It was busy signals on a phone line, disembodied voices droning through ductwork, whispers behind walls.

"I know what you're thinking, Harry," she said. "You're wondering about me. You're saying to yourself—first the drug bust, then I show up, and maybe there's a connection between the two. Take it a step further—am I on the level? Am I manipulating you for strange reasons of my own?"

He made a gesture of dispute. "You're wrong—"

"I don't think so. It's perfectly natural. After all, I just blow into your life." She touched the back of his hand. "You want to see my credentials? My Writer's Guild membership? My driver's license? You want me to show my plastic, Harry?"

He shook his head. He was uncomfortable. She'd divined his misgivings and her insight embarrassed him. He felt as if he'd been caught in an act of infidelity.

She said, "When it comes to me, what you see is what you get."

What you see is what you get. He wondered what it was he saw. He got up from the bed. The room stifled him. It brutalized him. He had to get away from this place. He considered the corridor beyond the door. Was it empty? Or was the killer of Sajac somewhere nearby? Killer, killers, singular, plural. He realized he was thinking exactly the way Bear Sajac had done. *How many others are with you? You got friends in the street?* He wondered if he was destined to spend the rest of his life the way Bear had tried—a demented recluse. Go underground, create a disguise, live a life of fear.

"Okay. Maybe it *is* my goddamn fault," Alison said. "If I hadn't come into your life, you wouldn't be here, would you? And maybe Sajac would still be alive, for Christ's sake. Maybe I am responsible for his death, Harry—"

"You can't think like that—"

"Why not? Why can't I think like that? I was the one who dug out the guy's address, I was the one who went looking for him, it was me that came up with the bright idea of doing a story on that goddamn photograph." She had tears in her eyes, and her small hands were clenched tightly.

"Quit," Tennant said. He drew her toward him and tried to calm her. "You can't blame yourself for any of this."

She clung to him for a time in silence. He stroked the back of her head gently. When she stepped back from him, she rubbed her eyes against her sleeve. She was working at being composed again. "Yeah. I'm fine. I'm a hundred percent now. I can't hang this shit on myself. You're right."

"I know I'm right," he said.

"Okay." She ran a hand through her short hair in a determined manner. "Okay. Let's get practical here. First thing, we move. We can't stay in this place."

The idea of movement was attractive. Do something. Walk, run, anything. Besides, this room wasn't his anymore. It belonged to the dead, who had that habit of disenfranchising the living.

"How far are we going to get before Sajac's devils catch up with us?" he asked.

"I don't think that's the question. They've already caught up with us. The real question is why they don't put a stop to us right now. Why let us go any further?" She glanced at the corpse. "If they don't want us to dig, why not do a disposal job and get it over with?"

Tennant had no answers. He began to stuff his few possessions into his canvas bag. He thought of the darkness outside; it had changed now, populated as it was by phantoms who had his private number. He took the gun from his coat and dropped it inside the bag, where it fell heavily among his clothes. He gazed at the weapon—half-concealed by the sleeve of a shirt—and he thought of Rayland Tennant.

He said, "My father knew where I'd been living. He knew my address for years. He's got a nose for keeping track."

"Sure, but it's quite a leap from that fact to the idea he might somehow be responsible for . . ." She gestured vaguely, as if she didn't know what she truly meant. "For us being followed. Why would he set people on our trail? And here's another biggie for you, Harry. If he *did* send spies, were they the same people that committed murder? If so, why?"

Around and around, Tennant thought. The carousel of problems. The teasers and the twisters. Around and around. You took a seat and you couldn't get off because the machine never stopped. When he thought of his father, he inevitably brought Colonel Harker to mind. It was all so undeniably clear, so reachable. Harker's bullet head, the military haircut, the absence of sideburns that gave him a sharp, terrifying, well-defined look, as if his face were constantly lit by an invisible lamp. Tennant remembered the implacable way the man had conducted himself in a court of law. Schooled and prompted by Rayland, Harker had hidden behind the veneer of duty. He was a soldier and X was the enemy and his function was to eliminate X and that was it. End of the ballgame. Tennant recalled, with biting clarity, a TV news report that pictured Rayland and the colonel strolling shoulder to shoulder from the court after the verdict had come down. Two self-satisfied men with blood on their hands. Absent from their expressions were any feelings for the dead women and babies Harker had left behind in Vietnam. Nothing of regret. Just graves. Just charred remains.

Another perfect memory. Something preserved. If he had amnesia, it was a selective sickness. It chose its moments. Now and then the clouds rolled off the horizon and you saw something: the prize of vision. The razor of insight.

He zipped his bag. He felt curiously callous: How could he walk away and leave the corpse in this room? Alison was already moving toward the door. "I only need to toss some stuff together," she said.

They went out into the corridor. Small pear-shaped lights lining the walls threw a dismal light that seemed sinister to him, as if the wattage had been reduced for a malignant purpose. Emptiness was spooky. He longed for crowded places, bright lights, clamor, all the things he'd spent the last nine years of his life avoiding. The strange lights diminished in shadows as the corridor stretched away. Ceiling and floor created parallel lines that seemingly met in infinity.

Alison went into her room and came back seconds later hurriedly thrusting things into a small leather overnight bag: tights, toothpaste, a red plastic hairbrush.

Tennant pushed the elevator button, then decided he didn't want to wait. He drew Alison toward the stairs. What lay in the streets? He felt he was rushing into blindness, into a deeper fugitive condition than he'd known before. Flight was a way of life, something to which you adapted quickly. If you didn't, you perished.

★   ★   ★

They encountered nobody on the way down. In the lobby there was only a night clerk and a uniformed doorman who eyed them in the way of doormen everywhere, assessing them for their tip potential. The man lost interest and turned away, coughing into a white-gloved hand. Outside it was raining, a soft drizzling rain that billowed down through the street lamps like strands of a broken silvery web.

The street was quiet. Alison's car, parked half a block away, was bright and conspicuous under the lamps. A red Cadillac convertible—why didn't she own something utterly nondescript, a Ford, a Dodge? When they reached the car, Tennant told her to drive—anywhere, it didn't matter for the moment.

Alison drove to the end of the street, where she made a left turn into one-way traffic. "Now what?"

"Out of this city for starters."

He watched the street, yellow cabs speeding down through their own violent spray, trucks clattering wildly. Traffic obeyed its own laws of gravity. The Hudson appeared, shivering, trapping fragments of light and dispersing them like glittering, distended fish. The random slipstream of things: Tennant had a sense of being caught up in an arbitrary universe. The bridge over the river seemed insubstantial to him, fragile as nylon, and yet it somehow supported the mass of traffic flowing over it. Like everything else, it could snap.

He needed space, quiet, a time in which he could collect himself. Speech was suddenly impossible. Words formed in his head, coagulated, fell apart in nonsense. He imagined he heard bells ringing in his head, and then the sound of demonic gulls screeching—and there was an uneasy familiarity in these noises, as if he'd heard them a long time ago.

Alison pulled the Cadillac over into the forecourt of a gas station, turned off the motor, sat for a time in the kind of silence that suggests frustration.

"The sensible part of me tells me this whole thing is fucked," she said eventually. "If we back off now, maybe we'll have some kind of chance. Maybe we won't end up like that miserable bastard."

"Is that what you want? To walk away?"

"I'm not the walking type, Harry. I don't always listen to the reasonable part of my brain. If I did, I'd be raising kids of my own in a ranch-style house in Tonawanda and cooking suppers for my workaholic husband. Something like that."

Tennant was quiet for a while, gazing at the darkened gas pumps and the solitary neon that said EXXON in a window. It was an eerie little pocket of civilization; each pump was a square motionless figure, the neon a malevolent formation of gasses.

"I hate this . . . this goddamn manipulation," he said. "Somebody's trying to tell me to stay away from my own past. I'm sick to death of threats. I'm up to here with people taking away things that belong to me." *And I'm scared*, he thought. He punched the palm of his left hand and sighed.

Turning, looking back, he saw the skyline of Manhattan, the light show. "Drive," he said.

He had no sense of destination, no purpose. He knew only that he'd underestimated flight. It was *more* than a mere way of life; it consumed you. He thought of nothing but distance, space between himself and the pathetic remains of Sajac.

10 The motel, a barren, balconied affair, was located outside the town of Bethlehem just across the Pennsylvania state line from New Jersey. Bethlehem: Christmas and old steelworks and German immigrants. In the 3:00 A.M. darkness the town struck Tennant as sad, as if it were dying, withering into itself. He and Alison checked into a single room with twin beds, a shabby box in which thousands of people had come and gone, leaving behind grease marks on the wallpaper, cigarette burns on the edge of the coffee table, a crack in the bathroom mirror. Happy days in Christmas City.

The drive had been tense, Alison constantly checking the rearview mirror, Tennant looking back every five minutes or so to scrutinize the dark highway. He wasn't aware of having been followed. And yet the sensation that he was somehow being *perceived* wouldn't leave him.

He sat on the bed that was situated close to the window. Alison drew the curtains. To keep out the night, he thought. To create an illusion of safety. He watched her switch on the TV, which played without sound. An underwater explorer floated silently among shivering sea plants while exotic fish moved away from him in translucent schools, like small flickers of electricity. Bubbles rose in a constant stream from the swimmer's mask. Tennant looked at the picture a moment, drawn into its placid quality. Alison lay on the other bed and stared at the ceiling. Her expression was remote, as if she were gazing into the future and seeing there absolutely nothing; the void at the center of a crystal ball.

He had the urge to hold her, to make a connection. He imagined, as he'd done in the hotel bar, that contact might defuse the menace surrounding them. But he didn't move. She got up from the bed and strolled into the bathroom. After she'd closed the door, there was the sound of the shower drumming upon tiles. He thought of water falling across her naked body, rolling over her breasts and her flat stomach and between her thighs—pictures going nowhere except into dead ends and impossibilities.

He gazed back at the explorer, who was surrounded by a blaze of pink coral. A large crab scuttled across the seabed, tossing up puffy little clouds of sand. He thought of a day when he'd gone to Pacifica where, stoned on some wicked acid, he'd sat on the beach and watched the sun set. People did that back then, a common ritual, a cool thing. Tripping on mushrooms, LSD, zonked on Thai sticks, any viable substance that would loosen the stranglehold of the senses, they gazed blankly into that great Californian orange disk of the sun, seeing all manner of patterns in light on water and thinking all kinds of disconnected cosmic thoughts, the intensity of which suggested they simply had to be *real*.

He remembered a blond, long-haired, doped boy walking past, muttering that he *was* the sun. Wowee! You oughta be there, man! Wasted, Tennant had experienced a deep, druggy lethargy that kept him motionless on the sand; in his torpor, he was detached from the world.

There was an oddity about the memory, a shadow of sorts. He'd gone to Pacifica with somebody, he was certain of that. Only he couldn't bring to mind the face of the other. No name, no face. Simply a presence. A spook. Another specter. A ghost in sunlight. He pressed his fingertips on his eyelids, as if he might force the image into view. Broken, he thought. My whole life is broken.

The bathroom door opened. Alison, wearing a gray silk slip, her hair wrapped in a damp towel, stepped toward her bed. She lay down without looking at him. "I needed that," she said. "God bless the therapy of water." She stretched both arms upward, her fingers extended. The graceful little movement suggested a passage in a dance. She pulled the towel free of her head and tossed it aside.

Her short hair sparkled with drops of water. A damp patch was visible through her slip at the thigh where she hadn't dried herself completely. Tennant was absorbed in this discolored area. He imagined feeling it, then raising the slip up and over her shoulders. Down into her flesh, her mouth, down inside her.

"I don't think it would help, Harry," she said. "You know that, don't you."

Perceptive little thing. "I guess I do."

"It would only be a complication, Harry."

"Some complications are easier than others," he said.

A droplet of water adhered to the shade of the bedside lamp, where it glowed before dissolving. "I can see where it would be a kind of escape hatch," she said, and she smiled at him. "On a temporary basis. Only I don't do temporary too well, Harry. I like commitment. But I don't need it in my life, especially in these circumstances. Does that clarify things for you?"

She rose from her bed and approached him; she sat, taking his hand, gently running her fingertips between the mounds of his knuckles.

"I like you," she said. "I like you a lot."

"Is this a tease?"

"Teasing you isn't in my repertoire, Harry."

"What you see is what you get."

"Right."

"Maybe you can tell me what I'm seeing right now."

"Somebody on the edge, Harry. Somebody who's become fond of you except she isn't sure what that involves because she doesn't really know who you are. Somebody whose future is a tad uncertain and who has a murder on her mind. Somebody who might be developing a really substantial paranoia."

Bad timing, Tennant thought. The room was filled, not with the breathless possibility of sex, but with the smell of Sajac's death. He looked into her eyes; the blackness there resembled one of those incredible starless nights in which nothing whispers, no wind shakes the trees, no animal forages. You could fall in love with those eyes alone.

"Have you ever been in love?" he asked.

"You come out of left field sometimes, don't you?"

"Curiosity, that's all." I want to know you, he thought. I want to reach a place where there are no secrets.

"I'm not sure I know how to define love, Harry."

"And I thought I was asking a simple question."

"Okay. Let's see. I had this mad passion one time for a guy called Stern. Charlie Stern. Class valedictorian in high school. Editor of the school paper. President of the student union. Mr. Big. We had some fumbling behind the bleachers. I thought my heart was going to shoot right out of my throat that night."

"What happened?"

Alison smiled. "Sad really. There I was all set to give up my suffocating virginity when poor Charlie Stern ejaculated in his pants. He avoided me after that. Embarrassed, I guess. Then, when I was in college, I had a fling with my professor, a married man by God. Swore he'd leave his wife and all that bull-shit. It came to nothing in the end. I was that semester's affair. He had a notorious habit of bedding his female students. I was one more conquest. Another notch. At least he gave me an A."

He had the feeling she hadn't answered his question, but had circled it instead, as if the subject of love was one on which she wouldn't be drawn. Secrets, he thought. Things she doesn't want to say. He was reminded of how she resisted his question about her parents in Buffalo. Okay. There were sides to her he didn't know. Live with the fact. You don't get to

know another person in a matter of days. It takes time, a lifetime.

"What about you, Harry? You been in love?"

The question stung him because he had no answer. He
stared at the ceiling. Had his life been loveless? There had been
girls in the Haight, there were always girls in the Haight
because sex was what everybody did—casual, carefree, going
through the motions of the deceptive new liberty. You fucked
indiscriminately because it was one way of saying, *Look, all the
old values are dead.* But love? He felt the panic of a man trying
to check his own pulse and failing to find it. I'd remember love,
he thought. Wouldn't I? I'd remember love. Something that
intense.

"Sorry. I shouldn't have asked," Alison said. She kissed
him lightly on the forehead—he smelled soap on her skin,
shampoo in her hair—then she rose and went back to her own
bed, where she sat with her legs crossed and hands clasped.
She arranged the slip as demurely as she could. If there was to
be anything between them, it had been put on hold.

The underwater diver on TV had surfaced, ripping his
mask off. He held something aloft in one hand, a trophy seized
from the deep, a gigantic shell, the former habitat of some poor
evicted gastropod. The man's life seemed very uncomplicated
to Tennant. He finned his way down through clear tropical
water and came back with a shell and that made him enthusias-
tic and happy. I must learn to dive. I must learn the simplicity
of shells. I would be a contented man.

Alison clicked her thumb and middle finger together. "Obe
might be the key," she said. "We've got to see him. We've got
to know if he arranged that particular group for a specific purpose."

"What makes you think Obe can tell us anything?" he
asked. "You said he'd lost it."

"His *wife* said he'd lost it, Harry. I didn't see for myself."

"And you want proof?"

"I'm addicted to proof."

"You said he was in Iowa. You know where exactly?"

"I know where his wife is."

"And we just go and ask for directions to Sammy? Where's the asylum? What's Sammy's room number?"

"Sure."

"If she refuses?"

"I'm a firm believer in not crossing bridges before I come to them."

Tennant reached out and switched off the bedside lamp. He'd never been in Iowa. But one place was as good or bad as any right now.

"As soon as it's light," she said. "We're out of here."

He slept in a superficial way, drifting in and out of awareness. He enjoyed the proximity of Alison, the idea that she lay only a few feet away. He dreamed of Chinatown, the fronts of tourist shops, gaudy silks, screens, paper lanterns. Somebody was beckoning to him, a figure in a shop doorway. He couldn't see a face, only an outstretched hand. At some point the sky over Chinatown was filled with screaming gulls flying across the sun.

The sound of a car in the parking lot woke him and the dream dissolved and he lay silent and tense, expecting to hear someone at the door. But nothing happened. Before daylight he woke again, this time with an erection, although he couldn't remember a dream that might have inspired it.

He looked at the curtains, which had begun to glow. On the other bed, Alison turned restlessly, asleep still but apparently troubled by specters of her own.

The parking lot of the motel lay beneath a skein of pale pink sunlight. The few other cars parked neatly in their slots shone in a dull way. So far as Tennant could tell they were unoccupied. He scanned them quickly as he got inside the Cadillac. It was going to be one of those glorious clear blue days of late summer, wonderful visibility; it was the kind of day in which his awareness of vulnerability could only be increased by the clarity of the landscape. He and Alison would drive back roads,

of course, but even so Tennant knew he wasn't going to be able
to subdue his tension. Where could you hide in this great blue-
sky continent? The sun was already huge by the time Alison
had driven twenty miles, and the pink had yielded to a fiery
orange that appeared to make trees and meadows blaze; a fero-
cious sun of unbroken scrutiny.

He took a road map from the glove compartment. Pennsylvania was a vast wedge of land that ended in one direction on
the shores of Lake Erie, and in another on the Ohio state line.
Youngstown, East Palestine, East Liverpool. In the center lay
the Appalachians, dotted by villages, small settlements, towns
that seemingly had no reason to exist other than as places on a
map. St. Augustin. Glasgow. Cassandra. What did people do
in a place called Cassandra? Feel sorry for themselves?

He and Alison shared driving, speaking only rarely to each
other. Tennant concentrated on the fields and woodlands that
breezed past. He rolled down his window, catching the sharply
delicious smell of fresh-cut grass. He tried to imagine he was
complete, that he had total recall of his past. The mysterious
dead were figments who had existed only in an old insignificant
photograph. I am not Harry Tennant, he thought. Harry Tennant is also dead. I am somebody else, a nameless fugitive. But
then he'd glance back too often, searching the road for any sign
of a car tracking the Cadillac, and the illusion, already so fragile, would dissolve. Where were they, he wondered, the pur-
suers, the followers? Why weren't they evident? Did they have
some improbable power that enabled them to merge with the
landscape? These questions worried him. Unanswered, they
seemed to give flight another, darker, dimension: What if
nobody was tracking them? What if everything were a complicated construct of the mind?

Alison stopped at a rural diner that sold chicken-fried steak
and biscuits with gravy. An American flag hung outside the
premises. The pole, blinding white in the sun, had recently
been painted. The flag itself had the look of a garment laun-
dered only ten minutes ago. Inside, where it was dark and cool
and fragrant with fried onions, Tennant, suddenly ravenous,

ordered two hamburgers and french fries and a Coke, roadhouse cuisine, greasy and magnificent. Alison nibbled on Tennant's french fries and drank ice water. She kept looking out the window. A spotty kid in oily coveralls stood by the pumps, arms folded, his expression as interesting as a donut. He turned once to look in her direction. His face remained impassive. He was eighteen, nineteen, but he seemed already old, as if pumping gas for passing tourists had wearied him beyond recovery.

"We need to get rid of the Cadillac," Alison said. "First used-car place we find, I'll trade the thing for something less conspicuous. Something totally *dull*. Black or beige."

"Wise move."

Tennant finished his food, pushed the plate away, and went to the men's room, where the smell of urine and pine disinfectant was overpowering. He closed the door and walked to the urinal. As he unzipped, a man entered the room. He was plump, wore black glasses and a short-sleeved Hawaiian shirt, a riot of bananas and parrots and palm fronds, a bad dream in rayon. He had a baseball cap with the logo of the Kansas City Royals. He went to the washbasin and turned on a faucet, holding his thick hands under the flow of water. He looked at himself in the mirror, which was when Tennant glanced at him.

The abrupt sense of recognition unnerved Tennant, who stepped away from the urinal. He watched the fat man turn toward the towel roll and dry his hands methodically, one finger at a time. Tennant—dispensing with doubt, galvanized by anger, frustrated—moved quickly, forcing his arm against the man's neck, pushing the head forward into the wall. The baseball cap rolled away and the fat man grunted. His neck was soft and fleshy and yielded easily under the pressure of Tennant's arm.

"Jesus Christ—"

"We keep meeting in toilets," Tennant said. "I don't like the intrusion on my privacy, fella."

The man squirmed, trying to turn his face around. The black glasses slid down his nose and he looked squashed, preposterous.

"What the fuck are you talking about, man?"

Tennant, who hadn't performed an act of violence since some pointless battle in grade school, two punches and a bloodied nose, said, "You were in the diner outside Albany. You followed me inside the john. Remember?" And he pressed harder, appalled by the way he was enjoying this moment. "Remember?"

"Albany? I never even been to the place. Jesus Christ. Look. If you want money, I got about seventy bucks, my hip pocket, take it, take it for God's sake. Just don't hurt me." The designer glasses fell and shattered on the hard floor, tiny specks of black.

"I don't want your goddamn money," Tennant said. "I want you off my back."

"Lookit, I never seen you in my life, go on, check my wallet, man, I sell insurance, I got my own agency in Williamsport, Walter Swin's my name, see for yourself," and he struggled to get the wallet out of his back pocket. Tennant knocked the hand away and seized the wallet from the pocket himself. He released the man, who rubbed his sweaty neck.

"My glasses. Lookit my glasses. Goddamn Ray.Bans. Lookit. You're outta your mind."

Tennant let the wallet dangle open. A plastic concertina of credit cards, a driver's license, membership in the Rotary Club, the Williamsport Chamber of Commerce, and a business card on which was written WALTER SWIN, INSURANCE BROKER. The wallet also revealed snapshots of an overweight blonde woman and two plump kids with flesh the color of white bread. He released the man completely and, still holding the wallet, stepped away. Under his feet the broken Ray.Bans crunched, a melancholy little sound. What had he done? What the hell had he done here? Confused, he saw his face in the mirror—scruffy, hardly recognizable even to himself. Harry Tennant, stranger. Violence was a new madness for him. He gazed again at the wallet; Walter Swin's self-contained world was so ordinary, so banal, and the man himself such a quivering bundle of apprehension, that Tennant didn't doubt the authenticity of the cards and photographs and memberships. He'd blundered into that bizarre world of plastic, that network of cards and documents upon which everyone's identity rested, that computerized, germfree universe in which you couldn't be the person you claimed to be unless you had evidence, credentials of yourself—as if constant reminders were needed because the country suffered from neurosis, an identity crisis too deep to understand. He remembered how Sajac had gone through Alison's purse, with the quick, greedy movements of a scared man. Had he behaved like that? Crazy, mindless, terrified into violence? *I am turning into Bear Sajac. A cruel metamorphosis.*

He handed the wallet back. "Listen, I don't know what to say."

"I oughta report you to the law. Guys like you shouldn't be running round. Guys like you should be locked up. Key thrown away." Walter Swin was indignant now. He'd escaped an encounter with a lunatic in a public toilet and he was reasserting himself. Didn't he have rights, after all? What was the Republic coming to? A man couldn't wash his hands without being assaulted? What kinda situation was that?

"I'm sorry, that's all I can say."

"Yeah. Right. Well. You may be sorry, guy. All well and good, yeah. But lookit my glasses, Christsake."

"Here, here," and Tennant took a bill from his pocket, a hundred, pressing it into Walter Swin's squablike hand.

"That covers the glasses, I guess. I gotta, I gotta, I gotta mind . . ." Suitably bribed, the fat man ran out of indignation all at once. Tennant, finding it difficult to breathe, his chest aching anew from Sajac's blow, picked up the baseball cap and handed it back, then stepped out of the toilet. Alison wasn't at the table. The empty space troubled him briefly, but then he saw her through the window. She was leaning against the Cadillac, staring off into the distance. She was wearing pale-tinted shades and running a hand through her hair. In the glare of sunlight, which reflected ferociously from the red car, she looked frail, diminished. He felt a protective urge toward her, but even as he stepped through the door and tried to dismiss the embarrassing encounter in the toilet, he wondered how he could safeguard somebody else when it was troublingly clear he had a frequent problem protecting Harry Tennant—that inscrutable entity—from himself.

11 It was late in the afternoon when Alison traded the Cadillac at a car lot in Columbus, Ohio. She chose a late-model black Buick, marvelously nondescript, twelve thousand miles on the clock. The salesman, dressed in a chocolate polyester suit and white shoes, wore a St. Francis medal against his furry chest. His simian hands were covered with black hair and he had a gold front tooth, which he fingered constantly. The deal involved some basic haggling, which Alison might have strung out because the car she was trading in was, after all, something of a classic. In her urgency to make the trade and move on, she accepted a straight swap. A great Cadillac convertible for a boring Buick, what the hell, sign the title papers, let's hit the road.

The Buick was equipped with a computerized dashboard that constantly issued digital information; the assumption in Detroit, it seemed to Tennant, was that all drivers, because they were morons, needed elementary electronic signals that might be as easily read as TV graphics. This thought dissolved into images of great abandoned car factories, broken

windows, unemployed men and women, the homeless; there
was a sorrow at the core of the country, a collapse into
despair and anger that spawned savagery, casual gunplay,
whimsical tragedies. He thought of all the old promise that
had existed so briefly in the Haight and how it had gone out
like a shattered light bulb. Martin Luther King. Bobby
Kennedy. Vietnam. Assassinations, coffins draped in flags,
men like Noel Harker who considered the war their private
killing ground.

He thought of poor fat Walter Swin in the men's room and
was embarrassed by his own outburst of violence. For a
moment he might gladly have broken some bones. What did
that make him? Had he ever been violent before? Had he
always been the hippie pacifist, the Haight dopehead dead set
against his father's world, the guy who walked in peace marches
stoned? He thought: I could have been anybody, anything, a
serial killer, a rapist, a monk, and I wouldn't know. He was an
unwritten book, blank chapters, a zero.

Alison said, "I just gave away a beautiful car for a goddamn
Wurlitzer on wheels. I have to wonder if it was worth it."

Tennant made a remark about the uncomplicated joy of
anonymity. Change a car, you're harder to find. He put no
great conviction into his words. Hope was a raft, and you clung
to it any way you could. You went under, came up again,
prayed for gentler waters.

Beyond Columbus, with twilight drifting lazily across the
landscape, he took over the driving. Alison fell asleep in the
passenger seat, her head inclined toward Tennant's shoulder. He liked the way she felt against him. Indiana lay ahead,
then Illinois. After that was Iowa, the heartland, and Sammy
Obe.

Night fell and the blackness of the highway was awesome.
The lights of oncoming cars dazzled him. Every now and then
his rearview mirror glared, and he imagined a spotlight being
turned on the Buick, illuminating both himself and Alison.
Once, overhead, he saw the solitary light of a helicopter cross-

ing the highway; with the window rolled down he could hear
blades thrash hot dark air. From above, from behind—where
did you look?

He drove one-handed, letting the free hand rest on Alison's smooth neck, where a small pulse beat. The digital
lights on the dash that informed you of gasoline usage and
mileage and outside temperature created a red glow, impart-
ing the strange impression you were traveling in a photographer's darkroom. When he could drive no farther and weariness had begun to distort his vision, he found a rest area and
parked the car. There were about six other cars in the parking spaces. He got out and stamped his feet to recharge his
circulation. He smoked a cigarette, his first in a long time,
and gazed at the small stone structure in which toilets were
located. A woman in a polka-dot dress came out, passed
beneath a lamp, and walked to her car. Tennant watched
her.

The woman—middle-aged, her dyed scarlet hair moussed
stiff and slightly ridiculous—took keys from her purse,
unlocked the door of her car, then paused. Momentarily she
turned in Tennant's direction, as if afflicted by a fear of brig-
ands and scoundrels in the lonely rest areas of America's free-
ways. Then she got inside her car and closed the door. Tennant
saw her back out and drive off. You suspect everyone, he
thought. It becomes habit, dreadful habit.

"Where are we?" Alison stepped from the Buick.

"Illinois. Indiana." He shrugged. What did their precise
location matter as long as their direction was generally the right
one? The flat, unlit landscape made geographical distinctions
vague. You moved, you kept moving, if you were going west
you were doing fine.

Alison said, "Let me drive for a while. I feel okay. You
rest."

Rest. That appealed to him. He sat in the passenger seat,
closed his eyes, felt a tide of fatigue wash over him, then
retreat, then return. His shoulders ached from driving. He

drifted for a few minutes, lulled into a thin sleep by the rhythm of the car.

He awoke—thinking of the room on Schrader and hippies painting in the sunlight. Scaffolding. The image panicked him.

He tried to relax, drummed his fingers on his knees, stretched his legs, switched on the radio. The music, riddled by static, was a song out of the past, "Good-day, Sunshine." He changed the station, found country-western, a loathsome little ditty about a man tired of crying over a woman called Ruby. He switched off the radio, thinking self-pity should never be set to music.

"You're antsy," Alison said.

Tennant looked at an enormous truck roaring in the opposite direction, blowing vast clouds of smoke from its stack. "I'm fine," was all he said. Why had he begun to feel this bad?

She reached out and placed her fingers in the palm of his hand. "You're sweating."

"It's hot in here."

"The windows are down, Harry."

"It's still hot." His heart beat was going fast. His pulse went at speed. He'd felt this way a few times on cocaine, slippage yielding to panic and then to a sense of your own doom. Coronary hour, an explosion in the old chambers. The downhill rush of the locomotive going out of control.

"Are you feeling sick?"

He shook his head. Sick, hell no, he was in fine shape, A1, first class, blue ribbon—except for the bothersome volcanic eruptions that every so often spewed lava and scattered ash inside his head. Help me, Alison, he thought. Get me out of this bummer.

"I'll pull over if you like."

"I'm fine."

"You don't have to shout. I'm only twelve inches away."

"Was I shouting?"

"Yeah. You were shouting."

"I'm sorry."

"It's okay." She looked at him quickly. "You want to talk? Or do I get some guff about a dizzy spell?"

"I was thinking about something, that's all."

"I'm listening."

"A room on Schrader Street in the Haight. That's what I was trying to remember. It bugs me. I can't place it exactly."

"Did you live there once?"

"I don't know."

"Do you think you could find the place again?"

Tennant shrugged. He couldn't be sure. He looked at the road ahead. A house on Schrader. What was the big deal anyway? A room, a few details, hippies splashing color on walls. He shut his eyes. Squeeze the brain, the headbox, force something out, for God's sake. Sweat ran over his eyelids.

He saw Maggie Silver.

Beneath the struts and planks of scaffolding, Maggie Silver raised her face in sunlight and smiled and waved her hand—and that was it, that was all, the image imploded and he opened his eyes. There was a confusion of leftover feelings he couldn't define—warmth, anguish, sadness: They swarmed through him furiously. But it was sadness mainly, the kind that runs dark and deep. What had Maggie Silver meant to him anyway? Down which culvert of his history had she walked? How had she touched him? There had to be a connection, something that linked himself to Maggie Silver and the house on Schrader.

"Harry," the girl said. "You didn't answer my question."

His throat was dry. The sensation of sadness wouldn't lift. "Maybe I could find the place. Maybe. I'm not sure. I get these flashes and they're not exactly precise." He wondered if he should mention the image of Maggie Silver. He dismissed the prospect; it was too ill-defined, and somehow too private, to speak aloud. "It's like messages from nowhere. Like a bombardment out of the sky. It's hard to explain."

Alison drove in silence for a mile or so. Tennant had the feeling they were traveling nowhere; west had become an abstract concept. Iowa was a word in a surreal collage. He was lost. He yearned for certainty. Other men led lives of self-assurance and quiet dignity, sedately organized existences recorded in diaries and notebooks and correspondence, in mortgages and checking accounts; they had life insurance and health insurance and car insurance, protection up the ying-yang. They understood where they were going and how to get there. They had wives who smiled and kids who went to college to become dentists or veterinarians. They constructed worlds of substance. Tennant, whose life in the Haight had been a form of disdain for these men, experienced a tiny envy of them now. What would it be like to live in a world of order and serenity? It didn't seem so dreadful to him after all. But how did you gain entrance, what dues did you have to pay?

He stared at the highway. In the headlights of the car it resembled some awful black predatory mouth into which he and Alison were rushing.

He must have slept again, because when he opened his eyes it was dawn and he was confused by his surroundings. The car was parked in the lot of a suburban shopping center, an expanse of empty concrete and unlit lamps. The place was clearly abandoned. The storefronts were empty. Some had old Going Out of Business sale signs in their windows. A commercial death had taken place here.

"Welcome to Iowa," Alison said. She looked and sounded bright, alert. He wondered about the sources of her stamina. Youth had everything except that which comes from experience: a tendency to weariness. "According to the address I've got, we're about twenty miles from where Karen Obe lives. We've got two options. Either we go there immediately or we find a motel and rest for a while."

"It's up to you."

"I'd like to see the woman first."

Tennant glanced around the parking lot. The place made

him feel exposed, conspicuous. "Let's go," he said, thinking how bad he must look himself, if the bitter taste in his mouth was any indication. He thought of swinging the rearview mirror so that he might see his own reflection. The hell with it. He didn't need to see Harry Tennant staring back. Some things couldn't be faced on an empty stomach.

Karen Obe's house was difficult to locate. Alison had to ask directions in a roadside café in a small village that consisted of a post office and five or six frame houses. Beyond the village the road was a narrow blacktop, badly cracked, neglected. It ran between flat fields that stretched as far as Tennant could see. A few of these fields had recently been harvested, but most lay barren, untilled dark earth and vigorous outgrowths of weeds. Here and there you could see FOR SALE signs and dilapidated farmhouses where porches listed and shingles had fallen from roofs, empty places that suggested more than mere abandonment of property; here, people had been uprooted and forced out of their lives, and now decay had taken the place of pride. The landscape was a bleak statement of its own. Tennant, seeing a rusted old tractor in a field, had a fleeting thought of his own woods, and his small white house, which would probably fall into ruin as certainly as these farmhouses.

Depressing dawn; a pink sun illuminated the relics of a way of life as though it were a spotlight in a museum of ancient artifacts. *What's a farmer, Daddy? They're extinct now, son.*

Alison drove a few more miles, then turned off the blacktop at a mailbox that had Karen Obe's name on it. At the end of a rutted dirt road the house came into view, a white-brick affair with an iron porch. Blinds were drawn on the lower windows. A pale blue Volvo with Iowa plates was parked to one side. A black dog, a hybrid of Labrador and hound, appeared on the porch, guarding the terrain with canine suspicion. The creature shuddered, barked a couple of times, then was silent; a certain sullen quality was evident in the animal's eyes.

The front door opened just as Alison parked, and a middle-aged woman in a long green dressing gown came out, her arms folded. Tennant thought her rather fleshy face was kind. Her hair was remarkable, a glorious red disarray that spilled around her shoulders. Uncombed, it had a vibrancy that couldn't have come from any bottle of conditioner. She tossed the hair away from her face as she stared at the car.

He and Alison got out of the Buick. The dog barked a few more times, then stepped back to stand at Karen Obe's side.

"Mrs. Obe?" Alison said. "We talked on the phone four or five weeks ago. Alison Seagrove?"

The woman smiled. "Sure. The journalist. I remember. You were interested in Sammy's work." She glanced at Tennant.

"This is Harry," Alison said. "He's helping me with my story. I hope we're not disturbing you."

"Hell, no, I'm an early bird. I just brewed some coffee if you want to come inside."

They followed Karen Obe into the house, which was furnished in a sparse way: a few items of scrubbed pine, a couple of Japanese prints. No photographs, Tennant noticed. None of Obe's work. She talked rapidly as she led them to the kitchen. I don't see many people out here, if it wasn't for the dog and the parrot I wouldn't have company, how do you take your coffee, I've got fresh cream if you like.

They sat together at a plain white table. In the window hung a large birdcage from which an oily green conure peered out morosely. The bird hopped suddenly from one spar to another, and a few feathers drifted in the air.

Tennant sipped his coffee. He was happy to let Alison ask the questions, to play the situation however she liked. She could be subtle if that was needed, forceful if she had to be. He admired her tenacity, even envied it. I need some of her stuff, he thought. I need an infusion of her kind of fortitude.

"It's such a pleasure somebody remembers Sammy's work, Miss Seagrove. Call me prejudiced, but I happen to think he was one of the best photographers of his time." Karen Obe had the air of a curator of a neglected museum taking delight in unexpected visitors.

Alison smiled in agreement with the woman. "This is the shot that intrigues us." She produced the clipping from her jeans. Straight to the point, Tennant thought. No waste of time.

Karen Obe took the picture and looked at it. "I could never forget this one. It's his most famous shot. I don't necessarily mean it's his best, of course, but it brought him a lot of money. A funny thing . . ." She paused, sat back in her chair, gazed at the parrot. "He never liked it himself all that much. I don't know why. He tended to dismiss it as an accident. But that's fame, I guess. Accidental. Maybe he thought it overshadowed some of his other stuff. The thing that brings you fame is the thing you sometimes come to resent."

She got up and poured more coffee. "I always thought the photograph brought him more bad luck than good."

"Bad luck?" Alison asked.

"There was the burglary, for starters." Karen Obe ran a hand through her lustrous red hair; a few strands of silver glistened. "A week after the picture was first published, somebody broke into our place in LA and stole Sammy's collection of negatives and prints. Devastating. Utterly devastating. A lifetime's work."

"Did you ever find the culprit?"

Karen Obe shook her head. "Never did. The thief stole some other stuff, but it was the collection that mattered most to us. Sammy took it very badly. He was never the same after that. About two weeks later, he began to believe somebody was following him. He was being watched. The phone was bugged."

She lit a cigarette, puffing on it twice before putting it out. "When it got to the stage where he imagined our water might be poisoned, I knew he badly needed professional help. I had a hell of a time convincing him, believe me. Sammy was always stubborn. Always went his own way. Anyway, he didn't get along with the first psychiatrist, who he decided was part of a conspiracy against him, so I talked him into trying another. It seemed to go okay for a couple of days." She got up from the table and fed a peanut to the conure. "So much for appearances. One morning I found him in his darkroom crying. He'd smashed his cameras with a hammer. The lenses were lying around broken. People were out to get him. There was nothing he could do about it. He just sat there crying. A complete wreck of a man. He began to lock himself in his darkroom for days. No food. Nothing to drink. Sometimes I could hear him singing these strange little songs. Tragic."

"And no explanation."

"No real explanation. What do doctors know anyway? The human mind. They don't know *that* about it, do they?" She lit another cigarette. The parrot squawked; a small bell rung in the cage. "They said he had symptoms of severe schizophrenia. What does that mean when you get down to it? All I know is this: I had a husband once and now I don't have anybody."

Tennant set down his coffee cup. He had all kinds of sympathy for Sammy Obe. "Is that all you were told? Severe schizophrenia?"

"Hell, no, they wrap it up in gobbledygook, don't they? Who am I to understand the kind of language these guys use? I know Sammy never came back to me. He never came back." She moved to the sink where she ran cold water over the backs of her hands, a reflex gesture, something to do while she struggled with an old grief that had clearly haunted her for years.

"What's the prognosis?" Alison asked.

"More of the same. He lives in his own limbo. And that's where he'll die, I guess."

The silence in the kitchen was interrupted only by the parrot's bell, which issued a thin metallic sound. Drying her hands, Karen Obe returned to the table where the photograph lay. She stared at it for a time but made no move to touch it, as if such an act might somehow transfer to her more bad luck. "What's your interest in this particular photo?" she asked.

"I've been trying to track down the participants," Alison answered. "For one of those 'Where Are They Now?' features. You know the kind of thing."

"Any success?"

"It's proving difficult. Except for Harry."

Karen Obe looked at Tennant, then back at the photograph. "That's you?"

Tennant nodded.

Karen Obe picked up the picture and squinted at it, as if she didn't believe the young man in the shot could be the one now sitting in her kitchen. "That's actually you?"

"I've changed," Tennant remarked.

"We've all changed, honey," the woman said. She put the photograph down and was silent for a time, walking between birdcage and table, nervously cracking the shells of peanuts and shoving them at the conure. She was clearly unsettled by Tennant's presence; the past might have been an unwelcome intruder in her own house. She turned from the cage and faced Tennant. "What do you remember about the day Sammy took that picture?"

"Very little," Tennant said.

"Nothing out of the ordinary, say?"

Tennant shrugged. He wasn't about to launch into an attempt to explain his situation. "Why do you ask?"

"I was kinda hoping you might enlighten me about something. A little mystery I've been carrying around for years."

"A mystery?" Alison asked.

"I don't know if it's such a big deal really." Karen Obe was hesitant. She brushed the fibrous remains of shells from the palms of her hands. She looked at Tennant again. "But since you were there that day, I'll show you anyway."

She walked out of the room. Tennant fidgeted with his coffee cup. Alison got up from the table and went to the window. She looked at Tennant expectantly. A little mystery, he thought. He wasn't sure he liked the idea of further puzzlement; but Alison did.

Karen Obe came back carrying a silk paisley scarf neatly

folded. "Before I show you this, I should tell you Sammy kept it in a safe-deposit box at his bank. It was the only thing in the box, so he must have considered it valuable in some way. I can't figure out why. But if it meant something to him, maybe it'll mean something to you."

She unfolded the scarf on the table. "I keep it hidden because it's the only thing of Sammy's I've got left. You understand, I wouldn't like somebody to steal it."

Concealed at the center of the scarf was a small white envelope, which she picked up very carefully and opened. With the tips of her fingers she took out a negative and held it up to the light. Tennant had one of those off-center moments, one of those imbalances, in which he knew he was going to see something significant. Karen Obe passed the negative to Alison, who studied it in silence for a while before she handed it to Tennant.

It was a black-and-white shot depicting, in the curious ghostly way of negatives, the same group of five hippies, but they were in disarray; something had happened off camera to make the group turn their heads and look to the side. *Harry Tennant, on the edge of the group, is pointing at something, hand in the air rather rigidly, a finger extended. The other faces are following the direction of his hand.*

Pointing at what? What had taken place across the street that day in Chinatown? What had interrupted the organization of Obe's composition?

"It must have been taken at roughly the same time as the shot that made your husband famous," Alison said.

"Minutes before, minutes after, it's hard to say," Karen Obe remarked. "I've looked at it a hundred times and every time I wish one of the faces would speak. I wish one of them would just step out of the negative and tell me what they were all so busy looking at. It spooks me. And why did Sammy go to the trouble of renting a safe-deposit box for one negative?"

Tennant thought: Minutes before, minutes after, it didn't make any difference, he couldn't bring it into focus anyway.

His head had begun to ache; his eyelids hurt. He thought of Chinatown, as if it were a nebulous place that existed only in the eye of the beholder. Look away, it's gone. All of it.

"And you don't remember, Harry?" Karen Obe asked.

Tennant said, "It could have been almost anything. The streets were filled with all kinds of activity back then. You name it, you could see it in San Francisco. Freaks, mimes, unicyclists, jugglers, fire-eaters, magicians, streakers, Frisbee tossers, musicians. Like I say, it could have been anything."

He held up the negative again. Stark white faces, black background—untethered white balloons floating in a midnight air. You are standing on a sidewalk in Chinatown, Harry. You are with a group of people you must have known. You are having a photograph taken. Across the street something is happening.

Across the street something is happening.

He thought: *A church on Grant and California streets.* What was it called? *St. Mary's?* It lurched toward him, like a framed picture whisked through the air by an earthquake. *St. Mary's.* Why would he be pointing at a church? He was infused by a feeling of expectancy, another little gate opening in his head.

"I wonder if it would be possible for us to visit your husband," Alison said.

"I don't see it would do any good," Karen Obe replied.

"Call it a shot in the dark."

"It might prove darker than you think, Miss Seagrove. He doesn't communicate. Even if he does—on rare days—nothing makes any sense. Not to me anyway. Still, if you're prepared to waste your time, that's up to you." She paused in an uncertain way. "He's in a place just outside Oskaloosa. The institute's called The Clinic. I like that, don't you? No Institute for the Insane. No asylum. Nothing revealing. Just The Clinic. If I called ahead and gave permission, they'd probably let you see him. It's going to depend on the kind of day he's having."

Alison thanked the woman. She was ready to leave; Tennant sensed her impatience.

"I wish you well," Karen Obe said. She picked up the negative, replaced it in the envelope, then folded the paisley scarf around it. "Both of you."

She walked them to the door and stepped out onto the porch alongside them. She held the scarf clutched to her side. She gazed across the fields.

Tennant followed her line of vision. Long-stalked grass grew, and weeds; a thin breeze blew through the blades, swaying them a little. It was easy to imagine people lying concealed in all that density, watching him. It was this place, that was all, this empty place, unsettling in its isolation. You could imagine anything here. A crow flew out of the grass, rising in ugly flight, as if aviation were a tremendous effort. It vanished over the house, feathers green-black in the sun.

"One thing," Karen Obe said. "If you ever turn anything up, let me know."

"Count on it," Alison said.

With a wave of her hand Mrs. Obe went back inside the house, moving with some reluctance. She didn't like her solitude. She closed the door. The dog slumped on the porch as if in dismay. Tennant and Alison walked to the car.

Tennant said, "Now I know one thing. Obe took his pictures across the street from a church called St. Mary's. Grant and California. Don't ask me why I know that, because I don't have an answer. But I know it anyway."

"You're *sure*?"

"As sure as I can be."

"That's something," Alison said.

"Something. Right. But what?"

"Never discount information, Harry. Now we've got a precise location, which we didn't have before, did we?" She switched on the engine, reversed the car, then swung it around toward the road. Tennant, thinking of the redbrick church in Chinatown, looked back at the upper windows of Karen Obe's house, which were reflecting the sun like mirrors too blinding to gaze at. Then the house vanished and the rutted dirt road gave way to the cracked blacktop.

Alison braked, studied the map, took a left turn. "Obe has a picture and he thinks it important enough to lock away, Harry. So he knew something. He *saw* whatever you saw outside St. Mary's Church. He must have. The next question is, what?"

What? Tennant thought. The biggie.

12 Twenty miles or so from Karen Obe's house, Tennant became conscious of a car traveling behind them, a pale blue Toyota. It could be perfectly innocent, of course. A farmer chugging along, a banker come to begin repossession proceedings on some unfortunate landowner. He mentioned the Toyota to Alison, who'd already seen it in the rearview mirror.

"If he's a watchdog, he's not up to the usual standard of performance," Tennant said.

"Maybe they've decided to become more visible. They want to make sure we behave."

"Keep driving. Don't take any evasive action. Don't suddenly turn up some sidetrack. I want to see what he does back there."

Mile after mile the Toyota stayed behind them. It made no move to pass, which might have been difficult anyway on so narrow a road. The blacktop finally came to an end on a wider county road; there was the option of turning either left or right.

"Which way, Harry?"

"It doesn't matter."

She went left. The Toyota took the same turning and

stayed behind. Tennant had the feeling that some invisible chain linked the Buick to the Japanese car; wherever the Buick went, the Toyota was sure to follow.

"He's persistent," Alison said.

"Maybe he just happens to be going in the same direction as us."

"We'll see."

Alison drove through a small town; a post office, a pencil-like memorial to war casualties, a grocery, a bar. The town was gone quickly, followed a few miles later by another almost exactly alike. A post office, a grocery, a bar. Solid frame houses, painted and maintained with great love, lurked behind ancient elms. America the peaceful. They sleep easy here, Tennant thought. They don't have crime and they don't have the dreariness of abandoned farmland to disrupt their view. A kid in a Megadeath T-shirt was delivering papers from a bike; a single touch of gothic in this pristine place.

The Toyota was still behind, a pale blue nuisance.

"Next place we come to we'll stop," Tennant suggested. "Find some breakfast. See if the Toyota vanishes."

It was fifteen miles further to the next town, which was different from the others they'd passed through. This was a run-down community of bleak houses, shuttered windows, rusted cars, uncollected garbage spilling from trash cans. Whatever industry had maintained this place had obviously shut up shop long ago. On the porch of a green shingle house, a black man stared at the Buick, as if the passage of an unknown car might be the high point of his day. *Saw a strange car today, hon,* he'd tell his wife. *Hell, no kidding,* the wife would answer. Life goes on.

Alison parked outside a diner, which specialized in the kind of food from which coronaries are constructed. Both she and Tennant ate hungrily, ignoring the grease in which strips of bacon floated and the single strand of hair Tennant found in his scrambled eggs. The blue Toyota had gone. It hadn't passed—Tennant had been watching from the window; either it had stopped some way back and the driver was watching the Buick, or it had taken a side road.

Alison shoved her plate aside. A fly swooped down into it. Tennant unfolded the map on the table. Oskaloosa was about thirty miles away, if you restricted your travel to back roads. He was suddenly sleepy, covered a yawn with this hand.

"Do you want to find a motel and get some rest before we go on?" Alison asked.

"I'll be fine."

"You don't look it." She reached across the table and brushed a fallen lock of hair from his forehead. "You need a shower and a haircut, Tennant. I don't want to be seen traveling around with a bum. I've got my standards."

"And I've got mine," Tennant said. Banter. Simple banter. Why not?

"A case could be made for some cologne, at the very least."

"Later." What a simple word, he thought. Later. People used it all the time without thinking that there might not be a later. He folded the map. "Let's get out of here."

They walked outside. There was no sign of the Toyota anywhere.

It began to rain on the way to Oskaloosa, a slow drizzle. The sun died in a flurry of clouds. The back roads were quiet, the countryside morose in the rain. Tennant, staring out at fields of stubble, had a sense of familiarity again, another of those quirky demonstrations of legerdemain his mind had a tendency to make. Iowa, gray fields, Oskaloosa. It was the feeling he'd had when he realized that Trebanzi was Bear Sajac. But why did he have it now? The feeling persisted weirdly, despite his efforts to cast it aside. He slumped down in the passenger seat, massaging his eyelids. He had no desire to look from the window. I don't know this place, he thought. I don't know Oskaloosa. I don't even want to imagine I do. My mind's a freak show. Stunted creatures parade back and forth and I watch them through bars. I pay my entrance fee, but I don't understand what I'm seeing. Misbegotten things waddle, hunchbacked monstrosities totter; a world of the grotesque. How do I get out of it?

"This is it, Harry," Alison said.

Tennant looked out. A long gravel driveway led to an unassuming brown brick building. Yes yes yes, he thought. If this was *déjà vu*, it was the strongest he'd ever experienced. He stared at the building. A discreet sign said THE CLINIC, INC. A medical corporation. Doctors busily turning themselves into limited companies. Entrepreneurs who just happened to have sworn to the Hippocratic oath. Another sign pointed the way to the office. Tennant opened the door, hearing his feet crunch in the gravel.

I have never been here before. Never.

Alison stretched her arms wearily. Tennant leaned against the car. Rain fell on his face, but he didn't feel it. It was as if there had grown around him a protective shell, shielding him from the world. It was perilously thin, this carapace, and already beginning in places to crack. Even as he walked toward the building and listened to the gravel, he was obliged to take Alison's arm for support. Why do I think I know this place? he wondered. But the question floated away from his mind, as if he'd never asked it in the first place. Suddenly he was fine again, steady on his feet. The faintness passed out of him. He was a man visiting a clinic, that was all. No more than that. Making a call, then going on his way. Yes.

He followed Alison inside the building. The foyer was painted a high-gloss white. A woman in a gray shirt sat behind the reception desk and smiled at Harry.

"What can I do for you?" she asked. She had perfect white teeth.

I wonder, Tennant thought. I really wonder.

Alison said, "We'd like to see Sammy Obe."

"Do you have an appointment?" The receptionist continued to smile politely. She'd been trained in the art of being pleasant. She'c say things like have a nice day. Take care. Come again soon.

"Not exactly," Alison said. "But we just came from seeing his wife, and she had no objections to our visit "

"I'll have to check that, you understand. Have a seat. Make yourselves comfortable. I'll be right back." The receptionist went inside another room.

Tennant sat on a soft beige sofa, while Alison remained at the desk. He studied the few illustrations hung around the room. They were mainly Constable prints, pastoral and placid, intended no doubt to induce in visitors a certain serenity. This place is no madhouse, you see. It's a quietly discreet institution where people can get well. Tender loving care is the main weapon in our arsenal. And drugs, Tennant thought. Let us not forget the drugs. Thorazine, diazepam, Librium, Dilaudid, all the other little downers that lulled the deranged inhabitants into lassitude. You didn't deal with madness, you numbed it. That made it easier for the handlers to manage the loonies.

Restless, he got up, paced, walked to the door. Through the glass pane he could see rain sweep the gravel driveway.

The rain. The driveway. He realized he was sweating, clenching his hands. The reactions of panic.

Alison smiled at him in an absent kind of way. The receptionist hadn't come back yet.

"She'll check with Karen, I guess. Then she'll probably have to talk to the resident shrink. Red tape."

Shrink. The word stuck in Tennant's head like a moth to a screen door. He sat down; Alison joined him. Her nearness was a comfort.

"I was thinking," he said. "Maybe I should turn myself in to a joint like this and see if they can fix me. Amnesia must be run-of-the-mill stuff around here."

"I'm sure," the girl said.

"I'll make an appointment. Maybe they can do it quickly, like those eyeglass places that grind your lenses while you wait." His voice was thin. The prints on the walls were having a bad effect on him. They changed as he gazed at them, colors seeming to mutate, lines losing their shape. They might have been the harbingers of migraine. He thought of that solitary negative in Karen Obe's house, the faces turned away from the camera, his own hand pointing. He'd gone to Chinatown that day because, because—

Just because.

Maggie Silver said Look look

But that didn't quite make it, the voice was disembodied. Instead, he was blindly plunged inside the room in the house on Schrader and somebody was screaming, a girl, Maggie Silver, why was she screaming so—

The receptionist had returned. "Everything seems to be in order." She produced a register in which visitors had to sign their names. Tennant stared at the book. The blank page accused him. He took the receptionist's pen and wrote down: Harry Rayland. She looked at him oddly, as if she'd seen through his need to be furtive. *A girl screaming*. The sound rolled through his head with all the piercing quality of a locomotive whistling in a black tunnel. I should be used to this. I should be accustomed by now to the synaptic explosions. But.

A man had come into the reception room. Tall, with a long jaw and tightly curled white hair, he said his name was Dr. Paul Lannigan. He was in his early fifties and wore a three-piece green tweed suit of an old-fashioned cut. The pants were a little baggy at the knees. His accent was hard to place; it had to it a lilt that suggested Irish origins tempered by many years in the United States. He shook Tennant's hand, then Alison's. Charm, bedside manner, a fine wide smile, honest blue eyes. You could put your trust in this Lannigan, Tennant thought. You could give him all your troubles and he'd conjure them away. Harry imagined telling Lannigan his problems, and the man would whisk him off to a peaceful room and have him lie down on a comfortable couch and say: *Now then, tell me what it is. What ails you.*

Lannigan, still smiling, said, "Rules are such a bore, but I should point out to both of you that we allow visits of no more than thirty minutes except for immediate family. Sometimes our clients become stressed by anything longer. What I'm saying is try to keep it short, if you will. I have the feeling you won't stay long anyway. Mr. Obe isn't a man you'd describe as, ah, well, communicative." The doctor smiled and sucked in air, a small sound of sympathy. He had about him the aura of a general practitioner of the sort you rarely saw any more, the kind that treated everything from syphilis to tonsillitis, and who knew the names of your siblings because he'd delivered most of them himself at inconvenient hours in inclement weather.

"If you'll be good enough to follow me," Lannigan said.

They went through a doorway and down a long corridor, a bright white rectangle lined with more pastoral prints. There were doors on either side of the corridor, all closed. They passed a large window that offered a view of a dining room, empty at present.

"We're quite proud of our facilities here," Lannigan said, and he glanced at Tennant as if he expected agreement. "Our cuisine is the finest. The link between nutrition and mental illness is significant. Food for the body is also food for the mind," and he tapped the side of his skull. He looked at Tennant again, rather expectantly.

Tennant felt compelled to say something. "Good-looking dining room."

"Ah," Lannigan said. "You haven't seen the half of it. Not the half of it."

From overhead came the sound of a piano being randomly struck. A woman's voice sang tuneless lyrics that had no meaning. *Ooobee ooobee doodah.*

"Our recreation area is upstairs," the doctor said. "Music, basket weaving, painting. Games. Some of our clients seem to respond well to simple card games. Some enjoy crossword puzzles." He paused, as if to consider something, then added. "A mind challenged is a mind on the mend, after all."

A mind on the mend, Tennant thought. Mend mine, Dr. Lannigan. Please.

A door opened and a white-coated nurse stepped into the

corridor, carrying a small triangular enamel pan over which lay a square of linen. Tennant wondered if a hypodermic syringe lay concealed there. An unruly patient given a suitable infusion of tranquility. He had the sudden urge to turn and run: What was he doing in this place of paper slippers, smocks, plastic forks?

They climbed a flight of stairs. Another corridor stretched ahead. Halfway along, Lannigan stopped outside a door. "Karen Obe gave you permission to see her husband. She was vague, but she led me to understand that the matter is, I suppose you might say, of a somewhat personal nature." Lannigan seemed to intend his last sentence as a question because he waited for Tennant and Alison to respond.

The girl said, "Personal, right."

"I have absolutely no objection. None at all. I don't think you'll get whatever it is you might be looking for, but anyway, anyway . . ." And he knocked on the door once before opening it.

"Sammy," he said. "You've got visitors. Your wife sent them along."

Tennant stepped inside the room, a white room with a small high window, a narrow bed, a chest of drawers. Newspapers, carefully sliced into strips for reasons only Obe could know, lay across the floor. Sammy Obe sat on the edge of the bed, huddled, shoulders hunched. His eyes had the singularly plaintive look of a man on a journey without destination, somebody who has been to places indescribable to others. His mouth was distended in a grimace. When he turned to look at Tennant, his expression didn't alter, as if his lips were sealed permanently in a look of contempt. But contempt wasn't quite the word, nor was disdain. The expression was a constant, without significance, a madman's vacantly sullen look.

"Remember. Thirty minutes." Lannigan touched Tennant's arm lightly, in a way that might have been solicitous. He was apparently reluctant to leave. Eventually he said, "Well. Things to do, things to do." He stepped out of the room.

Alone with Obe, neither Tennant nor Alison quite knew how to approach the man. How did you ask questions of some-

body reputed to speak only gibberish? How could any question
be the right one, if it were destined to remain unanswered?
Sammy Obe, in his loose-fitting white clothing, didn't move.

"I'm Alison Seagrove, Mr. Obe." A tentative opening, a
fumbling. Alison's voice, though gentle, was filled with uncertainty.

Obe turned his face to one side and looked up at the window, which was unreachable even if he were to stand on the
bed. You could imagine Obe's yearning, Tennant thought, for
a freedom that might lie beyond that taunting little glass pane.
If he yearned at all: How could you tell? Tennant studied the
strips of newspaper. Obviously they hadn't been cut with scis-
sors—Obe would not be allowed sharp instruments—but
they'd been torn fastidiously. Random columns, advertise-
ments, sports results, there was no logic to the papers. Did he
sit here all day and tear papers?

Alison walked to the bed, where she sat down alongside
Obe. She indicated Tennant and said, "You took this man's
picture once. A long time ago in the Haight-Ashbury. Do you
remember that?"

The ever-optimistic Alison, Tennant thought. She hopes
for sensible answers, memories, details.

"I tear the papers," Obe said, rather sadly. He sighed. "I
never find what I want."

"What exactly do you want, Sammy?"

"A sign, of course. What else would I be looking for? Are
you blind?"

"What kind of sign?"

Sammy Obe didn't hear the question. He was lost in a
world of his own making. How had it happened? Tennant
wondered. If one day he was allegedly normal, what had
occurred to destroy him overnight? People snapped; their wallpaper came unglued. But so abruptly?

Obe said, "Signs come in all forms, you know. I tear the
newspapers when I can't find them. There's a knack to it, I
think. I haven't quite learned it yet. But I will. I will. I swear to
God I will." He had his hands clenched tightly. "Newsprint

comes off on your fingers. Smudges. I once believed the signs might lie in the smudges, not in the papers themselves, but I was spending too much time looking at my own skin, you see. I got to know my fingerprints pretty well. But not the sign."

Dear Christ, Tennant thought. This rambling made him sad. It was clearly pointless to go on with this painful excursion, but Alison was undeterred. She dug like an archaeologist who believes, in the face of all evidence to the contrary, that a major discovery lies a few feet under the sand.

"I wish you could explain what you expect," she said quietly.

"It may come in the night, of course. Then I might miss it. It's dark then, you see. That's the problem. But there are all kinds of problems." Obe gazed at her. "Who are you?"

"Alison Seagrove."

"Who sent you?"

"Nobody sent me, Sammy."

"Mr. Obe, if you don't mind. I like respect."

"I'm sorry."

"See that you mean it."

Alison looked suitably chastised. She was silent for a time, staring at Tennant as if he might—by virtue of his own troubled history—have some insight into Obe's wandering.

"Somebody must have sent you," Obe said.

Tennant caught an echo of Bear Sajac in this remark. *Okay. I got one question. Who sent you?* What corner of Sammy Obe's brain suggested that Alison must have been sent? Messengers, those who controlled the messengers, dark agencies.

"I promise, Mr. Obe. I wasn't sent by anyone." Alison opened her purse. She took out the newspaper photograph. "Is the sign in this picture?"

Obe didn't touch the clipping. He got up and walked around the room in a stiff manner, wall to wall, back again, marching to a music he heard only in his own head. Alison held the paper toward him, a supplicant gesture.

"Please, Mr. Obe. Take a look."

"I look at nothing unless I want to," he answered. "I despise commands and directives. I'm a free agent, you understand. I do a thing only when I want to. You judge me wrongly, girl. You're an actress. You think you're showing me respect, but I recognize a facade when I see one. You're a facade, girl. You might not exist, for all I know. You might be some illusion they've brought in here to trick me. How do I know?"

"Touch me," she said.

"I might. I just might."

Alison held out her hand. Obe reached for it, caressed it. "You feel like flesh. But I understand—and so must you—that what I feel might not actually exist. I've been fooled before."

"Please look at this picture," she said.

"Obe agrees," he said. "Sammy Obe agrees to look. But only for a second. I have pressing matters that demand my attention." He took the clipping, then let it fall from his fingers. "I don't recognize the significance of it. You claimed it might be the sign. You lied to me. Obe doesn't like liars. Hah."

"You took the picture, Mr. Obe."

"What nonsense."

"You took it years ago in San Francisco."

"Deny deny deny. Look at the logic. If I took the picture, where is my camera? Search the room, you won't find it. You see."

Alison picked up the clipping and sighed. "You also took a photograph you locked inside a safe-deposit box. Does that mean anything to you?"

Obe shrugged, turned the palms of his hands up.

"Try this, Mr. Obe. What does the name Maggie Silver suggest?"

"Silver. Nothing."

"You took pictures of her."

"So you say."

"This is one of them."

"Silver. Maggie Silver."

"That's right."

"Silver and gold, my blood runs cold."

A riddle, Tennant thought. A crazed man's sorry riddle.

"Why does your blood run cold?"

"I lie."

"I thought you were concerned with truth, Mr. Obe."

"The truth is in the eating, girl. The pantry is the place where the food is kept. Look in the pantry."

Alison shook her head. Tennant hadn't seen her look quite so frustrated as she did now. What had she expected anyway— coherence, answers to her mystery? You didn't come to a sad lunatic for answers.

Tennant was ready to leave. This was going nowhere: A pantry, blood running cold, what did these signify? He was depressed by this room now, and by Sammy Obe's wretched condition.

"Mr. Obe," Alison said, still pushing for sense, "don't you remember anything about Maggie Silver?"

Obe stared up at the window, stroked his chin, opened and closed his mouth silently. He resembled for a moment a small desperate fish gasping for oxygen in a murky tank.

"Chinatown, Mr. Obe. San Francisco. Maggie Silver."

"San Francisco," Obe said. "Chinatown. Don't talk to me about Chinatown!" He became agitated, enraged, a spasm of anger passed through him quickly before he was calm again.

Tennant moved toward the door. The room choked him. He needed to get far away from here. Alison wasn't quite ready yet to yield. Christ, she could be irritatingly persistent.

"Do you remember *anything* about it?" she asked.

"Let's go, Alison," Tennant said. "I need air."

"Just wait, Harry."

Obe, whose calm hadn't lasted, walked to the wall and smacked his forehead against it. The wall, naturally, was padded. They took no chances about self-inflicted pain in this joint. He continued, rather frighteningly, to smack, back and forward, on and on, his movements those of a man ensnared in a bad dream. When he stopped, his face was red; looking quite exhausted, he lay down on the bed.

"Mr. Obe, let me ask you again. What do you remember of Chinatown?"

"Zero."

"And Maggie Silver?"

Some small light of understanding came into Obe's eyes, a momentary thing, as if a clear memory had come to him out of the general chaos of his mind. "Obe thinks of her as a Haight person. Frozen in time and place."

"What do you mean by that?"

"I refuse to prejudice myself."

Tennant opened the door. "Alison, for Christ's sake."

Alison sighed again; any small defeat annoyed her.

"Okay okay okay," she said. "I'm coming."

She walked to the door. Obe sat up suddenly, banging his forehead with a clenched hand. "It was almost the sign."

"Almost?" she asked.

"Almost." Obe turned his face to the wall. "Now go away."

Paul Lannigan was waiting at the end of the corridor. He looked preoccupied. Tennant wondered if he'd been waiting there all the time.

"Well? How did it go?"

"Just like you said," Alison answered.

"The poor man." Lannigan shook his head. "Sometimes I feel like a father. Some of my children come home, some go away forever. Sammy is seemingly one of the lost. We try. I admit we don't always succeed."

Alison asked, "What actually happened to him?"

Lannigan turned his attention to the girl, the full beam of his smile. "It's hard to say, my dear. He came here in a fearful condition. Oh, that was years ago now. At least he manages to talk every now and then, which you might say is some small improvement over his original state—"

"What is all that stuff with the newspapers?"

"That's Sammy's private little mystery, I'm afraid. Looking, he tells me, for a sign. A sign of what? All these years later I'm no wiser." Lannigan looked somewhat sad, as though the limitations of his professional ability depressed him. "Tell the truth, what I sometimes wish for is a wand. Some nifty little magic thing I might wave and, lo and behold, everybody is sound again."

A wand, Tennant thought. Sure, we could all use one of them.

"I'll see you both out," Lannigan said.

They followed Lannigan back along the corridor. They passed the window that overlooked the dining room, which was occupied now. Here and there people sat at tables in the big, pale green room. Trays of food, paper cups, plastic spoons; a few attendants, dressed in pale blue smocks, moved between the tables. The diners, for the most part, seemed indifferent to their surroundings and to one another. Tennant thought: They must sob in the lonely nights of madness, some shuffling and mumbling pointlessly to themselves, others holding conversations with imaginary companions or with devils, angels, gods. Frightened people too mad to understand why they felt as they did. Clinics like this, no matter how brightly painted, no matter how well endowed with rustic prints, no matter how much "creative therapy" went on, invariably failed to hide their true function—to keep the insane off the streets. If families could afford it, they shipped their unwanted, their schizophrenics, their depressives, their basket cases, to such facilities—not to be cured but to be forgotten.

Tennant felt clammy, his shirt adhering to his skin. The place was not only a clinic but a kind of prison. Even the pastoral prints of hayricks and peasants and women riding in horse-drawn buggies were unconvincing, stilted, bringing, not the sense of calm for which they were intended, but a cruel reminder of the freedom that lay beyond the walls, if only you could make your way out, if you could find a compass to sanity.

Sammy Obe had lost his compass. *Where is yours, Harry?*

He had to get away from this place. He didn't need to be here.

Down the stairs, another hallway, then the reception area. The receptionist was behind the desk, flicking through papers. She raised her face, looked at Tennant and the girl absently.

Lannigan walked to the front door, which he opened. Rain was still falling, the sky still gloomy.

"A hell of a day," Lannigan said. "The forecast is for more of the bloody same." He shook Alison's hand. "I hope you find what you're looking for." He gazed at Tennant and added, "Both of you." And then he grasped Harry's hand; his grip was warm, firm.

Tennant and the girl stepped out into the rain, which swept toward them, windblown and ragged now, changing direction whimsically.

From the doorway Lannigan called out, "Drive carefully, boyo."

13 When they got inside the car, Tennant said urgently, "Drive. Just drive. Anywhere. It doesn't matter." He turned and looked back at the clinic in the rain. *Boyo.* The voice in his head, the whispers that had come persistently surging up through consciousness: *boyo. Seek the calm center, boyo. Cope, boyo.* Yes yes Lannigan. You know me, don't you. You know me from another time. He stared out into the rainy landscape, feeling waterlogged himself, a soul rooted in swampland and struggling toward the light. Only the light was so goddamn far overhead, dimmed to little more than a slit.

"Speak to me, Harry," the girl said.

What was there to say? He shut his eyes. His breathing was strange, fast. "I met Lannigan before. Don't ask me when or in what circumstances. At the clinic. I'm sure of that."

"Why are you sure?"

"Because I am."

"Were you a patient?"

"Maybe."

"Try harder."

"Goddamn I'm trying."

"Take it nice and slow. Why do you think you were there as a patient?"

Nice and slow. "Drug abuse treatment. I don't know. What else could it be?"

"You want me to turn the car around and go back and talk to the guy?" she asked.

"No. I'm not going back there." That place. Lannigan's handshake. The faces in the dining room. The confinement of small white rooms. No way.

"If you've met him before, why didn't he say so? Why didn't he come right out and say it? If you'd been in that place as a patient, it would make perfect sense for him to say 'How are you now, Harry?' or 'How do you feel being back here?'— anything like that. But he didn't. He acted like he'd never seen you before in his life. Why would he do that?"

"I don't know his reasons. Maybe he's simply forgotten. Either that or he doesn't want to recognize me."

"Or the other way around. He doesn't want you to recognize him. Which is weird. Unless . . ."

"Unless what?"

"He thinks you've forgotten. You're not supposed to recognize him because because—" She peered through the windshield at the rain. "Because that's the way it was supposed to be. Maybe he thinks your memory's been suitably edited."

"Edited? Meaning what?"

Alison said, "What you call the black holes in your life, Harry. The great goddamn chunks of time gone just like that. You can't put all that down to drug abuse. I can't accept that. If you were his patient, and you were already blitzed by way too many narcotics when you came to him, hey, you'd be an easy target for the guy. You're practically a zombie to begin with. The rest of the trip is dead simple. More drugs, say. Some real extensive hypnosis. Manipulation. Who knows the techniques the Irishman has up his sleeve. Exit Harry Tennant, hippie. Enter Harry Tennant, dope farmer."

Your memory's been suitably edited. Tennant saw a distress signal go off inside his head, a flare that rose and fell in bright red disarray. The editing of memory. Snip snip. A recollection here. An image there. In with the whiteout, excise this, get rid of that: wholesale laceration, a larceny of sorts.

He had a maddening pain in his head. He imagined Lannigan going down into his skull, as if the man held in his hand a surgical probe, a fine sharp instrument, something that pierced bone and scraped the mind. He was nauseated by the idea that Lannigan might have achieved a kind of amputation inside him.

"I don't think it happened like that," he said. He was defensive, and yet what was he defending? His own state of mind? Lannigan? Both? "I don't think it *could* have happened like that—"

"Why not? Because you can't remember specifics? Is that why? Harry, think—you've been fucked over and stripped down and rebuilt, you've been distilled and refined and distilled again. You see the bind? You refuse to believe Lannigan did a number on you because *he really did a number on you.* Oh boy. It's perfect."

"No—"

"It's tragic and it's terrific," she said. "For some reason the guy wants to blank you out, which he does, only he's smart enough to build *your* denial into *his* creation."

"Why, for Christ's sake?"

"Why is what we're looking for."

"It doesn't make sense—"

"Sense, Harry? Try this one. Try this nice little coincidence. You and Sammy Obe, known to each other in the dim and distant past, patients in the *same place?* That's pulling the string a little too tight for my liking, kid."

Alison took her eyes from the road, and the Buick slithered along the rim of a drainage ditch a moment before she corrected her steering. "Oops."

Tennant slumped back in his seat. What to say, what to think. Alison stopped the car. Rain gleamed on the paintwork, slid across the windshield. She reached out and took his hand and pressed it between her own, a simple little touch, but it had an element of grace to it, an attempt to bestow peace on a troubled man.

"Harry, consider the connections between you and Obe. This clinic. Lannigan. The photograph. The fact that neither of you is capable of remembering much of anything. Both of you—wiped out. You at least have the benefit of sanity. Obe doesn't even have that."

"I wouldn't go as far as sanity," he said dryly.

"Okay. You're coherent. You lived on certain acceptable terms with the world. You got along day to day growing your plants. Obe, on the other hand, the guy's in orbit. He's not of this planet." She rubbed his skin in tiny circles with her fingertips. "The reason lies in Chinatown, Harry. It goes all the way back to whatever it was you saw outside St. Mary's Church."

Whatever it was, it devastated him. His headache raged as he stared out into the rain. He felt drained. Foundering, he listened to the jackhammers in his head. They had a pounding, crippling familiarity.

Nobody was following them, or so it seemed to Tennant. But there was always uncertainty. They drove through a series of more small towns, each of which was depressing.

"Get off the main road," he said. "Find a motel. Some backwater place. The more obscure the better."

The windshield wipers swept back and forth like two metronomes measuring the beat of the weather. Alison drove narrow highways for miles until she found a broken-down motel called The Crimson Motor Lodge, a group of small chalets that would have looked uninviting even in bright sunshine. The man at the reception desk had a walleye and smoky bad breath and wore a threadbare cardigan that had been darned at the elbows.

"Take your pick," he said. "Ain't nobody else staying here, that's for sure."

They got the key to chalet number 4, a damp little square of a room painted brown; here and there the paint had blistered. The ceiling was cracked, spotted with patches of plaster badly applied.

"Uplifting kind of place," Alison said.

Tennant lay down on the only bed, a sagging affair.

He gazed at the ceiling. The small bulges of plaster suggested goitrous eyes. He turned from the sight of them. Alison drew the curtain and sat on the edge of the mattress.

"Let's say Lannigan performed some kind of vanishing act with my memory," he said. "Where does that leave me? What does that make me? It's like I'm stunted. Something inside me's fucked. And part of me is still saying he didn't do anything. He *couldn't* have done anything. It's a voice that goes on and on. Lannigan's innocent. Lannigan's innocent. A drum, for God's sake. Bang bang bang." He put his hands to his head; Alison touched them lightly.

"You were happy before I came along," she said.

"Blissfully ignorant. Dumb. Unquestioning. Happiness never entered into it."

"Poor Harry. I'm sorry. I forced you out into the light. You could have spent some time in the country slammer on dope charges and come out a free man and you'd have been none the wiser, would you? My fault. All my fault."

"I'm not blaming you. In a strange way I ought to thank you. If you hadn't come along, I might have lived the rest of my life in the dark—"

"You might have had peace—"

"An overestimated commodity—"

"Maybe."

"Poor Harry," she said again.

They were silent for a time. The chalet felt frail to Tennant; the thud of rain on the roof was ominous. He had a sense of the fragility of things—not simply this half-assed little room, but of his life, his flight, delicate constructs unable to bear any great weight.

He got up from the bed, parted the curtain, looked out across the forecourt of the motel. The other chalets, neglected, peeled in the rain. The motel had all the atmosphere of a cheap carnival abandoned for the winter. Beyond the forecourt lay a field of weeds, a dark-green-choked place the emptiness of which appalled him. He pressed his face upon the glass, then stepped back, dropping the curtain. What kind of goddamn life was this, hiding out here or in some other grim little motel?

Alison said, "There's one easy way to bring all this to an end, Harry."

"I know it. I could walk away. I could skip. I could leave it alone."

"Slip away into the night," she said. "Good-bye and farewell. No more mysteries. Could you live without knowing, Harry?"

She stroked his hair in an absentminded manner, then drew him, somewhat coyly, toward the bed. "I've gotten used to you, Harry. Somewhere along the way you've started to mean something important to me. I never expected that. I wouldn't like you to leave."

He lay down, turned on his back, his face pressed to Alison's side. He could hear her heartbeat, the sweet sound of life. Suddenly he needed to be surrounded by life and light, embraced by it. He reached up and touched her breast. He wondered if the rhythm of her breathing changed. He wasn't sure. Making love to her seemed to him a way out, a fine release, flesh upon flesh, lips touching, vibrancy. But more than mere release, more than an escape hatch, a way of expressing feelings he had no memory of experiencing before. I could love her, he thought. I could tumble and go on falling and it wouldn't matter how far down I fell.

He drew her face down toward him and kissed her. He felt clumsy. Alison raised her arms, took off her T-shirt. Her breasts were small, firm with youth. Tennant laid her down on the bed, caressed the sides of her face tenderly. It was a moment in which all manner of magical things seemed possible, the closing of an intimate circle. He drew her jeans down from her narrow hips, laid a hand upon her flat stomach, touched the O of her navel.

She wore only underwear, pale blue.

"Take them off," she said.

He slipped the panties from her waist, over her feet. What did she feel? he wondered. What was she thinking now? What had happened to her earlier talk about commitment? He had to silence that inquisitor inside his head. All I have is this moment, nothing else. He could believe he was without beginnings and endings. He ran a hand along her inner thigh, felt her shiver. Her face was lovely, vulnerable. The desire in him was a bright white force. When he kissed her nipples, she laid one hand upon the back of his neck. The gesture was the most intimate he'd experienced in years. Kissing her, drawing her close to him, he felt her hand go between his legs, and she made a small sound of surprise, as if his hardness shocked her. She undid the buttons of his jeans—Christ, the awkwardness of clothing—and pushed his shirt from his shoulders. The intimacy overwhelmed him. She spoke his name quietly. He'd only ever heard it uttered quite that way once—and suddenly the past, like the wicked jaw of a predator, devoured him, and he was with another woman, he was lying alongside Maggie Silver. His mind buckled, veered away from him. *This wasn't Alison, this wasn't some journalist who had drawn him into a world of perplexity, she was Maggie Silver, she was Maggie beyond question. Maggie, Maggie. And this wasn't a godforsaken rundown chalet on the edge of nowhere, not now, this was a room in a house on Schrader.* The smell of incense made him dizzy. He imagined sunlight filling the window, illuminating the Indian rug. He imagined that if he were to open his eyes he'd see Bobby Kennedy and Dylan and Jimi Hendrix posters above the bed, he'd see her gauzy clothes strewn carelessly on the floor, he'd smell patchouli—Jesus, the musk possessed him—and he'd look down into her face at that characteristic expression she had during lovemaking, the eyes glazed as she moved inside her own world of abandonment, the mouth a wonderful opening he would kiss again and again, wanting to possess the unpossessable, to attain heights he'd sense but could never quite reach.

Sweating, he held hard to her. He entered her. She spread her legs, caressed his back, fingered the ridges of his spine. He made sounds that had meaning only in the context of love. Words, not words, phrases and fictions of the heart. Mystic utterances. The fact they lacked meaning was unimportant. He was beyond the embarrassment of failing to make sense. What did sense matter anyway?

I love this woman. He came with such force he imagined his skull exploding.

She pulled away from him abruptly and he opened his eyes and the illusion of Maggie Silver was gone. He was looking into the face of a girl called Alison Seagrove whose expression was one of hurt and grief.

"What's the matter?" he asked.

"Don't you know?"

"Tell me."

She sat, huddling her naked self, on the side of the bed. She was silent. He reached out to touch her but she pulled herself farther away.

"It doesn't fucking matter," she said, and her voice was flint.

"Tell me, Alison."

She looked at him and her eyes were chill. "Okay. You called me Maggie. You called out her name."

"I didn't know—"

"Why? Why Maggie?"

How to explain when he couldn't explain? "I had this, Jesus, this dream, this vision, I don't know what the hell to call it, and suddenly you weren't you, you were her, and this room was someplace else, Schrader Street in San Francisco, not here, and it was like I'd fallen into something, a slipstream . . ." His voice, in which there was a startled quality, trailed off. "I was dragged down into it. I didn't know what I was saying, I didn't hear myself. . . ."

She turned her face away.

"I've offended you," he said. "I've hurt you."

She got up from the bed. She walked back and forth, shivering.

He said, "I know it's weak, but I'm sorry. I'm really sorry."

She went inside the bathroom and shut the door. He closed his eyes, and the images of Maggie Silver filled him again. What weird thing had seared through him? The past, forceful all at once, had penetrated him. He listened to water running. A slip, a quirk. But he'd had no control over it. Something out of his history had blitzed him. He and Maggie Silver: lovers. Unless his mind had been playing another game. He and Maggie Silver. The intensity of the realization stunned him. A past passion so deeply submerged—Alison would say it was Lannigan's doing. The shrink had gone inside and excised it, but it had come back to the surface with such potency because you couldn't kill off every memory, they surged back when they needed to, as if propelled by a power of their own: The mind healing itself, was that it? He felt a muted little victory. He had recovered a part of himself.

Alison came out of the bathroom. She was dressed again. She folded her arms in a defensive posture as she walked across the room to the drawn curtains. There she paused. Her tension fanned out from her, filling all available space.

"I'm sorry," he said again. "I wouldn't have offended you for the world. You must know that."

Still she wouldn't look at him. He got up from the bed and went toward her, but even as he reached out, she stepped back. She said, "Don't touch me."

He stood in useless silence, shut out from the girl.

"So this is what you're saying. You and Maggie Silver were lovers. Is this what I'm getting?"

He didn't speak.

"More than twenty years ago you and her were an item, right?"

"I think it had to be that way—"

"Sweet Christ, Harry, can't you give me a straight answer for once? All you ever seem to say is I don't know or I don't remember. I'm goddamn sorry about what might have happened to you, don't misunderstand me, but just one time I'd like to hear *something* definite."

"Okay okay. This is about as definite as I can make it, Alison. We were lovers. What other explanation is there for the *thing* I just experienced? Why make such a big deal out of something so unintentional and unexpected? It wasn't like I started out to hurt you."

She sat down in a broken-backed chair set before a dressing table. She looked at herself in the mirror. Placing her hands on either cheek, she drew the skin back tightly, sharply revealing the structure of bone. She might have been trying in some odd way to change her appearance.

Tennant said, "I had a feeling about Maggie Silver before. I had this . . . this sense of sadness. There's something else. I have a memory of her screaming."

"Screaming?"

"It's out of place. Disjointed. My guess is we must have lived together, probably in the house on Schrader Street. I figure something good was going on between us that got badly damaged in some way." There—a flash of pain, of hurt. How could he deny that at some time in the past Maggie Silver had meant a great deal to him? A great love, say. One of those things you never get over no matter how blunted your memory is. No matter your amnesia. He felt suddenly hollow. He'd lost more than memory. Love was another casualty along the line.

"I don't know how long we were together. I don't know why we broke up. I'm sorry but that's it. I can tell you this because I know it: I loved her. And there's a major part of me back there." *I can tell you her scent, Alison. I can tell you the clothes she wore. I know what posters hung on the walls.* He forced a smile but it didn't work. The sadness was on him again like a fallen tree.

"I should have guessed something like this from the photograph, shouldn't I?" Alison asked. "I should have been able to read something into that picture. A sign I didn't see because I was too wrapped up in getting my story. Couldn't see the woods, huh?"

"I should have been able to read it myself, Alison. What does it matter now? It's past. Dead."

"Is it?" She dropped her hands from her face and stared into the mirror at his face.

She rose from the chair. He walked toward her, touched her shoulders. She drew away from him. He might have asked her why she was jealous of an old love, but he didn't. He wasn't even sure jealousy came into it. Maybe she was one of those people who overreact, whose responses run in the direction of hysteria—a part of her he'd never encountered. We're strangers still. Lovers, strangers, tossed together for the duration.

"Will you accept my apology?" he asked.

"You don't have to apologize. You're not to blame, Harry."

"Then I'm forgiven?"

She looked at him sadly. She didn't answer the question. "You ought to be happy, Harry. You just found something out about yourself. Another little piece of your private jigsaw just fell in place, didn't it?"

"Yeah," he said. But his earlier sense of a vague triumph had faded before the girl's manner. He wanted to hold her. He made no move, afraid of being rebuffed. "Look. If we're going on with this strange trip together, we ought to call a truce."

"Kiss and make up?"

"Something like that."

She looked at him for a long time, and now he couldn't read her expression at all and the understanding scared him. His only companion, his only ally, and he couldn't interpret her look. She stood on tiptoe and brushed her lips quickly on his cheek. Wrapped in a bedsheet, he felt suddenly silly, because the intimacy had drained out of the room. He was left with a forlorn sense, an abandonment. He wished he could exorcise the strain between them. A kiss on the cheek. He supposed it was better than a kiss blown off the palm of her hand, but not by much.

"I don't deserve the frost," he said. He found his clothes, started to dress.

"You're right. You deserve better. You deserve your life back." She approached him, her arms hanging loose at her sides. "Maybe that's going to be my gift to you in the end, Harry. Your life. Maybe that's what this is all about when you get to the bottom line. Not my stupid story. *Your life.* Harry Tennant, sealed and delivered. Put back together. Humpty-Dumpty."

Her tone of voice: Was it sarcastic? Slightly bitter? He couldn't be sure. He buttoned his shirt, glanced at himself in the mirror, saw a pale reflection. For a guy who just put back together some of the debris of his past, you don't look so good, Tennant. He sat on the bed, watching the girl.

She said, "One thing. Nothing happened between us. It was a mistake, that's all. We forget it and we go on."

"A mistake?"

"I lost control. You lost control. It can't happen again."

"I don't want it left like that." A mistake—what a terrible little word. An error of judgment. The hasty moment. Something existed between them, something had grown in a matter of days, how could she deny that? "I don't understand all this shit about losing control," he added. "Okay, so I had some kind of weird flashback, but what's that got to do with you and me? I'm talking about now, not twenty years ago, for Christ's sake. I'm talking about the fact that we're in each other's lives no matter what happened in the past. There are feelings here, Alison. Here and now. You know what that's like for me after all this time?"

She looked away from him. "Feelings. Sure there are. Except I don't know what they are exactly."

"They don't have to be precise, Alison. They don't have to be written in goddamn stone. You make me feel. I can't give you a definition, I can't draw you a map. This is all new to me."

"So what are you trying to say, Harry?"

"Only this. We don't write us off as some kind of mistake, Alison. We see where it goes. We see where it leads. But we can't just put it on ice."

She was silent for a time. Then, as if she didn't want to explore the situation further, she moved quickly, fussing, businesslike, gathering up stuff from the dressing table, a comb, a brush, bits and pieces of makeup. She shoved them into her bag. She didn't look at him as she moved. She talked as if to herself. "The next thing is to get out of here. I can't hack this place. We have to go to San Francisco because whatever connects you and Obe began there. Because that's where Maggie is buried. Because that's where everything begins and ends."

"You're changing the subject," he said.

"Right now there's only one subject, Harry. And it isn't you and me."

"You think Maggie Silver is going to be in San Francisco after all this time? You're chasing butterflies without a net, Alison." He caught her arms, forced her to remain still.

"Maybe she stayed in San Francisco because that was the place nobody would think to look for her. How do we know if we don't go see? We drive to Des Moines, dump the car. Catch a plane. San Francisco. A couple of hours."

"If we get that far. If we even make it out of this place."

"It's a chance we have to take. What's the alternative? Hiding out in this hole until they find us? I hate being cornered. I'm restless." She sighed, staring at him. He understood it was more than simple restlessness that was driving her out of this sorry little room; for whatever reason, she didn't want to countenance the situation between them, didn't want to talk about their relationship, she wanted to move and keep moving because if she stood still she'd be forced into examination. Okay, he thought. Leave it the way she wants. Let's just move.

San Francisco in a couple of hours. Haight Street and Ashbury and the Panhandle, a dead scene. The house on Schrader. The Conservatory of Flowers, the de Young Museum, the Golden Gate Park—if these still existed they did so in a dimension of which he was wary. But Alison was right in this respect at least: He had to go back. The options were running down. And the idea that Maggie Silver might still be in San Francisco—it was unlikely, but it tantalized him anyway. What would it be like to see her again? Would he discover more of himself in the sight of her? Would she have the key to his life? Of course she'd look different now; perhaps he wouldn't even recognize her, a possibility that troubled him. He shook his head and thought No way we're going to locate her. But what would he lose by looking? Nothing. Everything.

He went to the window, drew back the curtain a fraction, looked out. Nothing moved in the rain. He thought: San Francisco would be another world now. Old coffee shops and bars would have closed down. The street scene wouldn't be the same.

A car came into the forecourt, a small blue Toyota. Was it the same car that had tracked them before? Tennant couldn't tell. Apprehensive, he saw it swing in an arc, passing out of sight among the chalets.

When it came back in view, it rolled toward the Buick, then stopped. Nobody got out. The car looked both ominous and ordinary, mysterious and banal. Tennant, stepping quickly back from the window and allowing the curtain to fall into place, had an impression of two people in the front of the Toyota, but it was impossible to be sure. He went to his bag, took out the gun.

"Company," he said, whispering, as if by lowering his voice

he might convince the occupants of the Toyota that the chalet was empty. Yeah, that would really fool them. "It might be the Toyota from before. It's hard to tell."

"How many inside it?"

"Two. Maybe more. I couldn't see."

Alison looked at the gun. "What do you propose, Harry? Go rushing outside with your gun blazing? You think that would accomplish anything? Let them make the first move. If they're going to do anything, sooner or later they have to get out of the car. They have to expose themselves."

Tennant lingered to one side of the window. He wasn't good at waiting. All his years of solitude, which might have taught him patience, amounted to nothing. He peered through an opening in the curtain at the vehicle. Why didn't something happen? Why didn't somebody get out of the goddamn car, for Christ's sake?

"Why are they just fucking *sitting* there," Tennant said. "If they're going to act, why don't they do it now?"

"Maybe it's how they operate, Harry. Keep you on edge. Stick in the needle, then twist it."

How could she sound so *calm*? he wondered. The car outside the window represented the possibility of violence, destruction, death.

Tennant had the urge to tear down the curtain and smash the glass and fire the Taurus straight into the windshield. He didn't move. Waiting was a form of paralysis. When you waited like this, you ceased to exist. Your life was defined by a lack of motion. You were the sharp instrument of anticipation, nothing else. Everything else diminished.

He looked quickly out at the car again. Alison had moved near enough to the window to witness the Toyota herself. Nobody emerged. Nobody moved. Tennant was possessed by the sudden notion that the vehicle was empty, driven to this place by a will of its own. A blue Toyota, mundane, shrouded in rain, empty.

And still nobody got out.

Now a second car had entered the forecourt, a nondescript

brown vehicle that idled some way beyond the Toyota. Was this other car associated with the Toyota?

Tennant, consumed by the tension of inactivity, tightened his grip on the gun; his skin was moist on the metal. Come on, he thought. Do something. Make your move. Attack if you're going to attack.

The passenger door of the Toyota opened slowly. A man looked out but didn't emerge from the car. He was unknown to Tennant. He had squat ugly features; his face might have been accidentally compressed at birth by the forceps of some novice physician. He frowned at the window of the chalet as if he were uncertain of something. Tennant, tense, drew back into shadow. Through the thinnest of slits in the curtain he watched the man step out from the car. In his right hand he held a small dark object, an oval whose immediate significance was lost to Harry Tennant. But when the man arched his arm Tennant understood at once that the thing was a grenade, that it was going to be tossed as casually as a kid's ball through the window of the room, that when it struck glass it would explode instantly in flame and smoke, sucking all life out of the chalet.

Tennant pointed the Taurus directly at the figure. The man's arm was already halfway raised, the look on his face one of deadly determination, the kind of expression you might see in the features of a hunter taking deliberate aim. Tennant thought: *It's either you or us,* and he broke the window with his gun, his finger about to squeeze the trigger.

But he didn't fire. He didn't have to. The man with the grenade had doubled over and, clutching his chest, slumped to his knees. The grenade rolled under the body of the Toyota, and the squat-faced man lay still now, facedown in the dirt. Beyond, outside the brown vehicle, stood another figure, somebody holding a high-powered rifle. A moment of dark confusion, of inversions, as if tricks were being played out in distorting mirrors. The rifleman had fired a single deadly shot from the brown vehicle, and now he was stepping back inside his car even as the grenade, unpinned, roared beneath the Toyota, and a flash of red-yellow flame engulfed the blue car. Black smoke and broken glass and blinding flame; Tennant, dazzled, already smelling the wretched smoke floating toward him, moved back from the shattered window.

He went outside, Alison followed. The blazing Toyota, the dead guy on the ground, the driver burning in the front seat, the stench of melting rubber and flesh in the rain, the absence of the brown car—a landscape of sickening violence and confusion, a place from which to flee.

14 They drove in taut silence to Des Moines through increasingly sullen weather. Rain flooded the narrow highways. There was no sign of any vehicle lingering behind with conspicuous persistence. At a place where roadworks slowed traffic, Alison stopped at a red light behind which a disconsolate workman stood in a wet yellow mackinaw, as if his life were one of unbroken glumness. A line of cars formed at the back of the Buick. You couldn't tell if there were watchers in any one of them. When the light changed, she drove on carefully; the road was slick, treacherous, and her concentration poor.

She pulled over at a rest area and switched off the engine and laid her face in a weary manner against the steering wheel. Tennant lit a cigarette. He thought of the Toyota burning in the rain, the grenade that had never been thrown, the stranger with the rifle: the elements of a murderous equation.

"A guardian angel," she said. "Is it something like that? Somebody's looking out for us?"

"I don't know," Tennant replied. A guardian angel with a high-powered rifle instead of wings, a scope, a marksman's assurance.

"What else can it be? Two guys arrive in a car with the intention of blowing us all to hell, when out of nowhere comes a savior with a rifle? What would you call it, Harry?"

"Somebody wants us dead. Somebody else wants to keep us alive," he said. How uncomplicated it sounded when you said it that way. "The people who don't want us around don't approve of our little jaunt around the country—"

"So who's the killer angel, Harry? What's his motive?"

The search for motive, for purpose at the heart of obscurity. Tennant, shaking his head, drawing hard on the cigarette, looked at the parked cars in the rest area. He remembered the way he'd held the Taurus, how he'd been ready to shoot the man with the grenade, how he'd smashed the glass with the barrel of the gun, how the murderous intent he'd felt had formed in his head like a hard mass of blood. Harry Tennant, pacifist. He attacks innocent men in toilets, smashes their Ray.Bans. He longs to kill. But you were threatened, Harry. Your life was in peril. Somebody had your number. What are you supposed to say? Peace, bro? Peace and love? Lay down your arms? He wondered at the changes in himself, at the process of alteration, new sensations, fresh feelings. It was as if something fundamental in his chemistry had been transformed, and he wasn't sure what or how far the process could go.

He reached out and touched Alison's face. She said, "What happens if the angel isn't around next time, Harry?"

He had no answer for the question. But he had an unusual sense of confidence. He wanted to say, *I can protect you, Alison. I know that much now.* He stroked her cheek lightly; she shut her eyes. He thought of the small chalet room and how it had changed first from a place of love to a place of recrimination— and from there to violence. Transitions. Everywhere. A world in constant flux. He wondered if there might ever be stability again, such as the years he'd spent in the woods and the frame house. Could he ever go back to that kind of life even if he could find his way?

No. No, he couldn't.

★ ★ ★

At Des Moines International Airport, Alison drove into the long-term parking lot, gathered her belongings, and, followed by Tennant, bought tickets for San Francisco. Tennant put his gun in Alison's overnight bag because it had to be checked through in the luggage. Without it he felt vulnerable.

They had an hour to kill. Part of that time they drank coffee, saying little to each other, simply being anxiously vigilant—but how could you know who you were meant to be watching for? The cafeteria was crowded with people in wet raincoats; a smell of dampness pervaded the air. Tennant eavesdropped on the sporadic little conversations peculiar to airport terminals, where men and women fumbled with their belongings or kept examining their boarding cards as if to reassure themselves they were really booked on flights, that their destinations were the correct ones. Babies cried, farewells were made, lovers parted.

At the next table a man was speaking loudly into a cellular phone. He had that air of frantic self-importance of people who carry such things, people who live addicted to urgent business deals. *We gotta take a chance on this, John, if you wanna be a major player. It's one of those things where you snooze you lose.* Tennant finished his coffee, set down his Styrofoam cup, tore it into little pieces—remembering how Obe's room was filled with strips of newspaper. A sign, Obe had said. What kind of sign? You delve into madness, you look for signs, clues to something as basic as your identity. For Obe identity was lost in forms of babbling.

Tennant was sweating. He took off his raincoat, folded it over his arm, wiped his brow. A tall woman slid past him; her hair was upraised in a bouffant style that had gone out with Donovan records. He experienced dizziness, a longing for air. The warmth of the cafeteria, the smell of wet clothes—he was stifled.

"Let's go to the gate," Alison said. "It's about time."

They passed through the detector, found seats in the

crowded departure area. Crowds were safe. A clamor of inaudible messages came over the loudspeaker system. Flights for Omaha, Dubuque, New York La Guardia. The cacophony irritated him.

He thought about Maggie Silver, elusive Maggie, the ashes of old love. Had she ever thought about *him* down the years? Were there times when she'd taken out his memory and looked at it and wondered what had ever become of him? Maybe she lingered over the consideration of him, maybe she even had her own copy of Obe's photograph, something she looked at every so often to remember those days. *I wonder where Harry is now.* If she was alive. He had the realization that together they must have planned things in the way of lovers, talked about a future, discussed destiny. Whatever had become of that love anyway? Had it burned out in the Haight like everything else? The sound of her screaming filled his head all at once. *Somebody is pulling at her, pulling her hair, her clothes, and she doesn't want to go—*

Frustrated, a man deprived of an essential sense, Tennant silenced the noise. He stood up, walked around, tried to loosen his locked muscles. What had happened to Maggie Silver? Why was somebody dragging her away? And if you remember it, Harry, then it means you saw it, and if you saw it, why didn't you do something to help? Because you couldn't, because you weren't able to act, somebody or something restrained you—

If she was alive.

The flight to San Francisco was announced. He followed Alison aboard the plane, hating the notion of being trapped in a cylinder that would momentarily be sent implausibly rising into precarious space—up, up through rainclouds to the skies beyond. They sat together, Alison at the window, Tennant in the aisle seat. They were located next to the wing, which appeared too insubstantial to support the idea of flight. Tennant fiddled with the airline magazine, scanning articles about the pleasures of Biarritz and how to make home cider, then stuffed the magazine back in place. He had the notion that this trip was inevitable. He was simply doing, in his own way, what all exiles yearn to do—to return to a point, no matter how nebulous, of origin. And he had the confused feelings of the exile too, misgivings, intense curiosity, excitement.

And dread.

He stared down the aisle, watching other passengers board, cram their luggage into overhead compartments, take their seats, fiddle with belts. He gazed from the window, seeing puddles form on the tarmac under the wing. When the plane took off, rain scudded against the wing, and then the clouds were gone, evaporating rapidly; sunshine glistened on the damp wing. But blue skies and bright light and the smooth roar of the big plane didn't ease Tennant's anxiety. He adjusted his seat and closed his eyes, when an unexpected turbulence, which made the craft shiver, caused him to sit upright.

Flippantly he said, "I always preferred dope as a means of getting off the ground."

She didn't smile. She looked out of the window, her expression pensive, distant. He wondered if she was still thinking of their lovemaking in the chalet. More likely she was remembering the explosion of the Toyota. He was barred from knowing. She was drifting off into an inviolate space of her own, a privacy on which he couldn't intrude. It was as if some sudden mystifying force field surrounded her.

When cocktails were served—he had a double brandy—he made a few mild jokes about his fear of flying, but he struck no real response in her. He reached for her hand and took it; he might have been holding a lump of clay.

"I take it your systems are shut down in a general way," he said.

"I don't feel like speaking, Harry." She sipped her Bloody Mary and looked out at the blue expanses. The sun burned on the window. She drew down the blind with a brisk movement. He took his hand from her fingers, a little depressed.

The navigator, in the casually friendly way of men who feel mighty in the skies, announced that the Rocky Mountains could be seen to the left of the aircraft. Heads dutifully turned. Tennant finished his brandy; he had no great desire to raise the blind and peer at any rugged mountain range, which would only remind him of the terrible space between himself and the planet's surface. He ordered another brandy, which came in a miniature bottle. He sipped it slowly; the first drink was still rushing to his head.

He looked at Alison's face, the fine eyelids in which could be seen pale veins, the short black hair, the solitary earring. He let his fingers drift across the back of her hand. Her response was sudden, and the last thing he expected—tears; they slid from her closed eyes and over her cheeks. She covered her face.

"Alison," he said.

"I'll be all right in a second."

Other people's tears. Tennant felt helpless even as he wondered how he could possibly comfort her. What had brought the tears on? A delayed reaction to violence? You didn't see two men killed every day of the week. It wasn't your commonplace event to smell burning flesh and hear the explosion of a grenade. Or was it some other thing from which he was excluded?

She forced a mirthless smile. "See? The storm passes. It only lasts a minute."

He fingered the miniature of brandy, rolling it between his hands. Alison searched in her purse for a Kleenex, which she pressed against her eyes. She crumpled the tissue, leaned back in her seat, stared at the panel buttons overhead. "I get emotional sometimes. It comes out of nowhere."

Tennant wasn't buying. Tears didn't come out of absolute zero. He finished his brandy, got up, walked toward the toilet at the rear of the plane. He glanced at the faces of the other passengers: One man had a laptop computer on which he was diligently gaping at spreadsheets. Corporate man, never idle, white-shirted. An ink stain on his sleeve spoiled the little cameo of perfection. A small boy, squirming from his mother's embrace, reached out to touch Tennant playfully. The mother looked at Tennant as if she needed to apologize for her off-spring. Ordinary lives, Tennant thought, so goddamn normal. But somewhere lay a line dividing the mundane from the corrupt, except he couldn't draw it. It was the failure to recognize jeopardy that worried him.

Inside the toilet he washed his face, then looked at his reflection. Curiously, he thought he saw for the first time ever some resemblance to Rayland. It was slight, and depended on the angle of his head, but it was undeniable. An eerie moment, a correspondence between himself and his father. He wondered what other correspondences there were. Connections, membranes. He dried his face in a paper towel. If Paul Lannigan had taken his memory away, who had instructed him to do so? Who had paid him?

Who was it who'd kept tabs on Harry, who'd known he'd been in upstate New York the last nine years?

Rayland.

But did it follow that the old man must have known where Harry had been before that, during the lost years? Did it follow that some connection existed between Rayland and Lannigan?

Tennant had an image of a shabby transaction. This is my son, I want him to forget certain things, how much will it cost me? It was a squalid prospect. No, Rayland wasn't capable of any such thing. No father could harm his son so deeply. They had their sad differences, their relationship was tragically defunct, old angers had corroded it, true—but you couldn't jump from that breakdown to anything so dreadful as deliberately imposing amnesia on Tennant. *I want to remember my father as I knew him long ago. Childhood in North Carolina, the big Victorian house, endlessly humid, endlessly still summer afternoons, a hammock slung between oaks, Rayland and son lying together with books. I don't want to think about his association with Colonel Harker, his cronies in the sleaze of the arms business.*

He stepped out of the toilet. A middle-aged man in a long

black raincoat with epaulettes was waiting to take his place. Tall, stiff, with a look that suggested lockjaw and a haircut that might have been inflicted by an open razor, the man brushed past him.

Are you one of them? Are you a member of the club? Or are you an angel? How could you possibly tell anything now? If there were two sides, different parties with different goals, why didn't they wear badges so you could tell the good guys from the bad—if the distinction was that simple. Tennant had his doubts: Simplicity had no part in any of this.

He made his way back to his seat. He sat down, suddenly exhausted. Alison had her eyes shut. She opened them when she heard Tennant return. She looked at Harry a moment and smiled in a restrained way. He had a desire to draw her head against his shoulder and hold her, but she turned her face to the window against which the fierce sun lay. He thought of their lovemaking, the moment of unbearable intensity, the face of Maggie Silver, and then the fall from the dream. *I could love this girl, this Alison Seagrove, the way I must have loved Maggie Silver once.*

In San Francisco a ghostly afternoon mist, rolling in from the Pacific, obscured the sun. Tennant remembered those mists and fogs that turned the sun to milk. He remembered how they'd filter light from the streets, and then, as whimsically as they'd come, they'd be gone. Sometimes, when the mist fudged the lower parts of buildings, San Francisco had the appearance of a city on stilts. He'd seen Golden Gate Park vanish, watched the Bay disappear, strolled through the lingering haze of the Haight, thinking how the city seemed to come and go at will, in and out of existence, a fanciful place. Now, in the taxi that passed the boxed houses of Daly City and headed toward the center of the city, Tennant felt he was traveling, not toward his private past, but into the heart of a place unknown and unknowable, a city of vapors. A dream city, half-recalled, unfinished. Had he really lived here once? Why hadn't he let this whole business lie still?

The need to know. The driving force. But Maggie Silver would not be here. He was convinced of that. Even as the taxi headed toward Union Square, where a spectacular broadsword of sunlight perforated the mist, he felt the city was devoid of her presence.

Alison had directed the driver to Chinatown, to St. Mary's.

The taxi, whining, climbed. The driver was an old hippie with his gray hair worn in a ponytail. I might have known him once, Tennant thought. The hills of the city, impractically steep, made him wonder at the sheer nerve of men who'd chosen to build here: the ruthless dedication of construction. You tried to build something here too, Harry. Some kind of life once. Some kind of love. Devoted to a spirit, a phantom, a love from another dimension. Haunted, and not knowing how haunted he'd been.

He had a sense of strange physical imbalance, exacerbated by the unreality of San Francisco. It was as if gravity had been briefly suspended. Alison laid a hand on the back of his wrist, a sympathetic gesture. She understands what this place means to me, Tennant thought. She knows what's going on inside.

"I'm sorry," she said quietly. "About how I behaved on the plane, it was stupid of me. . . ."

"Forget it."

"Look. I care about you. But I don't know where it can go. I'm flying blind, Harry. And I don't like the sensation."

He wished some of the old utterances still had currency. *Go with the flow. Play it as it lays.* But these, if once they'd been vibrant and useful, were trite and feeble now. Flying blind. He wondered if a time would come when they'd know exactly what direction they were taking. Look into tomorrow and what do you see, Harry? You and Alison Seagrove living a life of growing love and contentment in some quiet town in the heartland? Unstalked, unthreatened, at peace? *Get real.* He had the whiff in his nostrils of human flesh on fire: Could you whittle idly on the porch of some clapboard house and listen to a spring wind shake the oaks lining the street and forget something like that? Shove it inside the closet where all the bad memories were stashed?

"Why the hell couldn't we have met in some other way at some other time, Harry? Why couldn't we have been two different people? I get this feeling the gods are not what you'd call charitable when it comes to matters of the heart."

"Charitable? They're a callous crew," he remarked.

"I don't want callous. I want something good. I want to think there's some justice at the end of it all. I want to think it balances out somehow. But I don't have a sense of the future when it comes to you and me." She sounded sad. Her eyes were dull with unhappiness. "You don't build relationships in the dark. You need to be able to hope for something. Anything. Any small thing you can just hold on to. I don't know what. Right now I feel this god-awful uncertainty. I don't know who you are or what the hell we're really doing together. What can we even *hope* for, Harry?"

"You said you care. So do I. I figure that's a beginning." *And more than I would ever have expected.*

She sighed and sat back. "A beginning to what? Maybe there's nothing for us at the end of all this anyway. Maybe you and me are coming in through different doorways, Harry."

"I don't want to think that way."

"We're being positive, are we? We're being optimistic?"

"We're trying." He thought: She doesn't even sound like herself. It was as if the grit had gone out of her. Let's have justice and hope. Some of that good stuff. Give us a rainbow. He wasn't accustomed to the idea of optimism because he'd never needed to think about it one way or another before. You didn't ponder such things as aspirations when your life was a mindless day-to-day affair and the heaviest matters you entertained had to do with whether your crop would flourish or fail. You had so few needs. Then somebody blows into your world and all kinds of sediments are stirred and suddenly nothing is ever the same. The map you thought flat was abruptly contoured. The landscape you considered featureless was filled with shadow.

He stared at buildings, swirls of mist, surreal outbursts of sunshine. From nowhere emerged a white-faced mime in top hat and tails pretending he was locked inside a glass box. His flattened palms pushed against imaginary barriers. On his face was an expression of exaggerated terror. Tennant watched him as the taxicab passed

Nob Hill now, and Huntington Square, and the Fairmont, and the Mark Hopkins where so long ago he'd had that outrageous altercation with Rayland. Peanuts and booze thrown and his father's sudden flare of violence. He could still feel the sting of Rayland's hand on his cheek. In the square, a group of men and women went through the strange slow motions of *t'ai chi*, balancing one-legged, stretching, reaching for invisible objects. Tennant had an urge to tell the driver to stop, he wanted to get out, didn't need to go any further because the city was impenetrable, he'd find nothing of himself here, the exercise was pointless. He restrained himself. There was a rough, dry sensation at the back of his throat.

When the taxi stopped on the edge of Chinatown, Alison paid the driver, who said, *Have a good one.* She and Tennant stepped out of the cab on the corner of Grant and California. The mist was unexpectedly cold even as it thinned. Tennant turned up the collar of his coat and shivered.

Across the way was St. Mary's Church. Poised on the rim of Chinatown, it had an incongruous look, a redbrick monolith besieged by Oriental forces, an outpost of Catholicism surrounded by Chinese souvenir shops and restaurants and Cantonese signs. The entrance to Chinatown. From somewhere came the sound of a guitar being strummed. A major, a minor, a seventh Tennant thought of his broken guitar in the house in upstate New York. He couldn't remember ever having played the damn thing. It belonged in somebody else's life.

Opposite St. Mary's Alison set her overnight bag on the sidewalk and took Obe's photograph from her purse. "I figure this is the precise spot where the picture was taken. The background's the same." She looked over at the church. A cable car sailed past, metal on metal, ferrying giddy tourists in the direction of Fisherman's Wharf.

Tennant, beset by an odd awareness that time had been charged with static electricity, gazed at the edifice of the church. An adjoining bookshop had a window filled with ecclesiastical volumes. Along the sidewalk a crazy man did a quick two-step, humming a tune as he went past. He glared at Tennant and Alison as if he considered them trespassers; then he danced on, still humming furiously.

"I don't remember," Tennant said in a flat way. He was disappointed in his failure. He'd somehow foolishly imagined that the past would come back like cavalry charging. "Nothing. Sweet fuck all."

"Five kids stood here. Obe took pictures. You saw something on the other side of this street. You pointed. Everyone looked. What did you see, Harry?"

The church yielded nothing.

"What did you see?" she asked again.

He stared hard at St. Mary's. Something happened over there. Something to do with the church. Long ago. He saw a woman emerge from the bookshop clutching a package. He strained for recollection, for clarity. It doesn't even need to be *clear*, does it? A spark would be enough. He turned his face away. Whatever had happened outside St. Mary's on a particular day more than twenty years ago was as closed as a miser's fist.

"I'm sorry," he said.

Alison picked up her bag. "It was worth a try," she said. "I hoped your memory might be jogged."

"Wait. Gimme a minute." He walked up and down, facing the church from different angles, as if he were himself a photographer assessing a shot—but it was a curious kind of photograph that could only be developed in the darkroom of his mind. Back down the years, Harry. Down anonymous little streets and lanes, past windowless houses, bolted doors, chain link fences. When the past faced you and you still couldn't remember it, you felt something more than despair—a heightened desperation, a fiery panic, because you were reduced to nothing. He wished he could set himself free, kick over the traces. He longed to be complete, but he would have settled for something less ambitious right then. A simple recollection; it wasn't much to want.

"Nothing," he said.

"Okay. Leave it. We'll go to the Haight. We'll take a look at Schrader Street."

He agreed, although he felt the need to linger here at the junction of Grant and California, an intersection where a key had been dropped and lost. The scent of Chinese food—ginger and soy and garlic—floated through the remnants of mist, and he was suddenly hungry.

She tugged at his sleeve. "Harry. Let's go."

He swung his bag from one hand to the other. The church was struck by sunlight briefly and the red brick assumed a warmth of sorts. A priest, defined by this abrupt brightness, came out of the place and turned right, heading down to the heart of Chinatown. Tennant watched him. A priest. Had there been a priest on that far-off day? A religious ceremony of some kind? He wasn't sure. He might have been trying too hard to convince himself of a memory. Self-delusion.

"I don't think we should hang around," Alison said. "Let's find a cab."

He followed her away from St. Mary's, glancing back once. But the church had absorbed the past and wasn't returning it, despite Tennant's longings.

They took a cab to the Haight. The mist had withered away now, the day was clear and sharp, a mischievous wind blowing unpredictably. Tennant rolled down the cab window. He heard voices in the wind, faint whispers. This way, Harry. Welcome back.

The sun was white like a damaged eye.

The cab crawled through slow traffic toward Haight Street. At the Panhandle, that large rectangle of parkland surrounded by trees, Alison and Tennant got out. For a moment he was reluctant to move. He might have been standing at the entrance to a maze, one of those elaborate labyrinths in which hapless strollers become trapped like flies in a fly bottle. Nearby was Golden Gate Park. What came back to Tennant suddenly was the exhausting humidity of the Conservatory of Flowers, the Japanese Tea Garden, the Oriental stone lions outside the museum, the flocks of pigeons that clustered there day after day in a manner he'd always found quietly malicious.

Now, as he walked through grass, he was flooded by recollections of Frisbees skimming between the trees, the scent of reefer, dogs running wild, boys and girls in headbands and sandals and beads, naked children decorating themselves with fingerpaint; he remembered flowers, guitars, the Diggers passing out spaghetti to hungry dopers and sundry derelicts' attracted to the Haight by free food. Bright days from long ago. Good vibes, as they once said in that time of bleak innocence. All the ghosts were agitated. He had come here to this parkland on the edge of Haight-Ashbury and disturbed them.

On the other side of the Panhandle lay the entrance to Schrader, which connected after a few blocks with Haight Street. He paused in his stride. He seemed to see himself across the way, an apparition that was a young Harry Tennant, long-haired, bearded, shuffling in a doped way along the sidewalk, his arm linked through Maggie Silver's, their heads together in the manner of lovers who have no more than a passing interest in the world outside their hearts. An idyll, a summer of light, and then an eclipse. Strange, terrifying.

The apparition vanished. There was nobody on the opposite sidewalk except for a man walking a yellow dog. It was Alison who had her arm linked through his, not Maggie Silver.

"We cross here," he said, looking into oncoming traffic.

They took one step off the sidewalk. A long gray limousine pulled alongside, blocking their progress. The back door opened. A man got out.

Another apparition.

Tennant said, *"Jesus Christ."*

Rayland Tennant—frail in the pale sunlight—moved toward his son.

15 The sun made the old man transparent, the way a flashlight held behind a hand will pierce flesh. Harry, who took a few steps forward from Alison, remembered when his father had been sturdy and healthy, his stride confident, his manner one that suggested the world was his personal fiefdom. The contrast between now and then amazed him. Rayland looked infinitely weary; the whites of his eyes were yellow, his thin lips colorless. Tennant had the sudden urge to hug the old man, to say that what lay in the past between them should be forgotten, grudges finally buried. He understood, as he'd always known on the level where the heart secretly operates, that he still loved this fragile figure, a realization that did nothing to dispel the surprise and tension he felt, and the odd little flicker of fear—which was focused on the understanding that another man sat in the back of the limousine, someone whose face he couldn't make out. Up front, the driver was concealed by smoked glass.

"Well, Harry," Rayland said.

"This is a hell of a place to meet," Tennant said. There was strain in his voice, a quality he tried to subdue. Pretend you're not surprised out of your mind, Harry. Pretend this is common, an everyday thing, meeting your father in the middle of San Francisco. Let's have coffee or a beer, son. Let's chew over old times. How's it been going? What's new?

"I suspect any place would be a hell of a place." Rayland stretched out a hand, touched his son's arm, then glanced briefly at Alison, who stood quietly some feet back

Tennant fought against the urge to move away from Rayland's hand. This is your father, Harry. This is the man whose blood runs in your veins, no matter what. "Your people must be pretty damn good hounds, Rayland."

"I could never stand amateurs." Rayland looked across the Panhandle. Birds rose out of a tree, startled by the abrupt backfire of a car, which rang like an assassin's gun.

Tennant looked at the limousine. The figure in the back was motionless and for that reason alone, sinister. Rayland, who flinched slightly at the backfire, had a faraway expression, that of a man who finds the taste of an old dream lingering. He still wore his wedding ring, a distinguished band of thick gold in which were inscribed his initials and those of his late wife. His hands had silvery hair upon them. The nails, flecked with white, were manicured as they always had been. Rayland had his vanities even now.

"Since I last saw you, Harry, I've entered what you might call, for want of anything better, the age of pathos. Winter of life, as they say." He smiled at his son, and there was the brightness of affection in the look. "I never dreamed I'd live quite this long. I thought I might see, oh, sixty, sixty-five, but when seventy came I began to consider infirmity a real possibility."

Tennant was crowded by too many questions. His head might have been an amphitheater in which a mass of people were clapping their hands discordantly in the dark. "Why are you having me followed?"

The old man ignored Harry's question. He said, "We used to be so damned close, you and I. I don't think I ever knew a father and son as close as we were, Harry. I think of that often. Too often. I get sick to my heart just remembering."

"You're evading me, Rayland."

The old man shook his head. "I'm far less interested in explaining the mechanics of how this meeting came about than I am in enjoying a sense of reunion, Harry."

"I don't think I have quite the heart for reunions, Rayland."

"Just seeing you again . . ." Rayland gestured vaguely with his hands, the act of a man who finds himself wandering along the limits of vocabulary. "I can't tell you how it makes me feel. I can't begin to tell you."

"You're not listening to me. I said I didn't have the heart for a reunion."

"You still can't get around it, can you, Harry? After all this time. I'm disappointed. Your outrage is passé." The old man looked solemn. "Everyone has the right to due process of law. A child molester. A serial killer. The most despicable criminals. I don't care who. They have the right to the best representation that can be found."

"Or bought."

"Harry, we've traveled this road before. Colonel Harker is past. He's history. All that was long ago."

"Harker's a monster, for Christ's sake," Harry said.

"I wonder how much effort it costs you to keep your heart this hard. All that energy wasted in something as negative as a grudge. Let it go, Harry. Don't resent me. I miss you. I miss you more than I can possibly say. This is the time to bury the past."

I miss you too, Harry thought. You were always there when I was a kid. But where were you later, Dad? Harry, who looked away from his father's face, had a childhood memory of a tree house Rayland had once built in the backyard of the family home. Hacking through branch and foliage with saw and machete, Rayland—who had no affinity for manual labor—had sweated and bled to construct this tiny fragile retreat for his only son. There had even been a sign done in bright red paint: HARRY'S PLACE. A sweet little image. Childhood had been a fine time, a great time, despite the premature death of Harry's mother. Rayland had striven to compensate for her absence, minimizing the extent of the boy's grief. Father, mother, friend.

True, the outrage Harry had felt years ago had lost some of its fire, but not to the point where he could slough it off and embrace the old man, as if nothing had ever happened. Rayland, no matter how you looked at it, no matter how you tried to conceal it behind talk of due process, had been the butcher's partner.

"You chose to take the side of the military, Rayland," he said. "I went in another direction."

"I don't call bad drugs a direction, Harry. I had hopes you might make something out of your life. You had opportunities, far more than most young people. You could have gone to the college of your choice. You could have done something useful. Achieved something You may call it a father's wishful thinking, but when you were born I remember saying to myself, 'This kid is going to be somebody special.' He's going to make a mark. Instead . . ." The old man looked sad, a figure disappointed by the expectations of love.

Somebody special, Tennant thought. Yeah. Somebody without a life. A hollowed-out man. I'd call that special. "You can't have ambitions for other people, Rayland. You can't impose your notion of destiny on anybody else. People live their own lives."

Rayland raised an eyebrow, an old courtroom mannerism, something to undermine the statements of some poor bastard in the witness box. He might have been asking: *Do they, Harry? Do people really live their own lives?* Then the look was gone, and he was glancing at Alison with an expression that might have been one of sympathy.

A breeze moved through the trees. The Panhandle was noisy with the roar of leaves. Rayland appeared to be listening to this abrupt green vibration in the fashion of a man who yearns for the simplicity of things, a life lived at a distance from the stressful complexity of cities. Was there regret in that look? Harry wondered. Did the old man yearn to turn back a clock and change the way his life had gone? Odd. Tennant would never have imagined his father to be the kind of man in whom regret would stir. Rayland had always made decisions and stuck to them. Age had changed him in more than the physical sense. Was it that simple?

In a voice that was strangely uncertain, he said, "I'll never forget the boy you were, Harry. My feelings for you have never changed. I've never stopped loving you, Harry. I never will."

"I don't doubt your love, Rayland."

"Then an amnesty is in order, Harry. I want your friendship."

"And the ledger closed."

"I want reconciliation. An embrace. I want my son back."

"I'm not ready, Rayland. One day maybe. Not right now."

"Harry, Harry. Don't you realize time is running out? I'm seventy-five. Sometimes at night when I close my eyes, I can see my own headstone. I see my name carved in granite. I see the date of my birth and death. You don't have any idea of what that feels like. How could you? Some nights I don't want to fall asleep because I think I'm not going to wake up again. I lie in the dark with my eyes open. Those are the worst times. That's when I start remembering. I see your face. And I cry, Harry. I cry. Rayland Tennant cries. He lies there and remembers the time he took you to the Grand Canyon and how goddamn hot it was, and how blue the sky was, and the way he was afraid you were going to fall off the edge somehow and how damned hard he held on to your hand because he didn't want to lose his little boy." The old man raised his face and looked up. His eyes were damp. "One time we were at a theme park somewhere in Virginia and we went on the roller coaster and I remember this dreadful panic I had because I sensed, I just *knew*, the whole structure was going to fall apart. I put my arms around you, Harry. I wanted to save you. I must have come close to a heart attack that day."

He shut his eyes a moment, rubbed them, smiled. "A father fears for his son. Every step of the way, Harry. Love and fear. You can't always separate them."

Harry Tennant remembered that ride. He remembered air rushing past him and his blood racing. He remembered people screaming as the cars plunged at terrifying angles. *Maggie Silver had screamed too once.*

"It's terrific to stand here and talk about the past, Rayland. But you're still evading me. You're still refusing to answer my questions. Like—why are you having me followed?"

Rayland Tennant didn't speak. He was clearly lost in the gloaming of recollection and had no desire to step out of that twilight into the present time.

"Does the name Sajac mean anything to you, Rayland? Or Paul Lannigan?"

Rayland shook his head. When he spoke he did so slowly, reluctantly. "You're in trouble, Harry."

"You mean the drug bust, which presumably you know about—"

"I'm not speaking of your legal difficulties, Harry. I'm not referring to drugs nor to a corpse in your hotel room and the fact that you jumped bail. I'm talking about another kind of trouble."

"Let's be specific."

"This is the bottom line: I'm not sure I can go on protecting you."

"Protecting me? What the hell is that supposed to mean?"

Tennant took a step back from his father. In the mire of perplexities, what was one more? When you split open the fruit of a conundrum, you were bound to find a proliferation of mysterious seeds.

"Did it never strike you as strange that you didn't go to Vietnam, Harry? You didn't have the excuse of physical disability. You didn't have the pretext of being an accredited student. You were hanging around San Francisco doing your drugs—yet you had a deferment. You never appeared before a draft board. What did you imagine, son? They'd lost your name and address? You'd slipped through the cracks in the system?"

In the haze of the Haight-Ashbury, in the fumes that clouded all the blown young minds, the noise of sabers in Vietnam had seemed a distant clash of metal, a senseless flexing of muscle in obscure jungles, young men dying for old men's causes. People who gravitated to the Haight in the days before the antiwar crusades gathered maximum force were stupefied by drugs, unlikely candidates for the abattoir in Southeast Asia. An illusion persisted in Harry's mind that he was immune to the draft because he inhabited the Haight, and no board would seek cannon fodder in such a place, amidst the dropouts, the freaks, people whose oars had long been out of the water. He'd been wrong, of course; but the fact the draft bypassed him hadn't surprised him at all. If you abandoned society, so did you abdicate your responsibility to society's wars. You smoked dope. You dropped acid. You were a lover, a poet, not a warrior.

"I had influence, Harry. And I'm not going to deny I used it. I wasn't going to see my boy die in some pointless war. Am I making myself clear? I protected you then."

Harry said nothing. The notion of Rayland's intervention had never occurred to him. He wondered why Rayland was telling him now. Was it to convince him that the father was worthy of the son's love? That a truce could be forged?

"While you were amusing yourself in la-la land, I was pulling strings in the real world. I didn't want you sent home from some jungle in a bloody bag. I couldn't have survived that." The old man appeared to sway. He had frail eyelids, the veins of which were suggestive of ink lines scratched on thin paper. "Later, when you moved to upstate New York, I knew the illicit trade you drifted into. I learned about your relationship with Bobby Delacroix. I found myself having to intervene on one occasion to prevent your arrest because agents of the DEA knew you were providing narcotics to Delacroix. This took a great deal of energy and persuasion on my part, Harry. Some of these agents can be bought. Others you have to coerce. Promises are made. Bargains struck. Do you understand me, Harry? I was your guardian angel."

Guardian angel? Alison's phrase for the sniper in the motel parking lot.

"Frank Rozak told you to sit tight, didn't he?"

"Frank Rozak is one your bloodhounds?" Tennant asked. *Of course.*

"Why the devil did you bolt before he even had a chance to get to the prosecutor? Why couldn't you have given it another few hours, time for strings to be pulled? Why didn't you listen to the man instead of jumping into this . . . let's call it a misadventure." Rayland looked forlorn. "Now I'm no longer sure I have the power to protect you. It may have been taken away."

"Taken by whom? I don't understand. I don't know what the hell you're talking about."

Rayland made a dismissive gesture with his white hand. "There are things I cannot explain, Harry. I can tell you only this," and he leaned forward, an old man who'd once known considerable power and who looked exhausted now, bone-colored, stripped of his authority. "If you participate in this quest of yours, I can't guarantee your safety. There are influential people involved. Do you understand?"

"What people, Rayland? What are they involved in? I hate this cryptic shit."

Rayland was quiet for a time. He stared at Alison, who, frozen out of this precarious reunion, looked anxious, longing to participate and yet not knowing whether she dare. "Let me spell it out for you. Stay away from the past. Stay away from that little girl."

"Why?"

"Because I have the feeling you may well come home to me in a bag. All these years after I tried to prevent it, my nightmare will finally happen."

"What are you talking about?"

"Take my advice. Leave the past alone. Discard your young traveling companion. That's all I can tell you."

"It's not enough," Harry said. "Why do I have to leave everything alone? What difference does it make to you what I do?"

"Because you have no future if you persist, Harry. I can't help you beyond this point, if you decide to ignore my advice. God knows, I had a hard enough time convincing my associates to give you one last chance. . . . They wanted you dead. They said, 'Why don't we just kill him and his young companion and get it over with once and for all?' So they sent down an order, and I managed to have it countermanded at the very last minute, but only at great cost to myself, Harry."

"The guy with the rifle," Tennant said. "You sent him."

Rayland made no response. Stress showed on his features, nervousness in the eyes. Whoever Rayland's associates were, they had clearly pressured the old man to his limits, and beyond. Tennant glanced at the limousine.

"Harry. I don't want you to die."

"I'm not in the mood for dying, Rayland."

"Harry, please." Rayland reached out, closing a hand around his son's wrist. "You've never seen me beg before, have you? I'm begging now. Don't get yourself killed over something that has no relevance. Leave it alone. Walk away."

"How can I walk away, Rayland? For God's sake, there are parts of myself I don't know, there are pieces of my life that don't fit. I want these things to cohere, Rayland. Call it wholeness. Does that make sense?"

"Survival's more important than wholeness, Harry. Better to live incomplete than die in some unpleasant manner."

"I don't want to live incomplete," Tennant said. "I want to know what the fuck is going on. Wouldn't you? Somehow I've mislaid twelve goddamn years of my life, and more—Jesus, would you walk away, Rayland?"

Rayland took out a handkerchief and rubbed it against

the tip of his nose. "I warn you, Harry. Don't persist. And keep this in mind. Your little friend is in the same claustrophobic pit as yourself, Harry. Would you want to see her damaged?"

"She makes her own choices, Rayland. I don't have any control over the girl."

Rayland looked at the limousine. A tractor-trailer, stacked with logs, rumbled past. The shadow in the back of the limousine shifted very slightly. Rayland took a step toward his son and held out his arms for an embrace. "Don't die on me. Please don't die."

Harry felt his father's arms go around him—a moment of old love expressed in the heart of a haunted city. He felt his father's frailty and smelled age upon him, and the sensation of love gave way to a terrible pity, as if only now did he really regret all the years of alienation. I could have ignored the differences between us, he thought. I could have set them aside. What the hell did it matter if you didn't agree with your father over certain moral issues—you could still maintain love, couldn't you? You could agree to differ. You could bypass rage. But you hadn't, Harry.

"I love you, Harry. I can't bear the idea of you dying." The voice was a whisper. This was a secret confession, hidden, words meant only for Harry and not for any potential eavesdropper in the limousine. "You mean everything to me. You always have. My heart breaks for you, son."

Harry didn't release his father. They held fast to each other, love and hurt, regret and reconciliation, a knot of emotions. Tennant cursed his own sullenness, the distance he'd kept from the old man. The trouble with love lay in the simple human failure to acknowledge it at times. You treated it with carelessness, disregarded it, silenced it, forgetting its rarity, its power to make life bearable. When you were neglectful of it, you harmed something essential deep inside yourself.

"If you can't give up this search, I can at least try to pretend that you have. I can report that you agreed."

"Report to whom, for Christ's sake?"

"I don't think for a moment the watchdogs will be pulled from duty on my word alone. I can't make any promises. I've played out my string, Harry. That's what it comes down to. All the cards I had are gone. All my markers have been called in."

"Who are they, Rayland? Your associates—who the hell are they? What are you all involved in? Maybe if I understood that, I might—"

"I can't say any more." Rayland stepped back. "I'm glad you've seen sense, Harry." He raised his voice for the benefit of the man in the limousine. Then he held out his hand, which Harry shook. There was a sense of finality in the touch, as if this were the ultimate good-bye. "Go. Live your life. Forget all this nonsense," and the old man turned, walking toward the limousine. The figure in the backseat emerged from shadow for a moment. Tennant had a sense of familiarity; nothing beyond a flicker. He tried to get a fix on it even as Rayland stepped inside the big car. The back door was immediately closed. The limo swung around and slid into the tide of traffic that rolled along the Panhandle.

Tennant watched it go. He was conscious of Alison standing beside him. He looked up into the sun, seeing a gathering of clouds float like a flock of malignant geese over the rooftops. He thought of Rayland sitting in the gray limo, thought of the old man being transported back inside a nightmare he couldn't explain to his own son.

Tennant turned his face to the girl. Pensive, hands in the pockets of her coat, she was walking around in a slow circle, staring at the ground. "I figure I was meant to hear what he had to say. I guess it was for my benefit as much as yours, Harry. Stay away from the past. Stay away from me. He can't go on covering your ass unless you're a good little scout and do what you're told—which explains why we haven't joined Bear Sajac yet. Daddy's looking after his boy." She kicked at blades of grass. "Okay. He loves you and he wants to do his best for you. But why is it so damn important to him that you don't go on? Why?"

Tennant reached out, squeezed the girl's shoulder fondly. He imagined looking down through the wrong end of a telescope, and what he saw were two very small people locked in a world too large for them. He faced Schrader Street. A part of him wanted to stop right where he was, avoid Schrader, avoid it all, obey the old man, take some of the obvious pressure off Rayland. But it wasn't enough. He'd come this far. He had to get to the end.

As he stepped off the sidewalk, he realized he knew the identity of the man in the back of the limousine. It had been Noel Harker.

16

On the corner of Schrader they paused. Uncertainly, Tennant looked up in the direction of Haight, a couple of blocks away. Which house had had the scaffolding around it all those years ago? He had the feeling of quicksands. At any moment the sidewalk would turn to swamp and swallow him.

Alison took his arm. They walked up Schrader. The houses, many of them large Victorian edifices carved up into apartments, were imposingly ornate in the sunlight; fanciful cupolas, eaves, bay windows that appeared to scrutinize you in the manner of great cameras. It was easy to imagine you were being observed, your movements recorded, if not by Rayland's watchdogs, then by unseen faces behind those windows. He thought about Noel Harker in the back of the limousine and wondered why his father maintained contact with the butcher, what it was that kept these two men circling in the same orbit. Of course, Rayland had lobbied for the arms makers, which in reality meant the Pentagon, and maybe he still kept up the friendships of expediency he'd developed before—but why had Harker been in the old man's company at that particular time in that particular car? There was a simple answer: Harker had to be one of Rayland's mysterious *associates,* but what did that loose term cover?

"Which house, Harry?" Alison asked. "Do you remember?" Her questions were asked in an anxious tone; she was hurried now. Why wouldn't she be? The encounter with Rayland, the warning contained in the old man's message—she wanted to move, to keep ahead of danger if she could. *I love you, Harry,* the old man had said. *I can't bear the idea of you dying.* Dying. Tennant wondered how long he and Alison had, if there was a timetable, a schedule of death, if it would come here in one of the streets of the Haight-Ashbury in daylight. How long could the old man protect them anyway? An hour or two? *I can't make any promises. All my markers have been called in.* Time had been rendered meaningless. Hours might have been diminishing into minutes, minutes into seconds.

He stepped into an alley. With a puzzled look Alison followed him. He unzipped his bag and took out the gun and, thinking how frail it seemed, how insubstantial against Rayland's associates, stuck it in the pocket of his overcoat. Alison watched him, said nothing.

They emerged from the alley and continued along Schrader. He gazed up at windows. Any one of them might have been the window from which he'd watched traffic slide down Schrader to the Panhandle. Any one of them might have been the room from which Maggie Silver had been dragged away by persons whose faces he couldn't recall. Windows yielded so little. Blinds, drapes, slats of plastic. Here and there a decal was pressed onto a pane, a bumper sticker. Or you could see a plant, flowers, the back of a piece of furniture. But what did these things really tell you about the inhabitants, the faces beyond glass, the shadows in dim rooms? He put his hand in the pocket that held the gun.

"Which house?" Alison asked again.

"I'm not sure. I need to think. Clear my head. We'll walk around, come back this way." So simple a pronouncement, he thought. Clear your head. People used it constantly and didn't need to think about what they were saying.

"Harry," she said. "I don't think we have the luxury of time to go strolling around the Haight like a pair of tourists—"

"What do you expect of me?" he asked. "You imagine I can just point to a house and say, Yeah, there it is, that's the very place. I wish to hell I could. I wish I could go straight up to some front door and ring a bell and everything would come back."

"Okay. Okay. I'm sorry. It's just that I'm getting jangled."

"You and me both."

She pressed her face against his arm. He liked the feeling: giving comfort and receiving it. He liked the sense of caring. "I spoke sharply," he said. "I'm sorry too."

She smiled at him, and he thought he caught a shadow in the smile, as if the expression were just slightly out of focus. She wants to look bright, she can't quite make it. That was all. This situation. This *business*. It wasn't exactly compatible with cheerfulness.

They reached the junction of Schrader and Haight. Tennant looked the length of Haight Street as if it were a menacing tunnel into his yesterdays. On the wall of a shut-down store somebody had spraypainted ABOLISH GOVERNMENT. Outside a donut shop a young man labored on the engine of his rusted jeep; his bare feet were black, his clothes filthy. When the boy raised his dirt-streaked face from the hood and glanced in an antagonistic way at Tennant, Harry looked elsewhere, embarrassed. He must have been staring.

Dazed young kids—summoned to the Haight by the siren of freedom past—sat on the sidewalk, passing paper-bagged Jack Daniel's back and forth. But they looked more like fugitives from parental authority, runaways from distant suburbs, than seekers after an illusory liberty. A whiff of pot, the aroma of coffee beans.

Tennant moved along the street, thinking he must have come this way thousands of times in a hundred mental conditions.

The stores were changed. They'd become self-conscious— expensive leather, holographs, 1940s clothing. He didn't notice any headshops, none of those crazy little places that had once proliferated in the neighborhood, selling hash pipes and roach clips and stash boxes, all the paraphernalia of the drug scene. The Weed Patch had vanished, and so had The Psychedelic Shop. There were no street dealers, formerly so prolific, offering acid, speed, lids. *I can get you anything.*

The people who wandered along the sidewalk didn't resemble the old crowd, unless you counted the occasional eccentric—a pale strung-out girl in Apache dress and headband, a tall black woman in velvet cloak and shades who chanted a mantra to herself as she passed. The place seemed to be a mixture of persevering residents who'd been in the neighborhood since the 1960s and a fresh influx of imposters who thought they'd find a freak show still. But the carnival had left town long ago.

When Tennant reached Roberts Hardware, he stopped. This at least hadn't changed. This at least was familiar. He'd gone in here once and bought something—what? Wooden shelves. Yes. Bookshelves. A sneaking little memory. Why could he bring back to mind such a trivial thing and yet fail to locate the house on Schrader? He'd hammered those shelves into a wall and they'd fallen down within days, but back then such trifles weren't catastrophes, they were something you just shook your head over and got stoned and said fuck it, it didn't matter in the cosmic scheme of things. A girl's laughter, yes, and books coming down in a heap, and a glass bong splintering—

"Something's missing," he said suddenly.

"What?"

"Noise. Music. You always had people with finger cymbals or bells. Somebody was always playing conga drums. I don't hear that now. It's a touch spooky. The street was always noisier than this. It used to . . . vibrate, I guess that's the word. But all the chaos is gone."

Empty. The Haight was empty.

They crossed the street. On the corner of Clayton the Free Medical Clinic was still in existence. Troubled, Tennant

looked at the sign; it pitched him back abruptly into the bad-
lands of memory—he'd been in this place, he'd been given
Thorazine here to bring him down from a vicious high when
he'd freaked out on STP. The universe had tilted that night.
Hooded figures stalked him. The stark moon over the Haight
had singled him out for scrutiny. He'd tumbled into a terrible
spiral of lights, a stroboscopic funnel at the bottom of which
he'd seen himself decomposing in a coffin, flesh honeycombed
with lice, his eyes red and staring into some godforsaken infinity.
All this rushed back at him and he was pained. What he
couldn't remember was how he'd made it to the free clinic. If
he'd been trapped in the violent seesaw of such a bad trip,
chances were good he hadn't found his own way. Somebody
must have brought him.

"I was in this place one time," he said. "Bogus drugs. Very
bogus. Thing is, I don't remember who treated me. The doctor's name, face, none of that stuff." He heard in his voice a
note of desperation. Had he *truly* been expecting a tidal assault
of minutia, of those small details from which an ordinary life is
forged? Nothing's ordinary, Harry. You can't have ordinary.

Alison looked at him with sympathy. "Ever since we started,
I've been trying to imagine what it must be like for you. All I
ever get is this impression of scattered bits and pieces. Fragments. Like a bomb exploded inside your brain." She
shrugged, her expression rather forlorn. Then she caught his
arm and drew him closer as they walked. "Nobody should have
to live that way, Harry."

Bits and pieces. Tennant looked away. He was thinking of
Schrader Street again. It was time to go back in that direction.
But he hesitated, studying the menu in the window of a health
food restaurant. Sprouted beans and cucumber and spinach on
whole-wheat bread. He gazed through glass, watched a waitress move between tables. She was lithe, dark-haired, in her
late thirties, early forties; it struck him there was some superficial resemblance between the waitress and Maggie, a chimeri-
cal thing that passed as soon as she turned her face. Similarities, small mockeries.

When they reached the intersection with Schrader, Tennant gazed down toward the Panhandle. He wondered where the gray limousine had transported Rayland. *Now go. Live your life. Forget all this nonsense.* He saw the old man climb back inside the big car, recalled the juxtaposition of his father's frailty upon sleek gray metal, the shadowed face of Harker in the back. Harker's features had once briefly been known throughout America from the cover of magazines, a face that had become a symbol of war's brutality, one that had forced ordinary Americans, people who went to church and were kind to their neighbors and who played with their kids in parks and sandlots, to confront the notion that savagery wasn't confined to the Vietcong. Harker's face was the maggot at the heart of the apple pie, scrutinized, removed, then eradicated, and in the manner of all such unpleasant things, totally forgotten.

I have seen Harker elsewhere, Tennant thought. At some other place and time. Not on TV, not in the pages of magazines, somewhere else. I have seen him.

They were walking down Schrader now toward the Panhandle. Tennant stopped. Across the way, located on the corner of a narrow street that intersected Schrader, was a large yellow house, Victorian, elaborate, something like a great cracked plaster cake. *Where did I see Harker?*

But then he wasn't thinking about the colonel because the big yellow house seized his attention. He stared at it long and hard. His head buzzed. "That's it. That's the one. I'm sure of it."

Alison caught his hand and started to move across the street.

"Wait," he said. He was reluctant all at once. He had a sense of trespassing.

"Why? All we have to do is go to the door. Check the names outside—"

"For what? For Maggie Silver? You're way off, Alison." And it struck him like the blow of a hammer that Maggie was dead. She wouldn't be here. Like Sajac, like Kat, like Carlos, she was dead. Only Harry Tennant of the group of five had been kept alive and functioning, if you could call it life. Diminished, reduced, it was an existence of sorts, sure, but it didn't add up to a life. He was suddenly furious. With himself for having been busted, with Alison for interrupting his hermetic world, with Rayland for keeping him under observation, with Lannigan for whatever it was the Irishman had done to him.

"Harry, I don't know what we'll find, but even if it only serves to jumpstart your memory, it's worth a look."

Tennant stared up at a score of windows. Which had been his? His eye roamed upward. Window after window, blank cartridges of glass. But then as he crossed the street, his perspective was lost and the shadow of the big house fell over him.

Alison studied the array of doorbells and nameplates. There were at least fifteen of them. More than twenty years ago people thumbtacked scraps of paper on which they'd written their Haight names. There were sometimes sundry rainbows and marijuana leaves inscribed lavishly on cards. But these had been replaced by small nameplates, all very tidy, completely at odds with the way things had been before.

Tennant struggled with his rage, which had nowhere to go; unfocused, it dwindled into blind frustration.

Alison gave up on the names. She tried the door in her usual direct way. It had been left unlocked, opening into a darkly painted lobby that led over exposed floorboards to a flight of stairs.

"We're in," she said.

Tennant followed her inside. He was having trouble breathing. The air was thick. A certain density hung in the shadows. He moved toward the stairs. On the landing above, light was filtered through a stained-glass window. A curious design, an abstract of simple slivers in reds and blues. He stopped at the foot of the stairs.

Give up all this nonsense.

He looked up toward the stained glass. Sweat from his scalp slid over his forehead, and he wiped it away with the back of his hand. The house was charged with heat. His past was all about him, yet it wasn't tangible; familiarity, yes, but nothing

on which he'd pledge his life. The stained glass—had that been
in place before?

No. It hadn't. It was recent.

He imagined climbing these steps years ago. He thought of
himself going up and up into the recesses of this huge house to
a room perched at the very top, where attic ceilings sloped
down to a window. The house had been raucous once, a
raunchy run-down place that vibrated continually with rock.
Doors were always open, rooms filled with boys and girls, the
laughter of freedom, the perfume of reefer. Day and night
hadn't mattered, time was a useless bourgeois device, nobody
cared: It was a world without appointments, without clocks.

He climbed, Alison just behind him.

When they reached the landing Tennant found himself
looking at the stained-glass pattern: a kaleidoscope effect. He
gazed up the next flight of stairs. His head ached. He felt raw,
unfinished around the edges of himself, someone on the edge
of disintegration. Keep climbing, Harry. Up and up.

On the second landing, corridors stretched off gloomily to
left and right. Here Tennant stood motionless. Left or right—
he wasn't certain of anything. He wasn't even sure this was the
correct house. Maybe he'd chosen it without any foundation in
fact because he wanted to please Alison, wanted to say, *Look I
remember this.* But now the house seemed to wrap itself around
him and propel him upward, as if he had no real choice in the
matter. He was at the mercy of a force he couldn't name.

I must have climbed these stairs with Maggie Silver. Hand
in hand we must have come this way. In the room I must have
touched her breasts, drawn her skirt up over her thighs. Was
any feeling worse than this—that love had become a fire blown
out, a collection of cold cinder? He had a black moment, a for-
getfulness of purpose. *I'm Harry Tennant and I'm trying to close
a circle that may not make it.*

"Left or right, Harry?" Alison asked.

"I think left." This decision was prompted by the sight of
an ancient lightshade that must not have been changed in more
than twenty years, a dingy fringed thing that was slightly famil-

iar. The shade had an intensity about it, as if it existed in a realm where all objects were infused with a heightened reality.

At the end of the corridor a door faced them. Tennant had the feeling it was about to be thrown open unexpectedly, exposing him to a rectangle of blinding light. But it didn't happen. He moved forward. He thought: In the old days the door hadn't been numbered—who cared about the gravity of numbers in those giddy years?—but now it was. Fourteen. One four. White plastic numerals from a hardware store. Screwed into the dark brown wood.

"Is this the place?" Alison asked.

Tennant didn't reply. Even if this was the room, what difference would it make? Some stranger occupied the place, a face Tennant had never seen in his life, what would it matter?

Alison touched his arm gently. Encouragement. "Do you think this is it?" she asked. She whispered her question eagerly.

Tennant imagined he stood on the edge of an unpleasant revelation—ill-defined, something half-glimpsed on a moonless night, scudding along the horizon of his recollection. He was shivering now despite the heat that pressed against him.

A toilet flushed somewhere. A domestic sound, the banality of which might have reassured Tennant of some commonplace reality, a humdrum universe totally manageable. But he was outside that structure, beyond ease.

Tennant stopped outside the door. Do you simply knock and see the face of a stranger and say, Sorry, wrong place? Alison reached past him and rapped her knuckles on the wood.

There wasn't an immediate answer. Tennant, breathless, waited. He might have been suspended in an airless pocket. Don't answer, he thought. I don't want anyone to come to the door.

Alison knocked again.

Tennant looked back along the corridor. It was strange how memory, like a net thrown randomly in the air, sometimes snared butterflies. He heard Maggie Silver laugh, and he saw her in shadow at the end of the corridor. She had her head tossed back, and the laugh was as flamboyant as the clothes she wore, the great floppy broad-brimmed hat under which her black hair flowed, the plum-velvet long coat, the strands of beads that sparkled against her breasts. The laughter roared in his head, smoky, uninhibited, genuine. He slipped through the grids of remembrance and imagination, the places where truth and fancy met, those intersections where what might have taken place and what had actually happened came together in remarkable collisions. Maggie Silver, Maggie Quicksilver—she had once said, *We'll love each other forever, Harry, no matter what, no matter what. You know why? Because some loves are a matter of destiny and you just can't fight against them.*

Destiny. People spoke of destiny and kismet in those times as if they were familiar objects you could buy in your local headshop along with glass coke straws and hash screens and Rizla papers. The stars were hip, baby. If they said you were to fall in love, that's what you did.

Tennant turned away from the empty corridor and faced the door where Alison was knocking a third time.

A sound of running water, a toilet being flushed, came from inside the room. Then the door was opened.

A woman, peering over the tops of steel glasses, asked, "Yeah?" Her long silver-black hair fell over her shoulders. She took off the glasses. She looked from Alison to Tennant. "You collecting for something? What is it?"

Tennant heard it clearly from some place way back in his head, old music, a chord plucked out of an arrangement of strings, a disembodied fragment of melody.

Alison said, "We're looking for somebody."

The woman took a step forward, peering in a myopic way. "Who?"

Tennant slumped against the jamb of the door, suddenly sure, as certain as he'd been of anything in his life.

"Maggie," he said.

He stretched out a hand tentatively, as if he might simply grasp the past like the head of a fragile flower.

17 The woman said, "You're out of your mind," and tried to close the door, but Tennant put a foot forward, advancing into the room. The woman, nervously pushing hair away from her face, continued to back up. Maggie, indisputably Maggie, the same but different, as he himself was different; his mind fogged, his senses reeled, he focused on nothing but this woman, who had raised one nicotine-stained hand in a gesture that mean halt, stay away from me. He kept going toward her, thinking how the differences in her were less than the similarities—there were lines around that fine mouth, and the eyes lacked some of the old vibrancy, but they were bright and knowing still. The waist was thicker, the clothing sensibly plain instead of outrageous, but she was Maggie. What hasn't changed is my heart, not in the slightest way. Breathless, he had the urge to hold her, as if by that simple act all his years of solitude and separation, all those forlorn spaces, might be erased.

"Maggie," he said again.

"Check out that telephone. You get the hell out of here or I call the cops."

"I don't think you understand," Tennant said. He'd hardly

heard a word she'd said. "I've been looking for you."

The woman appealed to Alison. "I don't know what's going on but you better get your asses out of here before I pick up the goddamn phone."

Tennant put a hand out toward her. One touch, he thought. It would take one touch and she'd give up this strange masquerade of ignorance. I love her the way I always have. Love was the constant, whether forgotten or not. It persisted even in neglect, in amnesia, it sustained itself in concealed corners and shuttered rooms, in damp lonely spaces.

She knocked his hand away. "Okay. That's it." She reached for the telephone, but Tennant stepped between the woman and the instrument before she could grasp it.

"Get out of my way Move!"

Alison said, "She doesn't know you, Harry. Can't you see that?"

"How could she not know me?" He snapped the question at the girl without taking his eyes from Maggie's face. He had the feeling he was on the edge of some awful madness, but insanity contained the elements of freedom, as if it were a harsh light suddenly turned on his past. Let it burn. Let it illuminate everything. "How the hell could she not know me?"

The woman said, "Simple. I never saw you before in my life, that's how."

Tennant shook his head. The fine thing about madness was how it focused your mind. You saw something and you went at it obsessively and nothing could sway you. "I know her," he said. "I know she's Maggie Silver, but for some reason she's lying."

"I don't think she's lying, Harry. I don't think it's that."

Tennant thought: Alison's protecting this woman. She's defending her. Taking her side. Why?

"You're both crazy," the woman said, and she laughed apprehensively.

For a second Tennant took his eyes away from Maggie and gazed around the room. A trickery had gone on. The walls, formerly hung with psychedelia, sizzling Fillmore Auditorium posters, Bobby Kennedy and Che and Bob Dylan, tie-dyed sheets in scarlet and orange, was painted a pale flat lilac. Here and there were placed small frames, under the glass of which dried flowers were arranged in prissy patterns. Maggie wouldn't have entertained such things, she'd have said they belonged in a spinster's attic somewhere in Nebraska or South Dakota—geographical regions she once referred to as American Siberia. Up there, Harry, where they sleep eight hours and eat three square meals a day and have their lives all figured out and what are they but prisoners of the system?

The afternoon light upon the window was the color of whisky held to a bright lamp. It flowed inside the room, striking the place where once a threadbare Indian rug had been located; now a simple purple carpet lay in the spot. Purple carpet, lilac walls, pressed flowers. Against the windows hung flimsy lace curtains, caught back in a bow, fussy, unlike anything Maggie had ever put there.

He had the puzzled response of a man faced with a counterfeit. He felt his heart drop as though it were a dead coal in his chest. If this woman wasn't Maggie Silver, why did he feel the yearning to hold her and tell her they were back together again, everything was going to be fine, everything resolved? Was it truly madness in the end, the kind from which no return was ever possible?

"Show her Obe's picture, Alison."

Slowly Alison took the clipping from her purse; the woman shook her head and wouldn't touch it.

"Listen, I live here in peace, I mind my own business, the last thing I need is for a couple of loonies to come barging in calling me Maggie."

Alison moved toward the woman, still holding the photograph out. There was uncertainty in Alison's step. When she spoke she did so in a tone of tenderness and concern. "Please. Look at the picture," she said.

"Screw your picture."

"Look at it. Please." Alison laid a hand on the woman's wrist in a curiously gentle manner. For a moment it seemed to

Tennant that he existed outside of these two women, that some kind of sharing was going on, a situation in which he could never intrude. Maybe a sign has passed between them, one woman to another, a light in the eye invisible to him, as if between them they'd decided that Tennant was sick, a man to be humored. He dismissed this thought at once. But the feeling of having been excluded lingered in him.

The woman shrugged and took the clipping from Alison. She put her glasses back on and gazed at it. "Well?"

"Keep looking," Tennant said.

"What's to see?"

"Just look."

Alison said, "Give her time, Harry. Don't rush her."

The woman shook her head. "Five kids. The old days. So what?"

"The one in the middle is you," Tennant said.

"No way. Hey, no way."

"I'm standing at the edge of the picture."

She stared at Tennant. "Look. I admit there's some kinda similarity between me and the girl there, but you can hardly see her face for that hat. In any case, I'd remember if I had my picture taken. I'd remember you, right?"

"Would you?" Alison asked.

"Sure I would. I've got a terrific memory for faces."

Alison took the picture back and looked at Tennant in a resigned way. "If she's Maggie Silver, Harry, face it. She doesn't remember."

"She's got to remember—"

"Did *you*?" Alison asked.

Tennant was silent. If Maggie couldn't remember, what did it mean? He knew the answer. He was numb. His muscles might have been lead. He thought of Lannigan.

The woman said, "Listen. My name's Gill. Barbara Gill. You've come to the wrong place if you're looking for this Maggie Silver." She gazed at Harry Tennant in such a manner that for a moment he was optimistic, as if the sight of him in this room—this altered room where he and she had been lovers—might kick some faint recollection out of her.

There was nothing.

"How long have you lived here?" Alison asked.

"Years."

"How many exactly?" There was no inquisitorial edge in Alison's question. She phrased it quietly, as if she were conscious of trespassing. The expression on her face was one of consideration and patience. Why isn't she pushing? Tennant wondered. Why isn't she going after Maggie Silver?

"I don't keep count." The woman pushed her long hair back from her shoulders. "Long enough. I happen to like it here. Until a few minutes ago what I liked most was privacy." She looked at Tennant again. *Long enough*, he thought. He was charged with the same expectancy, but then she turned away from him and walked to the door. "Now if you're through."

"We used to live here," he said. "You and me. We lived in this place—"

"I think I've heard as much as I want to hear."

"Listen to me goddamit." Tennant went toward her, grabbed her wrist, held it tightly. "You and me. Maggie and Harry. We lived here together."

"Yeah? Like I'd forget something like that? Look, I know a lot of drugs used to float through the neighborhood, mister, and maybe you took one flight too many. Let's be good about it, huh? Let's just call this thing quits nice and quiet and get on with our lives, okay?"

Tennant ignored her. "We had posters on the walls. Che Guevara, Hendrix. And right over here"—he drew her away from the door—"this is where you had all those old Fillmore things and here, up here, this is where I hung those goddamn bookshelves that fell down—"

"You're babbling," she said. "You scare me, friend."

"They fell down and you thought it the funniest thing, don't you remember?" Tennant, dizzy, angry, sad to his heart, a storm of sensations, wouldn't let her go, he'd force her to remember, he'd make her bring it all back. "We had this old four-poster bed up on cinder blocks and some kind of patchwork quilt that belonged to your great-aunt or something—"

"Jesus, let go of my arm—"

"Harry," Alison said "For God's sake. Leave it."

"Your great-aunt, her name was Harriet or Henrietta and the quilt was an heirloom—"

The woman pulled herself free and looked at Alison. "Make him stop. Get him out of here."

Tennant was surrounded by the debris now, the broken bookshelves, the big decrepit bed that had creaked to the movement of their bodies, the posters on the walls, the music they'd played endlessly on an erratic stereo system.

"Maggie, we loved each other. We were lovers." And he thought: *You meant everything to me. You still do.* A devastating sorrow went through him. This was the place where his life began and ended. This was the room where he lay buried. The corpse of Harry Tennant.

"I don't know where you get your ideas from, but they don't mean anything to me," the woman said. "Lovers! You're deranged."

Alison touched Tennant's arm. "Give it up, Harry. Give it up. She doesn't know what you're talking about."

He shook his head furiously. The madness was a high fever. "One night somebody came and took you away, Maggie. Two men. I remember that. They just came in and grabbed you and you struggled and one of them hit me with I don't know what—" He'd make her believe him. "I don't remember what happened after that because I must have been hit pretty damn hard, but it happened maybe a few weeks after the photograph was published, that was when everything went to shit."

"Quit, Harry," Alison said. "Before you lose it totally. Don't you see? She isn't going to remember anything."

"She will. She will." Trying to calm himself, seeking some control, he reached out with both hands and tenderly caught Maggie's wrists. For a moment she allowed herself to be held this way, and her eyes encountered his, and he spoke softly. "We saw something in Chinatown we weren't supposed to see, Maggie. The day the photograph was taken we witnessed something we weren't meant to see. You and me and the others in that picture. The guy who took the photograph too. We were sacrificed, you understand me? Try, Maggie. Please try."

"Chinatown? I don't know what you're rambling on about." But she looked at him as if she might just have flashed on some sense in what he was telling her, and her eyes lost their hard little light of alarm. Her mouth softened. The lines around the lips disappeared. I met you in the Haight, he thought. You came into my life out of nowhere, you stormed me. Come back to me, Maggie.

"I've missed you," he said quietly. "I never knew how much until I saw you again." In his chest was a terrible dry pain. He heard his own heart beat. His pulses were out of control. His veins might have been ferrying mercury, not blood. All his life came down to this one place and time, a room in the Haight, a woman he loved who said she'd never seen him before. What have they done to us? What in God's name have they done to us?

She stepped away from him. "You know, I feel real sorry for you, whoever you are. I feel this great pity." And she turned to Alison. "Get him out of here. I've had enough."

The woman was trembling.

Alison said, "Let's go, Harry."

"Maggie, listen to me, for God's sake hear me out. We used to live here. We partied, we got stoned—"

"I never did drugs." She looked at him with a determined expression. "I made it a point to avoid them. They wrecked too many lives."

"Okay okay, if that's the way you want it, we didn't do drugs, but we lived here together."

"No."

"We met in this neighborhood, Maggie. I remember I first saw you in the park. You were lying in the grass. You were alone. I must have been wasted. I walked over and I lay down beside you. We started talking."

The woman, exasperated, made a long sighing sound. Alison stepped toward Tennant and tugged at his sleeve. He didn't feel the touch.

He had a memory of a bright summer day on what had once been known as Hippie Hill. A kite had fluttered through the air, a dragon in the sky; in the absence of any true wind it had fallen feebly into the trees. "You were wearing velvet pants. They had these little flowers stitched into them. The blouse you had on was dark red. I asked you your name and you said guess and you made me go through the alphabet before you told me. Remember? I went from Abigail to Linda before you stopped me."

The woman stood in the window, her arms folded. Alison, frowning, watched her closely. The woman turned and gazed at the girl—almost as if she perceived some connection between herself and the younger woman. There might have been an invisible arc of low electricity linking them. Tennant thought: *Whatever passed between them before is happening again.* But then the woman looked away and stared through the window down into Schrader Street. Below, some piece of heavy traffic rumbled, and the window frames shook.

He said, "Believe me, Maggie. I hadn't remembered any of this stuff until a minute ago."

"You're completely insane," she said. "Velvet pants. Flowers. Red blouse. Where the hell do you come up with stuff like that? You've got some kind of imagination there."

Tennant saw himself through the woman's eyes. A loony. A poor deluded madman. Somebody to be listened to quietly, and with a show of patience, because violence wasn't far away. He was unpredictable, a guy on the edge, he could go in any direction. He glanced at Alison and wondered if she were perceiving him in the same way. Poor Harry. Stop bothering this woman. Leave her the hell alone.

He fell silent, his energy run down. He was depleted. He couldn't move. Somebody might have taken a hammer to his glass heart and pounded it without mercy. The woman walked to the door and opened it and said, "Okay. Show's over."

Alison said, "Harry. Let's go."

He looked at the open door, the corridor beyond. In the shadows stood Maggie Silver of more than twenty years ago. She leaned against the wall, a hand on one hip. *Harry, I know where we can score some real good opium if we go to Chinatown, a guy called Lee, lives above this grocery, he's got some real nice shit.*

"Like I said. The show's over. Leave."

And still Tennant didn't move. The ghost in the corridor was laughing. *Come on, Harry, get your ass in gear before Lee sells out of the stuff.* I remember, he thought. But what good was memory if it turned out to be a worthless prize? Here's your reward, Harry. Nothing. Tough shit, kid.

"I've met some people in this neighborhood," the woman said. "But you, hey, you really get the blue ribbon for sheer weirdness."

Sheer weirdness. Of course. Tennant walked slowly across the room. He had come all this way for what? To be rejected. Crushed by the density of the past, that dead iron weight. He stepped into the doorway. There he turned to the woman.

"Maggie." He wanted to hold her face between his hands. He wanted to feel her against him. It's all over, we've come through it, he would say, we've buried it, it's gone, we're back together, they can't force us apart again. Sure, he'd say that and more. Except she didn't have any way of hearing him.

The woman looked at him warily. He was aware of incalculable loss; sadness was an infinite thing. If you had an abacus on which to estimate grief, it would consist of an immeasurable number of beads on wires that stretched to the ends of the universe.

"I'm sorry," the woman said in an unexpectedly sympathetic way. "I hope you find whatever you're looking for, Harry. If that's your name."

Tennant didn't say anything. He'd pretend he'd discovered nothing, he'd go away, forget what he'd learned, drift and drift. He was about to leave this room and the woman called Maggie Silver. But he knew it wasn't finished yet. It wasn't over. That was what memory did—it attached you unshakably to your life.

You asked for it, Harry. You pursued it. Now you've got it. Maggie Silver. A memory of Chinatown. Now you're just about to nail it all down and you don't want to.

He stepped into the empty corridor. There were no ghosts hanging in the shadows. Everything was silent. He took a few paces, turned, saw Alison lingering in the doorway with the woman, watched how light from the room beyond created a frame around the two women. He had a moment in which he thought he saw them somehow merge together, but this was because Alison moved slightly and the strip of light that separated their bodies was eclipsed; a strange illusion—two women becoming one.

It was the same deranged perception he'd had when he made love to Alison, that she was Maggie Silver.

He heard Alison say, "Listen . . ."

There was a very long silence. The woman tilted her head and looked at Alison in an attitude of waiting.

"I just want to say . . ." and Alison faltered in an uncharacteristic manner. There was a break in her voice, a loss of words. More. A loss of language, of meaning.

The woman didn't speak. Alison reached out and touched her arm briefly, then withdrew the hand and said, "Nothing. It's nothing. I'm sorry we bothered you. Okay."

The woman hesitated, glanced at Tennant, then shut the door. She had closed more than a door, Tennant thought.

He went down the stairs and out into the street. Alison followed in silence. The sun had gone. The sky was gray and cold. A wind blew down Schrader Street, rolling toward the Panhandle. There it would diffuse itself among the trees.

They walked toward Haight.

"They got to her," Alison said. She was angry and sad. Her face was without color. Moisture formed in her dark eyes. "The way they got to you. I feel . . ." Alison hesitated. "I don't know. Hatred. Despair. I want to hurt them, Harry. That's what I really want. I want to destroy them."

Tennant nodded bleakly. How could you hurt them? How did you begin? On the corner of Haight he looked left. The

wind made him shiver. How could he leave Maggie Silver like
that? With her delusions, her lapses, her own failures? On the
other hand, how could he even start to bring her back? Yeah,
they got to her. They did their number well. You had to hand it
to them. You had to pat Lannigan on the back. Well done,
boyo.

But they weren't infallible. There was a weakness in their
operation. They hadn't counted on Alison Seagrove turning up
and prodding Tennant toward hard answers. And he almost
had the answers now. He'd go back to Chinatown and open
the last door. He should have been uplifted, but he wasn't. He
was hollow. Even as he glimpsed that day in Chinatown and
remembered Sammy Obe hustling with his camera, orchestrat-
ing his pathetic little group of five, even as he recalled raising
an arm and pointing across the street where a small crowd had
gathered outside St. Mary's, even then he didn't feel any sense
of achievement. He would be complete when he could see why
the crowd had congregated at that place and time. But no.
There would always be a void if he didn't have Maggie Silver.
That was the worst understanding of all.

They moved in the direction of Golden Gate Park. The
wind made trees shudder, the sky turned toward rain. He hesitated. He'd go back, make her see the sense in what he had to
say. He'd lay out before her the skeleton of the past. Bone by
bone he'd show her how her life was filled with mystifying gaps
she couldn't fill, how she'd been transformed from flamboyant
Maggie Silver into this other person, this Barbara Gill. How
long would it take?

"I'm sorry, Harry. About everything."

Tennant stared into the traffic. You're sorry, I'm sorry, let
the whole fucking world be sorry, what did it matter? He
kicked at the sidewalk in despair. "This is the bit I don't get.
Why did they let Maggie live? I can see how my father protected
me, but why wasn't she killed like Carlos and Kat? That's the
bit that evades me." He paused, his mouth very dry. "If I push
myself I can see the kind of thinking that goes like this: They
can't murder everybody in the photograph, it's too much, it's

overkill, so you make one look like suicide, another an accident, and one is made to look like a total schizoid. The other two—well, they get their shutters pulled down on their windows. They get their shades well and truly drawn. Only Sajac got away. For a time."

Bitterness in his voice. A couple of blocks away Maggie Silver lived out her life in awful ignorance of her history. What did she do with her days? Work in a public library? Sling cocktails? Whatever it was, she'd go through the motions without ever asking questions, the way he'd tended his doomed farm in New York. Ignorant, plodding, never examining the past to see what it contained because neither of them was supposed to have a past.

"It would have been simpler to have killed us both," he said.

Alison frowned. She said nothing as they wandered through traffic to the edge of the park. Her expression was strange, regretful, and apprehensive. She was about to tell him something, except she didn't want to. It was obvious to him.

Tennant stood still. The wind blew at his coat, flapping it.

"I think I know why they didn't kill Maggie," the girl said.

He looked at her face and thought: I don't want to hear this, whatever it is. He was balanced on a dreadful moment.

"Be patient with me," she said. "Try to understand. Don't be angry with me."

He waited. The collar of his coat blew against his cheek. A spot of rain hung in the air. Alison took a creased piece of paper from her purse.

"Here."

"I don't want it," he said.

"Take it. Look at it."

He reached for it with great reluctance. He read the words typed on it, but they didn't mean anything to him.

"What is this?" he asked.

"A birth certificate."

He looked at it again. Words had a way of escaping before your eyes. You stared at one word long enough and it shed the skin of its meaning. It lost all relevance. "My birth certificate, Harry."

He gazed into her face and wondered why he'd been too dense, too blind, to perceive it before. He might have felt it in some uncertain way, but now, dear God, it was obvious. From a certain angle, with the light touching her in exactly the right way, she looked like Maggie.

18

Bewildered, head down against the squall that had begun to shift through the trees, Tennant walked quickly. There has to be a way of dealing with this and all its implications, something nice and easy. An opiate against comprehension, a prophylactic to prevent understanding. When he raised his face, rain blew into his eyes and against his lips. With his canvas bag thumping against his leg, he stepped under a tree for shelter, seeing across the grassland the entrance to the Conservatory of Flowers. It was an elaborate structure of glass whose panes were wet and glossy. A group of tourists stood outside, huddled under bright umbrellas. A birth certificate, he thought. She gives me a birth certificate with her mother's name typed in the appropriate column.

And zero under *Father.*

He saw her hurrying to catch up with him. He didn't want to hear explanations, excuses, he wanted nothing more than to stand beneath this goddamn tree and listen to the way rain beat on leaves and branches. A tree house, that was what he needed now, his old tree house—he'd climb up into it and hide and keep the world away. He recalled Rayland perspiring in the upper branches, his hammer driving nails into planks of wood, the occasional yelp of pain when Rayland struck his hand with the head of the hammer. Harry's Place. Where was Harry's Place now? Rotted, slats weathered, nails rusted and loose, a shell overgrown with foliage.

The girl stepped under the branches. "Harry, listen to me."

"You lied to me." It's more than a lie, but you don't want to confront it.

"I didn't lie."

"What would you call it, Alison?" He moved, heading quickly toward the conservatory. At the entrance desk he paid his fee and stepped inside, where the atmosphere was humid and the air smelled of green things growing in damp soil. His last time here he'd been out of his mind on acid, and the place was filled with monstrous menace. Now he was sober and straight and wished he wasn't. He passed under a giant overhanging philodendron that looked as old as the planet itself.

The girl was still tracking him. He walked away, deeper into the conservatory, the tangled vines, roots, mosses, flying fronds. A jungle, steamy and ill-lit, trapped under vast panes of glass, a controlled experiment in growth, temperature, and humidity neatly maintained. He was sweating hard, moisture running across his face. When he found a bench he sat down, exhausted by the lack of air.

"Harry, please listen to me."

The girl approached him slowly. He turned away, seeing two men in raincoats study the tangled roots of an enormous philodendron that resembled more a mutated prehistoric bird than a plant. Two men in raincoats, he thought. But they weren't looking at him.

The girl sat alongside him. "Listen. Maggie had me adopted at birth. Something I only learned about eighteen months ago. I spent most of the last year looking for her. I didn't have an address. I only had Obe's photograph, Harry, and the names in Cygnet's files. I went after them. You know what I found. And then I came across you."

"And I led you to her."

Alison drummed her fingertips on her thighs and sighed. Tennant undid the buttons of his coat. His jeans were damp, clinging to skin. "The story's all bullshit," he said. "There's no magazine assignment."

"Yes and no."

"I don't like that kind of ambiguity."

"I work for the magazine, sure—"

"But not on this."

She shook her head. "Not on this."

He stood up. The humidity was smothering him. "This is what you'd call more *personal,* right?" He remembered the chalet, the room, her thin body pressed against him, the moment of intimacy that had broken down under the weight of Maggie Silver's intrusion. He felt remote from himself all at once. The birth certificate, no father's name. I don't want to think. But there had been undeniable feelings, there had been caring, even—God help him—some naive consideration of a future in which this girl might have played a part. How sightless he'd been. How goddamn *unseeing.*

She was watching him. He met her eyes briefly, then looked elsewhere. There ought to be birds in here, he thought. Not just these great silent growths and the sound of running water—but birds, life, song.

The girl stared down into her upturned hands. "I didn't tell you about Maggie because I figured you wouldn't help me. You wouldn't want to become involved in my personal, whatever you call it—okay, my private fucking obsession. You'd probably tell me to leave you alone. The search for my mother had unhinged me: Consequently I was reading too many wild things into a photograph. You wouldn't have listened to me, would you? I was just some young bimbo up from the city pathetically chasing a ghost. You wouldn't have time for me."

"So you edited it," Tennant said.

"I edited it."

Find the lady, Tennant thought. What you see is what you get. "How convenient I was facing a drug rap."

"I had nothing to do with that. That was pure coincidence."

"Yeah, but you used the situation, Alison."

"Okay. I used it. I'm sorry."

"And how convenient I had no goddamn memory. Harry Tennant, a criminal, a blank page. Let's fill in the gaps, Harry. Let's hunt the big white whale of the past, Harry. Let's harpoon that sorry sonofabitch."

Alison looked at him sadly. "I wanted to find my mother, goddamit. That makes sense, doesn't it? I was desperate, Harry. I didn't set out to uncover all the other shit. I wasn't expecting dead kids and lost memories. And I didn't mean to drag you into anything like this. How could I have known where it was going to lead? How?"

Tennant stuffed his hands in his pockets. She wanted to find her mother, he thought. And so did I. So God help me did I.

He stared up at the vaulted glass roof. Ribbons of condensation slid down the panes and dripped into deep foliage. He thought of the chalet again, the way he'd held the girl even as he called her by her mother's name. He shook his head. Connections he didn't want to make. Thickets of the past, entanglements that threatened to choke him. He stared at the roof. Rain fell on glass.

"I don't need to think this through," he said. "You and me. Maggie and me."

"I understand. But you must understand this: I didn't know, and you didn't know."

"So that makes us innocent?"

"It doesn't make us guilty."

Tennant said, "I don't care about innocent or guilty. I just don't like the idea of sitting here trying to do calculations in my head. Your birthday. The last time I saw Maggie. I don't need the arithmetic of all that. I don't want to think about it. What good would it do you or me?"

A kid. A daughter. Was she all he had left of Maggie Silver?

The question shocked and depressed him. And yet there was some mild undercurrent in him he didn't want to explore right then: some muted sense of—what?—having reclaimed a lost part of himself. But then he was back in the chalet again, and the vague feeling that had lifted him turned bleak. I don't need to know, he thought. I don't need the burden of proof. I don't want evidence. Maggie Silver might have been unfaithful. Another lover. But he didn't want to believe that any more than he wanted to entertain the idea Alison might be the hapless offspring of a fated liaison between himself and a woman totally lost to him. So which way do you go, Tennant?

"There's a name for this," he said.

"Forget the name—"

"It runs around and around inside my head, Alison."

"And you feel what? Disgusted?"

"I don't know if that's the word. I don't know what the word is. This isn't one of your everyday situations, is it?" He saw her stand beside the bed, saw the tight bare breasts, the triangle of underwear, heard the way she'd said, *Take them off*. He remembered sliding them from her hips and the sensation of her flesh under his fingertips. Alison, Maggie, one and the same. You once loved the mother, and you still do.

And now the daughter. The daughter.

She asked, "Suppose we'd never found out? Suppose we'd gone on without discovering Maggie? We'd go deeper and deeper, Harry. You and me. We'd have gone on. We'd have been together. I feel that. I *know* that. If we hadn't found Maggie, we'd never have known, would we? And if we'd never known, and if we survived all this . . ." She gestured around the conservatory as if the foliage itself were the enemy. "We'd have tried somehow to stay together."

Yes, he thought. We might have tried. We might have amounted to something. Alison and Harry, a couple, going on blindly into the sunset. Sheer happiness.

Hunched in his overcoat he studied the massive leaf of the philodendron in front of him. He considered the vast mystery of the plant. Controlled and yet finally untrammeled, it forced its way up toward the glass roof, and when it could grow no further it coiled back in on itself, twisting, twining, as if intent on devouring itself. He had the urge to move now, to pick up his bag from the bench and walk.

"I've never been happy with hypothesis. What do we really know anyway? We can't be sure of anything. Leave it that way." But you do know, Harry. If the child hadn't been his, would Maggie Silver have been allowed to live? Rayland's granddaughter. Your own daughter. Maggie Silver had been protected too. She'd had her life taken away, sure, but she'd been spared because of the child. He felt an enormous sadness. He was being pulled this way and that, with no more control over his responses than an object adrift on a rough tide. Too many strands here, too many blood echoes he hadn't known existed. Breakdown. Collapse. Systems unraveling.

Alison covered the back of his hand with her own. "It doesn't disgust me, Harry. That's not where it leaves me. Sad, sure. More sad than you'll ever know. Because we can't be. Because we don't have a future of the kind we might have considered. But disgust, no, I don't feel anything like that."

He enjoyed her touch a moment, even the small contrary stirring of godforsaken desire he felt, before he took his hand away.

She said, "We can still have something, Harry. We can still have some kind of love."

Love? The word had too many meanings, every one elusive. Did she love him as a lover? A father? What did it matter now? He was suffocating in this humid place. The past had betrayed him. The future was obscure. He looked at the girl and he thought: *I can't have you. But maybe I can have something else. Maybe I can still have Harry Tennant.*

Grabbing his bag, he stood up.

"Where are you going?" she asked.

He didn't answer. Walk away. Do what you have to do on your own. Leave this child out of it. She came after him, tugging at his sleeve. Outside the conservatory, where rain drizzled among the trees, he stopped.

"You don't walk out on me, Harry. No matter what."

He said nothing.

"I have every right to go wherever you're going," she said.

What had Rayland said? *Would you want to see her damaged?*

"You can't leave me now, Harry."

"Wait here. I'll come back for you."

"Screw it. I go where you go."

He shook his head, but he already knew the depths of her determination, he already knew he had lost the conflict before it had even begun in earnest.

"Don't do this to me," she said. "I won't put up with it, Harry. I'm in this with you. All the way."

He started to walk in the direction of the street. She followed. All the way, no matter where. On the sidewalk he scanned traffic for a taxicab. When one finally arrived through the rain, Tennant opened the door and the girl skipped inside before him. She was impossible to restrict. How could he even begin to try?

He told the driver Chinatown and sat back, his eyes closed.

Chinatown. Where Obe had clicked his camera. Where a crowd had gathered more than twenty years ago outside St. Mary's Church. Where the roots of treachery and murder lay. Where a child, a girl, was already forming in Maggie Silver's body.

It was no longer raining by the time the cab dropped them at the intersection of Grant and California. A watery sun hung in the sky, and dark clouds, blown by a breeze from the Bay, streamed above rooftops. Tennant stood on the corner and looked at St. Mary's. A cable car crammed with a laughing tourist party clanged past. Smiling people hung precariously to handrails.

He walked past the church a little way, past the place where

Sammy Obe had taken his photographs, down into Chinatown. Alison was keeping up with him. He stopped outside a souvenir shop whose window displayed silk robes and kites and chairs made out of bamboo. A Chinese woman stood in the doorway and regarded him with mild interest.

I came this way with Maggie, he thought. To buy opium. And then a chance encounter with Sammy Obe. A group shot, quickly assembled. *Gimme a knowing look, kids. Gimme the kinda look that says you know something your parents wouldn't begin to dream about. Yeah yeah yeah that's it that's better.* He'd plotted their positions, making Carlos stand here, Bear Sajac there, Maggie in the dead center. *Quit giggling, kid. I want this picture to be kinda solemn. I want you all to look wise.* Tennant pressed his forehead against the window of the store. To look wise. He remembered Obe's hands on his body, pushing him into place. *This is a composition, kids, this isn't some kinda souvenir shot you send your granny. Gimme the look, gimme the look!*

Yes. The look.

Tennant stepped back from the glass as if electrified.

"What is it, Harry?" the girl asked.

He hurried back to the street corner and faced the church from the exact position in which Obe had taken his photograph and he said, "There was this crowd outside the church. They just seemed to come out of nowhere. One minute there was nothing, the next, guys in dark suits, then after that, a small bunch of people began to assemble."

"Why?"

Why? Why, Harry? Tell her. Tell the child. This child. He frowned. A light was burning in the church bookshop. The door to the church was open. A man stood there in shadow, motionless. He raised a hand to his face, touched the side of his scalp as if adjusting his hair, then he moved slightly, deeper into shadow.

"The crowd, Harry. You were saying something about a crowd."

Yes, he thought. He kept his eyes fixed on the open door. The figure was very still now.

"Harry," the girl said.

"We stood here," he said. "Maggie and me and the others. Right here. Obe had his camera—"

"And what happened?"

"Somebody came out of the church."

"Tell me who."

He lapsed into dumb silence because he was back more than twenty years ago and he was looking at people emerging from St. Mary's. "The guys in the suits were security people," he said.

"Security for what?"

Tennant had a moment in which his brain, like a bad tent, collapsed on him, and he couldn't see anything. And then this cleared and he was watching two people come out of St. Mary's and the way some of the security men formed a loose circle around this pair while the others spread out into the crowd. People were singing, *We love you, Bobby. Oh yes we do.* Maggie had raised her fists jubilantly. He remembered that, the glow on her face, the smile lit like a Christmas tree.

He said, "Bobby and Ethel Kennedy came out of the church. They started to walk up toward the Fairmont Hotel on Nob Hill. It was the day before the California primary, Bobby was campaigning here. I guess he'd been to mass in the church. There were all kinds of people round him and his wife. Well-wishers. Security. People singing. We love you, Bobby."

He thought: Bobby looks young and haggard, as if a premonition of his violent death, a little more than twenty-four hours away, already weighed on him. Ethel is bright, buoyant, and yet in some fashion somber at the heart of her appearance. They are doomed, both of them, but they don't know it yet. Tomorrow, in the pantry of the Ambassador Hotel in Los Angeles, Bobby will die from gunshot wounds.

The pantry.

But that isn't it either. That isn't what caused you to raise your hand and point. You weren't pointing at Bobby and Ethel Kennedy.

"I saw something," he said.

"What, Harry?"

Something. Somebody else. He stopped talking. The memory wouldn't come. He remembered only this: raising his hand, pointing a finger, faces turning, Obe swinging his head around to follow the direction of Tennant's finger.

"What did you see, Harry?"

"I can't get a bearing on it—"

"Harry."

"I can't—"

"One last step, that's all."

The crowds, the security people, some of them with walkie-talkies, others with small listening devices attached to their ears, Bobby and Ethel emerging from the church. He saw all that, but he couldn't grasp what it was that had drawn his attention across the street. He remembered the negative in Karen Obe's house, and he thought: There is an accusatory quality in my gesture, and surprise. And cold cold recognition.

But I can't see now what I saw then.

He was aware of a dark brown car edging up to the sidewalk outside the church and idling there. The man in the doorway glanced at the car, moved one hand. It was hard to tell what the motion meant. Quick, surreptitious, a gesture that alarmed Tennant. This is the wrong place, he thought. The wrong time. The vehicle started forward toward the intersection, where it was boxed in by traffic moving on Grant. The man in the shadowy doorway was still again.

"Try, Harry," Alison said. "Try."

Tennant's memory was a shipwrecked thing. I lift my hand, I extend a finger, at what? They sweated it out of me, he thought. They made me forget. They went inside my head and killed me.

He leaned against the wall. His legs were weak. I was instructed not to remember this. This is forbidden territory. There is barbed wire hung all around it, and warning signs. I touch the wire and I will bleed.

He watched the dark brown car cross the intersection.

"Harry," the girl was saying.

Tennant felt her shake his arm. He fought for the memory. He strained toward it. Nothing. Bobby and Ethel, security goons, cheers, we love you Bobby oh yes we do. Beyond that nothing.

He looked at the girl. His head was filled with silences. He tried to speak. Turn the page, Harry. Look again. What did you see that day?

The man in the doorway had taken a step forward and gray light struck him now

Something is wrong with this, Tennant thought. There was a confusing juxtaposition of past and present, time had gone all wrong, cogs and wheels had come undone and were rattling uselessly inside the clock. The man on the other side of the street walked to the edge of the sidewalk and stopped, gazing across at Tennant, who was no longer sure of the boundary separating now from then. It was an indistinct borderline badly etched in his brain. Past or present, did it make any difference? He had no way of knowing what the date was, whether he was suspended in a distortion of time—had he fallen through cracks in the flimsy edifice of the years?

Rayland Tennant was crossing toward him.

Harry, beset by confusion, heard the crowd sing, saw Bobby and Ethel besieged by supporters, saw the security men whose limitations would be tragically exposed twenty-four hours later in Los Angeles—all this clamored in his head as Rayland crossed the street. And then his father was standing a mere two or three feet away, his expression mournfully reproachful.

He knew now what he had seen on this street on the day Bobby Kennedy had gone inside St. Mary's to celebrate his last mass. He knew.

Rayland said, "I told you to keep away, Harry. I warned you."

Tennant didn't hear his father. "I saw you here," he said. "I saw you in the crowd."

Rayland looked impassive. "So you saw me. What else?"

"You and Harker. You were together that day."

Tennant looked toward the intersection. The chocolate-colored car had made an arc and was coming back. He jabbed his finger into his father's chest. He prodded hard and the old man stepped back, wincing slightly.

"I must have thought—what the hell is he doing here? What's Harker doing here? They aren't Kennedy people. They aren't supporters. They're opposed, like all their cronies in Pentagon circles, to everything Bobby stands for. So what the fuck are they doing here?"

"And what were we doing, Harry? Do tell."

Tennant saw the picture clearly now. The glass sparkled, the images shone.

The dark brown car was moving slowly.

"You and Harker were standing on the edge of the crowd, Rayland. You were talking to a couple of security guys. One of them had one of those walkie-talkie things in his hand."

"Yes, Harry?"

"You saw me. You happened to look across at Obe taking his photographs, and you saw me. Exactly at the same time as I noticed you and Harker." Tennant paused. *Rayland has his head inclined, the security men are listening as he talks, Noel Harker, in a felt hat, is standing in the manner of a man who fears discovery, recognition, Rayland turns and looks in the direction of Obe, and Harry Tennant, who shouldn't have been there, raises his arm, Obe's shutter closes, something is captured then and for all time. Five kids in a picture. A collision of realities. A murderous alignment. An accident of geography and history.*

"And then Harry?"

"Next day Bobby was dead."

Rayland Tennant turned his face in the direction of the brown car. He appeared anxious, stressed. He looked a moment at Alison before turning his face back to his son. "And you draw some conclusion from my appearance on this street and Kennedy's murder?"

A conclusion, Tennant thought. That was the easy part, and the most difficult. "You had a foot in the door, Rayland. You had people on the inside. I don't give a shit about the mechanics, but somehow you and Harker managed to buy your way into the circle. So the security guys look the wrong way. Or maybe they react too slowly. I don't know. But they sure as hell weren't doing their job, were they, Rayland? They took their eye off the ball long enough for Sirhan Sirhan to do his thing in the Ambassador Hotel."

"Sirhan was a sick man who acted alone, Harry."

"Yeah yeah. Here's the way I see it. He was one of yours. Maybe you had Lannigan fuck with him the way he did with me and Maggie Silver. Maybe. I don't know. But I'm not buying into this, Rayland. You and Harker and your associates did the spadework. Sirhan was the cannon."

Rayland caught Harry's hand tightly. "All you have is some pretty wild stuff, Harry. Faces in a crowd. Ancient history. Nothing you can substantiate."

"Substantiate? Jesus Christ, what kind of word is that? How can you stand there and spout crap, Rayland? Kids are dead. Lives have been ruined. All because you had to cover your bloody tracks. Don't talk to me about proof. I don't want to hear about confirmation. I saw what I saw. And so did those other miserable bastards who just happened to be passing along a street when somebody says, 'Hey kids, I want to take your photograph.'" Tennant, who could no longer stand Rayland's touch, pulled his hand away.

"You blame me for them, Harry?"

"Yeah, I blame you. What do you expect? An award?"

"You don't understand, Harry."

"What's to understand? You were involved in Kennedy's murder. You tried to cover your tracks. You killed. You wrecked lives. What is there to understand? What can possibly justify the things you did? And don't feed me bullshit about how you weren't in this alone, you had *associates*, the decision wasn't just yours—"

"You can still be very naive," Rayland said. "You have no grasp of reality at times."

"Fuck off, Rayland—"

"Try to see it from another angle, Harry. Certain parties

felt, quite rightly, that Bobby would be a complete disaster for this country."

Quite rightly. A good Rayland phrase. "What parties? Your chums in the Pentagon? Noel Harker's crowd? Your friends in the arms business? They didn't like Bobby, did they?"

"A lot of people didn't like Bobby," Rayland said. "But the lines are not quite as clear as you might wish, Harry. You're looking for simple answers, but you aren't going to find them. It's far more complicated than you'll ever understand."

"What's complicated? I think it's dead simple, Rayland. Bobby wants us out of an idiot war. Right? He's running on that platform. No more Vietnam. And that means no more profits for your friends. No more fancy expensive weapons for Southeast Asia. This is what I understand, Rayland. You killed people. Directly, indirectly,' you think I give a damn? You're a fucking monster."

"A monster, Harry?" The old man gazed at Harry with a look of profound sorrow. "Would a monster have protected his son the way I've done for years? Would a monster have spared Maggie Silver because she happened to be carrying your child?" And here he smiled in a forlorn way at Alison. "I don't think so, Harry. A monster would have disposed of you long before this. That's what Harker wanted, Harry. He wanted you—what's his nice expression?—deep-sixed? He wanted you out of the way once and for all. I fought hard against that. For you. For your child."

Your child, Tennant thought. Maggie's little girl. "Protection. Is that what you call it? Is that the nice antiseptic name you give to fucking with other people's minds?"

Rayland Tennant said, "I did what I could, Harry. I did what I thought I had to do."

"Yeah. You're a terrific father all right. A prince. Couldn't have asked for one better."

Alison touched Tennant's hand. In other circumstances, vastly different ones, Tennant thought that this might be quite a reunion. But it was tainted, and dreadful, and all the life had gone out of Alison's face, all the vibrancy vanished. He put his arm around her shoulder and drew her against him. She turned her face into his shoulder.

The brown car was coming toward the place where they stood. Tennant watched the wheels come up over the sidewalk, saw the back door open.

The men who emerged from the vehicle were not strangers. Noel Harker stepped out first, his face dark and angry and determined. Noel Harker, who had been that day in China-town with Rayland, conspiring among the crowds. Behind Harker was fat Walter Swin, without sunglasses. Walter Swin, insurance agent. The man with good plastic credentials. And then there was Frank Rozak, fake attorney, Rayland's man in upstate New York; Frank Rozak, whose big arthritic hand concealed a pistol.

Rayland gave a quick little signal. The men spread out, moving in Tennant's direction. Tennant pushed the girl aside and said *Run,* but she didn't move. She had once said she was going all the way. And this was it. This was all the way. There was no place left to go.

He drew her closer to him and gazed at his father. The old man's look was of inexpressible regret.

"I am going to ask you and Alison to get into the back of the car," Rayland said politely. "I don't want a scene."

All this would lack the necessary refinement for him of course, this unseemly situation on a public street. He would feel exposed here. Indelicate matters were best dealt with in less obvious places. Back rooms, clinics, private clubs, locations where men met to decide the course of history, who would live, who would die. The brokers of power, the corrupt, the criminal.

"Where are we going, Rayland?"

The old man didn't answer. Tennant knew anyway. He was crowded toward the car, Alison and himself jammed between Rayland's people. He thought of the gun in the pocket of his coat. He'd go for it because there wasn't any alternative. He'd drag it out and use it here on this street corner with cable cars clattering past and people moving along the sidewalk into the heart of Chinatown. He put his hand in his pocket quickly and fumbled the pistol out, but Noel Harker struck him with a fist to the side of the neck, and dizzied by the blow, he slackened his hold on the gun, which tumbled to the ground. Rozak picked it up quickly.

Noel Harker struck him again, a short, sharp, angular punch directed to his throat. It was as if Harker had been waiting years for this opportunity to inflict pain on Tennant, a personal matter, a grudge grown out of the strategic differences between himself and Rayland Tennant. *I want to hurt your boy, Rayland. I want to kill the sonofabitch.*

"No more," Rayland was saying. "Enough, for the love of God. Enough, Harker."

Harry went down on his knees. His voice was all but gone, his senses in disarray. He raised his face, looked at Alison, tried to say something to her, he wasn't sure what. Noel Harker dragged Tennant to his feet. For a moment Tennant found himself looking directly in the colonel's eyes, and what he saw there was the light of rage, the kind of fire in which conspiracies are forged and murders elaborately plotted. Tennant was afraid because there was no bottom to Harker's expression, no place where you could say: *This is it, this is where the rage dies.*

He was being hustled inside the car. Frank Rozak's pistol was stuck into his ribs. Resentful, Tennant found strength enough to bring his elbow up and thrust it into Rozak's chest, and for a moment the man lost his balance, but the moment wasn't long enough for Tennant to grab the girl and run, because Harker brought up a fist again and, despite Rayland's cry of protest, struck Tennant in the side of the face. Tennant's mouth filled with the bitter saliva of nausea. Somebody gripped him under his shoulders and dumped him into the back of the car. He was dimly aware of Alison—protesting, swearing, kicking out in angry gestures that were ultimately futile—being pushed in beside him. She raised a hand to the side of his face. He thought he saw his own blood on her fingertips.

Through the zigzagging waves of his pain he was conscious of a figure in the front of the car. The man turned.

"This time we'll heal you properly, Harry," Lannigan said and smiled his graceful solicitous smile.

Tennant heard doors close. Not just inside the car, but everywhere. Door after door after door.

19

He didn't know where he was, or how long he'd been sleeping. When he awoke he was stunned by the searing whiteness of his surroundings. He twisted his head, seeing a small window set high up, gray light beyond.

Then he knew.

He tried to rise but couldn't. A straitjacket confined him to the bed. In frustration, he thrashed against it, a useless pastime. His face throbbed. The inside of his mouth was intolerably dry, his gums adhering to his inner lips. He'd been given drugs. Painkillers. Painkillers to begin with. Then some kind of massive downer.

He drifted off to sleep.

When he awoke next, he had a faint recollection of somebody standing over him and sticking a needle into his arm with great care and consideration. He hadn't felt the injection. He slept again. Later, he was given water to sip through an angular straw and injected again. He had no idea how long this routine went on because time had imploded, broken into fragments of dreams in the course of which Lannigan appeared—friendly, cheerful, shirtsleeves rolled up in the way of a man who means business. Lannigan talked to him quietly. He used the tones of a schoolmaster speaking to a difficult child.

Sometimes a man goes to the edge, then goes a step further, boyo, and before you know it, why, he's fallen over the goddamn cliff.

What we have to do, Harry, is take you apart and rebuild you like you were a car. We lubricate this, change that, make an adjustment to your suspension—just like a car. And then you're whole again, you're off and running.

Tennant swore at the man and kicked against the restraints of the harness that tethered him to the bed. He kicked until his muscles ached painfully. Fuck you, Lannigan. Fuck you. I'm not a goddamn machine.

Ah, you're wrong. We're all machines, Harry. Wonderful machines. Intricate and lovely. And repairable. That's the best part. We can salvage ourselves.

I know your kind of salvage, Lannigan.

Sleep easy, boyo.

I don't want to sleep, you sonofabitch.

A needle punctured Tennant's flesh. His anger disintegrated. He slept, didn't dream. When he awoke, dehydrated, bound to the hard narrow bed, he thought: I know what I saw in San Francisco. I know what happened there. They can't exorcise that. I will hold on to that. During everything that follows, I will hold hard to that.

He wondered where Alison might be. He asked Lannigan once or twice, but the shrink merely made reassuring noises. You'll see her soon, boyo. Trust me.

Trust you?

Lannigan had an easy manner. *Sometimes we suffer delusions, Harry. We think we see things that don't exist. And sometimes we experience what I'd call false memories. We believe such and such happened but in reality it didn't. And that's where your problem lies.*

Tennant kept his eyes shut tight and thought about Alison. If he concentrated on the girl, he'd stand a chance against the drugs and the sweet persuasiveness of Lannigan's voice and those periods in which he drifted out into a warm welcoming ocean of sleep. Sometimes, when Lannigan came into his room and Harry cursed him, the Irishman would sigh, a prolonged expulsion of air, a weary sound. *Dear oh dear oh dear.* Lannigan had a way of seeming to blame himself for the shortfalls of his patients; his sighs were little arrows of despondency, as if the limitations of his profession made him despair.

At night Tennant fought narcotic sleep, concentrating on the moon on the high window or the sound of rain. He would focus on Alison's face, sometimes with such intensity that he'd lose sight of it, his memory would disintegrate, he'd be left with nothing. And then the panic kicked in. The night sweats. The tremors and palpitations. When he shouted for attention, nobody came. His voice died, without echo, against the white walls.

One morning Lannigan said, *What do you remember of Maggie Silver?*

I loved her, Tennant said.

If I told you she didn't exist, what would you say?

I'd say you were full of shit.

What would you say if I told you we spent a great deal of time here, you and I? We used to talk for hours. We talked about your problems.

I don't remember, Lannigan.

Do you want to see your file? Shall I show you your records? Would they prove anything? Harry, you were here for more than a year.

Tennant shook his head. He'd never been here. He was determined to deny it.

You'd just say the records were false anyway, wouldn't you?

Yes.

Oh, laddie, you were in a truly bad way when you came here first. You said you heard bells, gulls, you were terrified of telephones. You wouldn't believe the half of it. We gave you drugs, and we counseled you, and we took damn fine care of you here, even if I say so myself. And I should know, Harry. I run this place. I know everything that goes on. We heal tortured souls at this clinic. We spread a little balm on the awful pain people feel.

You didn't get enough of that special balm, boyo. We let you down, I fear.

You can't touch me, Lannigan. I won't let you get inside my skull.

Lannigan soothed him gently, comforted him. Drugs were injected three or four times daily; then Lannigan would appear in the room to offer some encouragement, telling Harry he wouldn't have to lie in this little bed forever, soon the straps would be removed and the bedpans—oh, they're such humiliating things—taken away and he'd be able to get up and stroll around, and won't that be absolutely grand?

Days elapsed in the changing colors beyond the high window. People came and went with water, medication, soft foods. Sometimes a nurse changed his clothing, one loose-fitting pale green smock for another. His concept of time was altered. It was a matter of light, not clocks. He continued to concentrate on the girl. He wouldn't let that go, no way.

He sometimes didn't listen to anything Lannigan said. He closed his eyes and the Irishman droned on—but every now and again the soft lilting voice would sneak inside Tennant's head, insidious, ingratiatingly authoritative, a sly melodic voice unerringly controlled.

Once he asked Lannigan: What do they pay you for this? Or do you do it for political motives? Is it a matter of belief for you?

Lannigan used a bony hand to massage Tennant's shoulder a moment. It was one of his techniques, the laying on of hands, a guru distributing calm among his troubled followers. *Nothing's for free, Harry.*

So what do they pay you, Lannigan?

The Irishman had a way of answering questions obliquely, another of his techniques. *I'm interested in what makes people tick. Their clockwork, if you like. I think of myself, ah well, as an explorer.*

A well-paid explorer, Tennant said. Mountains of blood money.

It isn't cheap to keep this clinic together. And I'm not a political creature.

So it's hard cash.

Let's say there are benefits, Harry. But that stuff shouldn't concern you. You're only here to get better.

Or worse, Tennant said. Then he asked about Sirhan, about whether Sirhan had ever been a "client" of Lannigan's country retreat.

Paul Lannigan smiled, and sighed, and massaged with slow circular movements. *I don't think that name would be anywhere on our records, Harry. You surely get some very strange notions.*

One afternoon—was it early evening? how long had he lain in this bed? his body ached and he had sores—Lannigan told him that Rayland Tennant hadn't been in San Francisco the day before Robert Kennedy was gunned down. He massaged Tennant's neck. His smooth skin smelled medicinal. *What you think you saw didn't happen, Harry. Do you understand that? Your father wasn't there, not on that day, not at any other time. Am I getting through to you, Harry? Neither your father nor Noel Harker. Is that clear?*

Tennant felt the big fingertips dig into his flesh. He couldn't get away from Lannigan's hand. He tried to move his head aside but the restraints prevented him. He thought: I saw Rayland. I saw Harker. I saw them in 1968 and I saw them again—

When? When?

What day of the week, what month, what year. The idea of maintaining a calendar inside his brain was useless. He didn't have the arithmetic.

Somebody had hung a blind on the small window high above his head, and he wasn't sure of time passing at all. The room was dark and stayed dark. Darkness became his life. He might have been submerged in a tank of murky water. He couldn't feel his limbs. Couldn't hear his heart. When they came to inject him, he didn't feel the penetration of the needle.

And still he fought. He fought to keep his eyes open. He fought sleep. He even fought dreams when sleep finally overwhelmed him as it always did. He would whisper to himself. I am Harry Tennant. I am Harry Tennant. I know what I saw. I remember Alison. I remember Maggie's poor ignorant face. You can't erode that, Lannigan. Not this time.

You see, Harry, I am only interested in your well-being, your mental health. You're a mess. You're back on the highway to dementia with both feet working. Take a detour, Harry. Come with me. Get off that bloody road and come with me. Be cooperative, Harry. Be good to yourself.

Hold on tight, Tennant. Don't listen to him.

There were more injections, many more. He lay in a listless state, suspended in the permanently dark room, where he longed for any kind of light to appear in the window. He was thirsty most of the time, but they didn't bring him water the way they'd done at first Weakened, parched, forever groggy, he found it harder and harder to differentiate between illusion and reality. People came and went in the room but they lacked substance. They drifted in a spectral manner, lingered over his bed, pulled his eyelids back or prodded his flesh, then left. He had the strange delusion he could levitate, but when he tried to will himself upward from the bed, nothing happened. His bedsores had begun to bleed. His flesh smelled of death.

One time he heard a bell ring in some distant tower and a black-headed sea gull, razor beak clacking, flapped violently in his room, hovering over his face with all the concentrated malice of a famished creature. He shouted for help, nobody came. He thought: I have to hold on. But what was he supposed to be holding? Alison? Maggie? A nebulous notion of self? Self was an odd little word, he thought. It broke when you hit it, like flawed crystal.

Lannigan whispered in his ear. *Let me make you better, Harry. I know the way.*

Did he dream that? A fever raged through him, flames through a condemned building. He sweated until the pale green smock was saturated. He'd sink into his sweat and drown.

Lannigan whispered in his ear, *I want to be kind to you,*

Harry. But you have to trust me. You understand what I'm telling you? I can make you better. You've taken too many bad drugs in the past. They've hurt you badly. But if you leave it to me, Harry, I can take the pain away.

Yes, Tennant thought. I want to be better.

One day they let him walk around his small room. His legs were strange, liquid, not entirely his own. *See, Harry,* Lannigan said, *you're on the mend. Soon you'll be out of here. On your way. Not yet. Not quite yet. We still need to talk.*

And so they talked. Tennant was taken to Lannigan's office, a big room with plants and leather chairs. They talked every other afternoon for an hour. Each time Tennant was taken back to his white room, he could never remember anything Lannigan had said. But the straps and buckles had been removed from his bed and the blind was gone from the window and he was grateful for that kindness. The barren branch of a tree rapped upon the glass.

What season is it? Tennant wondered. He didn't know. The sessions with Lannigan became longer. The Irishman used a pencil-sized flashlight every so often, shining it into Tennant's eyes and speaking quietly. We have to unburden you, Harry. We have to make you whole. But it takes time, you see. Everything takes time. This isn't a walk in the park, Harry. This is a long process. We have to trust each other. We have to take that long walk together. Hand in hand, if you like.

Do you trust me, boyo?

Yes, Tennant said. He couldn't think of a reason not to; in this friendless place, where corridors rang at night with the cries of strangers, and distant hands constantly thumped the keys of an untuned piano, Lannigan had become his only ally.

Sometimes after the sessions, Tennant would give in to depression, a deep black place from which escape was impossible. Sometimes he'd sit on his bed and cry uncontrollably for an hour or more and not know why he was weeping with such ferocity. He had the sensation of breaking apart inside, as if

someone had taken an ice pick to his heart. He would bang his
hands upon his thighs; sometimes he struck the walls for no
good reason. I did too many drugs, that's what happened to
me. Bad drugs. Street drugs. LSD cut with cyanide. Angel
dust. Anything going That's the problem.

Lannigan helped him over the tears and the depression.
You'll come out of this, laddie. You're going to get well again.

Yes, Lannigan. Yes, of course.

One day Lannigan asked him if he'd like to see Alison, and
Tennant had to strive to remember the name. He almost had
it, but it slipped away into nothing, and Lannigan looked
pleased. You're coming along nicely, Harry. You're doing very
well. Soon we'll have you walking in the fresh air.

Days later, Lannigan asked about Alison again. Tennant
looked at the shrink blankly.

After that, he was allowed to stroll in the parkland, accompanied by a male nurse whose name was Charlie. Charlie was
pleasantly talkative, and the weather, though sharply cold, was
sunny. Tennant liked these walks, although they tired him out
and ultimately confused him.

He dreamed of his father. He couldn't quite remember his
father's face. He accepted this loss of memory casually because
Lannigan said it was good to forget certain things about the
past; if he kept them alive, he'd never get better. I have to get
better, Tennant kept telling himself.

The sessions with Lannigan grew longer, sometimes two or
three a day. One afternoon, while he sat in the big leather chair
in the Irishman's office, Tennant had the thought: *I like this
man. I owe him a debt I can never pay.*

And one memorable morning, when the small high window
was frosted with flakes of snow, he was escorted into a room
filled with tables and shown how to weave a basket. The work
was intricate at first, and frustrating, but Tennant learned. He
watched his fingers work the cane as if they were somebody
else's. He got considerable satisfaction out of the task.

—Would you like to see Alison? Lannigan asked on a certain evening.

—I don't think I know anybody of that name, Harry replied.

Lannigan took him out of weaving and put him into the gymnasium. Total health, Harry. That's the concept. Sound mind, sound body. It's nature's own equation. Harry worked weights, pumped iron, felt good. He suffered no further depression, no outbreaks of tears. It wasn't a bad life in its way.

Now when he went on walks, he was accompanied not only by Charlie but by another man, a small Oriental called Sammy something. Sammy was insane, babbled endlessly about signs and omens. Tennant didn't speak to Sammy; he had nothing to say. The man was a sad case.

He told Lannigan that Sammy made him uneasy, unnerved him. He didn't want to be in Sammy's company. After that Sammy didn't appear for the walks.

Just before Christmas, when decorations had been hung in Lannigan's office and mistletoe pinned above the door, the Irishman asked him about his past, what did he remember?

Harry said, I remember having a house close to some woods. I remember I grew marijuana.

—And after that?

—After that I came here.

—Why did you come here?

—I had a breakdown.

—But now you feel better?

—I feel terrific now.

—Did you enjoy growing dope, Harry?

—It was a living, I guess.

Lannigan went away.

Tennant didn't dream so much anymore. His life had become comfortable in a routine kind of way. Talks with Lannigan. Sleep. Medication. Working the weights. He was physically stronger than he'd ever been, but a certain restlessness had begun to invade him. One morning he asked Lannigan when he could look forward to his release.

—You want to get out, Harry?

—Yeah. I think I'm better than I was. I'd like to get back to what I was doing.

—Growing stuff, d'you mean?

—Something like that.

Lannigan said he'd consider it. A month, perhaps six weeks, after Christmas the Irishman said, You really think you're well enough to go it alone, Harry?

—You know better than me, but I'm beginning to feel, I don't know, restricted. I don't want to sound ungrateful, you understand. You've done a lot for me.

Lannigan sat on the edge of the bed. He said, I know where there's a small house with some land not far from here. It's available, if you're interested.

—Sure, I'm interested, Tennant replied.

—I ought to caution you. No dope this time.

—Right.

—I mean it, Harry. You want to grow things, grow cabbage, something people can't smoke.

—Sure. Cabbage. Corn. I can see that.

—That keeps you legal, Harry. You don't want another breakdown, do you? You don't want to go near dope of any kind.

—No.

During the third week in February, when the fields were covered with snow and the trees looked as if they might never live again, Lannigan drove Tennant to a tiny frame house that stood on eight or nine acres of mixed woodland and fields. It was a twenty-minute drive from the clinic. Tennant explored the small rooms. The house had good light from the west and the paintwork wasn't bad. The furniture was functional. All in all, he liked it.

—I might get a dog, Paul.

—I think that would be helpful.

—And if I don't feel good, I know where to find you.

—Down the road, take a right. You know the way.

—Who owns this house?

—Oh, some corporation in D.C. I don't remember the name offhand, boyo.

The following week, after days of intensive talks with Lannigan, during which the Irishman constantly interrogated him about his family, his past history, Harry moved in. From a nearby breeder he bought a Great Dane pup. He couldn't think of a name for her.

He walked the fields, enjoying the way his feet sank through the crust of snow. He walked in the woods, delighting in the barren melancholy of the trees. From a certain angle he could see the small house between the trees. Something in the perception touched him: He felt at home here.

Lannigan had loaned him a shortbed truck. Every now and then he'd drive it into the nearest hamlet—a place called Shelbyville—and buy groceries and beer and dog food. The store had everything he needed. Once or twice he lingered outside the public telephone located in front of the shop, possessed by the odd idea that he had a phone call to make, but he didn't go inside the box. He couldn't think of anyone to call, and he wasn't sure why he had such an irrational urge in any case. I will have to make a friend, he thought. Just so I have somebody to call. But he wasn't lonely.

One morning when he was stepping out of the store, he saw a gray bus parked alongside his truck. He knew it was the private bus that sometimes ferried the clinic's clients here and there—therapeutic outings, day trips to one place or another. Lannigan believed in exposing his patients to what he called the real world. Otherwise, he always said, they feel more cut off than they should.

Tennant gazed at the windows of the vehicle. A pale-skinned girl looked at him through the window. Some aspect of her impassive face provoked a sense of curiosity in him. He wondered why. He got in the truck and drove back to his house, thinking of the girl all the way. The black hair, the big sad empty eyes. Her image troubled him for the rest of the day. She was one of Lannigan's patients: What had happened to her? Why was she sick? He took one of the tranquilizers and lay down, the Dane at his feet. Then he forgot about the girl.

He lived quietly.

He lived quietly for weeks before he awoke one dawn with a sense of panic. He'd dreamed something menacing, a situation crowded with figures who meant to harm him. A girl dressed in black had entered the dream. Sweating in the unheated house, he dressed quickly and drove the truck to the clinic, where he asked to see Lannigan.

The Irishman calmed him down, gave him some tranquilizers, massaged his shoulders in that comforting way he had.

Tennant didn't describe his dream in detail. Dreams were sometimes too obscure to talk about. He told Lannigan he'd woken up with a bad feeling. He just didn't know why.

—Don't worry about it. Don't get stressed. Go back home. Take a pill and relax.

—Yeah. I'll do that.

Tennant left the clinic and drove back to his small house. The day was cold and bright. He shivered when he went indoors. He stacked logs and kindling and lit a fire in the living room. He sat on the sofa, watching smoke drift. He had a feeling of satisfaction. House, fire, dog. What could be better?

Crazy question. I have it all. All I'll ever need. He rose to lift the poker. The logs had to be prodded. A few sparks disappeared into the blackness of the chimney. Wood crackled, spat. A flying chip, burning fiercely, adhered to the back of his hand. Moaning, he brushed it quickly away. He went inside the kitchen, ran the hand under cold water, dried it gently. He returned to the old horsehair sofa and sat down, hunched forward. He watched the fire, the sparks. His hand ached. He looked at the scorched mark on his flesh and found himself for some reason thinking of the girl he'd seen on the bus. The image was quickly gone, leaving him with an unfocused sense of pity.

In early spring he decided to plant his first seeds: corn, green beans, peas. He cleared an overgrown plot of land at the back of the house, hacking away diligently at weeds and nettles. He pricked his fingers; blood ran down the palm of his hand. He placed the tips of his fingers in his mouth, tasted his own blood, felt a quick sharp jab of pain. He was thinking of the girl, that forlorn face imprisoned behind the window of the bus, dark eyes, short black hair. It was perhaps somebody he'd dreamed, or somebody he'd met once. He wasn't sure. He felt a jab of loneliness.

He sat down on a grassy bank and surveyed the soil he'd just turned over. The dog came from the house and stood alongside him. I have to find her a name, he thought. The bright yellow sun lay flat on the landscape, the sky was cloudless. He picked up a stick, thinking he'd throw it for the dog to fetch—the Dane hadn't learned to play this game—but instead, forced by an impulse he didn't understand, he inscribed a couple of lines in the earth, two diagonal lines that formed the sides of an incomplete triangle connected one to the other by a short bridge. He looked at what he'd done. The letter *A*.

It signified nothing. He erased it with his foot.